BY JOSH MALERMAN

MALORIE

A BIRD BOX NOVEL

JOSH MALERMAN

ORION

An Orion paperback

First published in Great Britain in 2020
by Orion Fiction,
This paperback edition published in 2021
by Orion Fiction,
an imprint of The Orion Publishing Group Ltd.,
Carmelite House, 50 Victoria Embankment
London EC4Y 0DZ

An Hachette UK company

1 3 5 7 9 10 8 6 4 2

A CIP catalogue record for this book is
available from the British Library.

ISBN (Paperback) 978 1 4091 9314 2

Printed and bound in Great Britain by Clays Ltd,
Elcograf S.p.A.

www.orionbooks.co.uk

Malorie is for Kristin Nelson.

THE JANE TUCKER
SCHOOL FOR THE BLIND

Malorie stands flat against the brick wall of a classroom. The door is locked. She is alone. The lights are off.

She is blindfolded.

Outside, in the hall, violence has begun.

She knows this sound, has heard it in nightmares, has heard it in the echoes of a fallen house full of sane people tearing one another apart as she gave birth to her son.

Tom is out there in the violence right now. Malorie doesn't know where.

She breathes in. She holds it. She breathes out.

She reaches for the door, to unlock it, to open it, to find her son and daughter among the screams, the hysteria, the frenzy. Something cracks on the other side of the door. Sounds like someone slamming their head against the hall wall.

She pulls back from the doorknob.

When she last saw Olympia, the six-year-old was reading braille books in the Tucker Library. A dozen others were there, listening to the classical music played through the school speakers by way of the record player in the office.

Malorie listens for the voices of those people now. She needs to know if this violence has reached the library. Reached her daughter. If it has, she will look for Tom first.

She listens.

Her kids have taught her a lot about listening since arriving at the Jane Tucker School for the Blind. And while Malorie will never hear the world they do, she can try.

But there's too much noise out there. Chaos. It's impossible to discern one voice from another.

She thinks of Annette. The blind woman, much older than herself, whose name she heard screamed, moments ago, as Malorie, hungry, walked the hall to the cafeteria. Before Malorie had time to process the nature of the scream, Annette herself came around the corner, blue bathrobe and red hair trailing like spinning sirens, knife in hand. Malorie had time to note the woman's open, unfocused eyes before closing her own.

Malorie thought, *She's blind . . . how is she mad?*, then she went still. Annette passed her, breathing heavy, moving fast, and Malorie, hearing the first guttural howls from deeper in the school, stepped blind into the nearest classroom and locked its door behind her.

She reaches for the knob again now.

The last she saw of Tom he was in what was once the staff lounge, pieces of a new invention at his knees. Malorie is responsible for those pieces. Only six, Tom the boy invents like Tom the man, his namesake, once did. Often Malorie's instinct is to humor this impulse. She feels a mother must. Or perhaps, a mother *should have,* in the old world. Now, here, she always destroys what Tom's made and reminds him that the blindfold is the only protection any of them will ever need.

Yet, Annette is blind.

And now mad.

Malorie hears a sudden obscenity from the other side of the locked door. Two people are fighting in the hall. It's a man and a woman. And it's not difficult to put visual images with the sounds they make. Clawing, scratching. Fingers in eyes and fingers down throats and the cracking of a bone and the tearing of what sounds like a throat.

Bare-handed?

Malorie doesn't move. A body slams against the wood door and slides to the tiled floor. Whoever's won the fight, he or she is panting just outside.

Malorie listens. She breathes in, she holds it, she breathes out. She knows there's no stopping the panic. She wants to hear farther up the hall, past the breathing, to the screams of the people who live here, to the exact things they say, to the exact location of her kids. She remembers giving birth in the attic of a home, a place much smaller than this. She recalls a cry from below: *Don tore the drapes down!*

Who tore them down here?

In the hall, the breathing has stopped. But the distant sounds of fists on wood, fists on fists, and the last vestiges of sanity are getting louder.

Malorie unlocks the classroom door. She opens it.

There is no immediate movement in the hall. No one erupts toward her. No one speaks at all. Whoever won the fight, they are gone now. Howls erupt from deeper in the building. Muffled death knells, last words and wishes. There is the smacking of fists, the cracking of wood. There is yelling and gibberish, doors slamming open and doors slamming closed. Children cry out. The music from the office continues.

Malorie steps over the body at the open door's threshold. She steps into the hall, keeping to the wall. An alarm sounds. The front door to the school is open. The rhythmic throbbing is so at odds with the classical music that for a confused second Malorie feels like she's already lost her mind.

Her kids are somewhere in this furor.

Shaking, she tries to close her eyes a third time, behind her already closed lids, behind the fold wrapped tight to her head, closing her mind to the idea of what this all must look like.

She slides along the brick wall. She does not call out to Tom or Olympia though it's all she wants to do. She breathes in, she holds it, breathes out. The bricks prickle her bare shoulders and arms, tugging at the fabric of the white tank top she wears. The alarm gets louder as she approaches the end of this hall, approaches the very place from which redheaded Annette came rushing with a large knife in hand. People scream ahead. Someone is close. Heavy, clumsy boots on the floor, the grunt of someone not used to this much effort.

Malorie goes still.

The person passes her, breathing hard, muttering to himself. Is he mad? Malorie doesn't know. Can't know. She only slides along the wall, finding herself, incredibly, feeling a slim sense of gratitude for the two years they have lived here. For the respite from the road. But that indebtedness is a marble fallen to a beach of glass orbs, never to be found again. A horror she's long expected has arrived.

Don't get lazy.

Her three-word mantra means nothing now. Proof: she's already gotten lazy, she doesn't know where her kids are.

A metallic bang thunders throughout; the music and alarm get louder.

Malorie doesn't try to calm the children she hears. She doesn't reach out in her darkness to help them. She only slides, so flat now the bricks draw blood.

Movement ahead, coming at her, quick, flat steps. She holds her breath. But this person does not pass.

"Malorie?"

Someone with their eyes open. A woman. Who?

"Leave me alone," Malorie says. "Please."

She hears the echo of her own voice pleading, six years ago, in the attic in which she gave birth.

"Malorie, what's happened?"

Malorie thinks it's a woman named Felice. All that matters is whether or not this woman is mad.

"Did they get in?" the woman asks.

"I don't—"

"Everybody's mad!" the woman says.

Malorie doesn't answer. This woman may be armed.

"You can't go that way," the woman says.

Malorie feels a hand on her bare wrist. She pulls back, cracks her elbow against the bricks.

"What's *wrong* with you?" the woman says. "Do you think *I'm* mad?"

Malorie walks from her, arms out, prepared to be hurt. She moves toward the end of the hall, where she knows a glass case dominates the wall, a thing that once held trophies, accomplishments, proof of progress in a school for the blind.

She connects with it before she can stop herself.

Her shoulder cracks it first, the cuts coming fast and warm, the pain loud. She cries out but her voice is inhaled by the rising chaos in the halls.

She does not stop moving. And she still doesn't call their names. Touching the wall with fingers painted freshly red, she approaches the wailing, the shouts, the metal on metal, the fists on fists.

Someone brushes against her shoulder and Malorie turns quickly, pushes at them, shoves nothing.

Nobody is there. But she feels cold. Doesn't want to be touched by anyone.

By anything.

She thinks of Annette, blind but mad.

Yes, a person could go mad in the old world way. But Malorie knows the look of the particular madness delivered by the creatures.

Annette did not simply snap. And if the woman cannot see . . . what happened?

"Mom!"

Malorie stops. Is it Olympia? The urgent but distant cry of the girl she did not give birth to but has raised as a daughter all the same?

"Somebody turn off that music," Malorie says, needing to say something, needing to hear a familiar, sane voice as she drags her fingers along the bricks, as she feels the pegboard where community notices alerted people to school events for the last two years.

Ahead, a scream. Behind, the cracking of wood. Someone bounds past her. Someone follows.

Malorie does not cry. She only moves, her knees weak, her shoulder bright with the fresh injury. Her ears open for an echo of the voice that cried *mom*, one of her own, perhaps, rising to the surface for air, before sinking back into the raging waves ahead in the hall.

She tells herself to move with purpose, but slow. She needs to be sharp, needs to be standing.

A boy cries out ahead. A child. Sounds like he's gone mad.

She breathes in, she holds it, she breathes out. She walks

toward the maddening volume, the sounds of an entire community losing their minds at once. A second child, perhaps. A third.

"They got in," she says. But she doesn't need to say it. And this time her own voice brings her no comfort.

To her right, a door rattles. Ahead on the left something on wheels crashes against the bricks. People scream profanities. Malorie tries not to allow herself to imagine what these scenes must look like. The expressions on the faces of the men and women she has shared this edifice with for two years. The chips in the bricks. The wreckage. The bruises and the blood. She tries to deny herself even the memory of sight, as if imagining what happens in the space might drive her mad.

She refuses to imagine a creature. She will not even allow herself that.

Something clips her bad shoulder. Malorie covers it with her hand. She doesn't want to be touched. Is thinking that Annette was touched. Is worried, horrified, that the creatures have begun . . . *touching*.

But this was a piece of wood perhaps. Another brick. A finger sent sailing from a hand.

A woman howls. A child speaks.

Speaks?

"Mom."

A hand in her own.

It doesn't take more than a second for her to recognize the hand as Olympia's.

Mania fattens ahead.

"This way," Olympia says.

Malorie doesn't ask her daughter why they are walking toward the violence rather than from it. She knows it's because Tom must be on the other side of this scene.

Even at only six years old, Olympia leads.

Malorie cries. She can't stop it from happening. As if, in her personal darkness, she is being lowered into the house at the moment when Don tore the drapes down. As if she never took the river to the Jane Tucker School for the Blind. As if she is falling, on her back, through the attic floor, into the hideous events below.

Tom the man died that day. The namesake of her son. Yet Malorie did not bear witness. She was removed, if such a word applies, safer in the attic than those below. But here, now, she hears the carnage up close, no floors between her and it; ordinary people turning. Once civil men and women now cracked, cursing, hurting each other and hurting themselves.

Something enormous crashes. Glass explodes.

Malorie wouldn't be able to hear her daughter if she spoke. They are in the eye of it now.

Olympia's grip tightens.

Someone thumps against Malorie, shin to shin. Then, bricks again, against her bad shoulder. She recognizes some of the voices. They've spent two years here. They know people. They've made friends.

Or have they?

As Malorie steps deeper into the madness, she hears a distant question, asked in her own voice, her own head, asking if she was righteous in her staunch safety precautions, the fact that she was often chided for wearing her blindfold indoors. Oh, how the people of this place were offended by her measures. Oh, how it made the others feel as if Malorie thought herself better than them.

"Tom," Olympia says.

Or Malorie thinks she hears it. The same name of the man she most admired in this world, the optimist in a time of impossible despair. Yes, Tom the boy is much like Tom the man, though the man was not his father. Malorie can't stop him from wanting to fashion stronger blindfolds, from covering the windows with layers of wood, from painting false windows on the room they've called their own for two years.

But she can stop him from doing it.

Someone hits Malorie on the side of the head. She swings out, tries to push the person away, but Olympia pulls her deeper into the derangement.

"Olympia," she says. But she says no more. Cannot speak. As now bodies press against her, objects break above and behind her, words are sworn close to her ear.

It can sound like a celebration if she wants it to, the screams no longer of terror, but excitement. The heavy thuds only heavy feet upon a dance floor. No anguish, only cheer.

Is this how Tom the man chose to see this world? And if so . . . can she do it, too?

"Tom," Olympia says. This time Malorie hears it clearly, and she understands they are on the other side of the violence.

"Where?"

"Here."

Malorie reaches out, feels the doorjamb of an open classroom. It smells of people in here.

"Tom?" she says.

"Mom," Tom says. She hears the smile in his voice. She can tell he's proud.

She goes to him, crouches, and feels for his eyes. They are covered with what feels like cardboard, and Malorie thinks of Tom the man wearing a helmet of couch cushions and tape.

The relief she feels is not tempered by the chaos in the halls. Her children are with her again.

"Get up," she says, her voice still trembling. "We're leaving."

She steps farther into the room, finds the beds, removes three blankets.

"Are we taking the river again?" Tom asks.

Beyond them, the madness does not quell. Boots clamor up and down the halls. Glass breaks. Children scream.

"No," Malorie says. Then, frantic, "I don't know. I have no plan. Take these."

She hands them each a blanket.

"Cover yourselves from head to toe."

She thinks of blind Annette, blue robe, red hair, the knife.

"They can touch us now," she says.

"Mom," Tom says, but Malorie reaches out and takes his hand. The violence swells, swallowing the questions he was close to asking.

Olympia takes Malorie's other hand.

Malorie breathes in, she holds it, she breathes out.

"Now," she says. "*Now* . . . we go."

They step, together, out of the classroom and into the hall.

"The front door," she says.

The same door they entered two years ago, Malorie's body and mind then ravaged by rowing and the constant bowstring terror of navigating the water blind.

And the fear then, too, of a man named Gary.

"Malorie?"

Malorie, under the blanket, grips the hands of her children. It's a man named Jesse who speaks to her. Malorie knows Jesse, when sane, had a crush on her. He does not sound sane now.

"Malorie? Where are you taking the kids?"

"*Go,*" Malorie says. She does not turn around. She does not answer Jesse, who now follows close behind.

"Malorie," he says. "You can't go."

Malorie makes a fist, turns, and swings.

Her fist connects with what she believes is Jesse's jaw.

He cries out.

She grips the hands of her children.

Tom and Olympia move in concert with her, the trio making for the open front door.

"My blindfold worked," Tom says. Still, despite the horror, there is pride in his voice.

"It's here," Olympia says, indicating the door.

Malorie places a palm against the doorjamb. She listens for Jesse. For anyone.

She breathes in. She holds it. She breathes out.

"How many are out there?" she asks. "How many do you hear?"

The kids are quiet. The frenzy continues deeper into the school. But it feels far now. Farther. Malorie knows Tom wants to answer her questions exactly. But he can't.

"Too many to count," he says.

"Olympia?"

A pause. A crash from far behind. A scream.

"A lot," Olympia says.

"Okay. *Okay*. Don't take the blankets off. Wear them until I tell you otherwise. They touch us now. Do you understand?"

"Yes," Tom says.

"Yes," Olympia says.

Malorie tries to close her eyes a third time. Tries to shutter her imagination to what lurks outside.

A lot.

She tries to close her eyes a fourth time, a fifth, a sixth. She wants to say something about how unfair this is. She wants to tell someone her age. Someone raised before the creatures came. How it shouldn't be that a mother and her children have to flee the place they call home, so suddenly, to enter a world where the threats are worse than those they leave behind.

She grips the hands of her children and takes the first step away from the Jane Tucker School for the Blind.

This is the new world. This is how things are and how they have been for many years.

From hysteria to the complete unknown.

The three of them, blind, draped in cloth, setting out.

Alone.

Again.

TEN YEARS ON

ONE

Tom is getting water from the well. It's something he's done every other day for the better part of a decade, the three of them having called Camp Yadin home for that long. Olympia believes the camp was once an outpost in the American frontier days. She's read almost every book in the camp library (more than a thousand), including books on the history of Michigan. She says the camp lodge was most likely once a saloon. Cabin One was the jail. Tom doesn't know if she's right, though he has no reason not to believe her. It was a Jewish summer camp when the creatures came, that much is for sure. And now, it's home.

"Hand over hand," he says, taking the rope that connects Cabin Three to the stone lip of the well. He says it because, despite the ropes that tie every building to one another (and even link Cabin Ten to the H dock on the lake), he's trying to come up with a better way to move about.

Tom loathes the blindfolds. Sometimes, when he's feeling

particularly lazy, he doesn't use one at all. He keeps his eyes closed. But his mother's never-ending rules remain firm in his mind.

Closing your eyes isn't enough. You could be startled into opening them. Or something could open them for you.

Sure. Yes. In theory Malorie is right. In theory she usually is. But who wants to live in theory? Tom is sixteen years old now. He was born into this world. And nothing's tried to open his eyes yet.

"Hand over hand."

He's almost there. Malorie insists that he check the water before bringing it up. She's told him the story of two men named Felix and Jules many times. How his namesake, Tom the man, tested the water the two brought back, the water everybody was worried could be contaminated by a creature. Tom the teen likes that part of the story. He relates to the test. He even relates to the idea of new information about the creatures. Anything would be more to work with than what they have. But he's not worried about something swimming in their drinking water. The filter he invented himself has taken care of that.

And besides, despite the way Malorie carries on, even she can't believe water can go mad.

"Here!" he says.

He reaches out and touches the lip before bumping into it. He's made this walk so many times that he could run it and still stop before the stone circle.

He leans over the edge and yells into the dark tunnel.

"Get out of there!"

He smiles. His voice echoes—the sound is a rich one—and Tom likes to imagine it's someone else calling back up to him. For as lucky as they are to have chanced upon an abandoned summer camp with numerous buildings and amenities, life gets lonely out here.

"Tom is the best!" he hollers, just to hear the echo.

Nothing stirs in the water below, and Tom begins to bring the bucket up. It's a standard crank, made of steel, and he's repaired it more than once. He oils it regularly, too, as the camp giveth in all ways; a supply cellar in the main lodge that brought Malorie to tears ten years ago.

"A pipeline that delivers water directly to us," Tom says, cranking. "We could put it exactly where the rope is now. It passes through the existing filter. All we'd have to do is turn a dial, and presto. Clean water comes right to us. No more hand over hand on the rope. We wouldn't have to leave the cabin at all."

Not that the walk is difficult. And any excuse to get outside is a good one. But Tom wants things to improve.

It's all he thinks about.

The bucket up, he removes it from its hooks and carries it back to Cabin Three, the largest of the cabins, the one he, Olympia, and Malorie have slept in most of these years. Mom Rules won't allow Tom or Olympia to sleep anywhere else, despite their growing needs, a rule that Tom has so far followed.

Spend all day in another one if you need to. But we sleep together.

Still. A decade in.

Tom shakes his head and tries to laugh it off. What else is there to do? Olympia has told him in private about the differences in generations that she's read about in her books. She says it's common for teenagers to feel like their parents are "from another planet." Tom definitely agrees with the writers on that front. Malorie acts as if every second of every day could be the moment they all go mad. And Tom and Olympia both have pondered aloud, in their own ways, the worth of a life in which the only aim is to keep living.

"Okay, Mom," Tom says, smiling. It's easier for him to smile about this stuff than not. The few times outsiders have passed through their camp, their home, Tom has been able to glean how much stricter Malorie is than most. He's heard it in the voices of others. He saw it regularly at the school for the blind. Often, it was embarrassing, living under her thumb in public. People looked at her like she was.... what's the word Olympia used?

Abusive.

Yes. That's it. Whether or not Olympia thinks Malorie is abusive doesn't matter. Tom thinks she is.

But what can he do? He can leave his blindfold inside. He can keep notes and dream of inventing ways to push back against the creatures. He can refuse to wear long sleeves and a hood on the hottest day of the year. Like today.

At the cabin's back door, he hears movement on the other side. It's not Olympia, it's Malorie. This means he can't simply open the door and place the bucket of water inside. He needs to put that hood on after all.

"Shit," Tom says.

So many little dalliances, so many quirks of his mother's that get in the way of him existing on his own, the way he'd have it done.

He sets the bucket in the grass and takes the long-sleeved hoodie from the hook outside. His arms through the sleeves, he doesn't bother with the hood. Malorie will only check an arm.

The bucket in hand again, he knocks five times.

"Tom?" Malorie calls.

But who else would it be?

"Yep. Bucket one."

He will gather four buckets today. The same number he always retrieves.

"Are your eyes closed?"

"Blindfolded, Mom."

The door opens.

Tom hands the bucket over the threshold. Malorie takes it. But not without touching his arm in the process.

"Good boy," she says.

Tom smiles. Malorie hands him a second bucket and closes the door. Tom removes the hoodie and puts it back on the hook.

It's easy to fool your mom when she's not allowed to look at you.

"Hand over hand," he says. Though really now he's just walking alongside the rope, bucket in one hand. Malorie's told him many times how they did it in the house on Shillingham, the house where Tom was born. They tied the rope around their waists and got water in pairs. Olympia says Malorie talks about that house more often than she realizes. But they both know she only talks about it up to a point. Then, nothing. As if the ending of the story is too dark, and repeating it might bring it back upon her.

At the well, his arms bare below the short sleeves, Tom secures the second bucket and turns the crank. The metal clangs against the stone as it always does but despite the contained cacophony, Tom hears a foot upon the grass to his left. He hears what he thinks are wheels, too.

A wheelbarrow pushed past the well.

He stops cranking. The bucket takes a moment to settle.

Someone's here. He can hear them breathing.

He thinks of the hoodie hanging on the hook.

Another step. A shoe. Dry grass flattens in a different way beneath a bare foot than it does the solid sole of a shoe.

A person, then.

He does not ask who it is. He doesn't move at all.

A third step and Tom wonders if the person knows he's here. Surely they had to have heard him?

"Hello?"

It's a man's voice. Tom hears paper rustling, like when Olympia flips pages while reading. Does the man have books?

Tom is scared. But he's thrilled, too.

A visitor.

Still, he does not answer. Some of Malorie's rules make more sense in the moment.

Tom steps away from the well. He could run to the cabin's back door. It wouldn't be difficult, and he'd know when to stop.

In his personal darkness, he's all ears.

"I'd like to speak to you," the man says.

Tom takes another step. His fingertips touch the rope. He turns to face the house.

He hears the small wheels creak. Imagines weapons in the barrow.

Then he's moving fast, faster than he's ever taken this walk before.

"Hey," the man says.

But Tom is at the back door and knocking five times before the man says another word.

"Tom?"

"Yes. Hurry."

"Are your—"

"Mom. *Hurry.*"

Malorie opens the back door and Tom nearly knocks her over as he rushes inside.

"What's going on?" Olympia asks.

"Mom—" Tom begins.

But there is a knock at the front door.

The door is thin and old. Malorie has expressed worry before; it isn't enough to stop anything, or anyone, from coming in.

"It's a man," Tom says. But Malorie has already tapped him on the shoulder. He knows what this means. He knows also that Olympia received the same tap.

Tom doesn't speak again.

"Hello in there," the man says on the other side of the cabin door. "I'm with the census."

Malorie doesn't respond. Tom thinks of the rustling papers he heard. A barrow full?

"Do you know what the census is?"

Malorie doesn't respond. Tom thinks he might have to do something. If the man tries to break the door down, he's going to have to do something.

"I don't mean to frighten you," the man says. "I could come back another time. But it's hard to say when that will be."

Malorie doesn't respond. Tom knows she won't.

He wants to ask Olympia what a census is.

"I just wanna talk to you. However many there are in there. It could save lives."

Malorie doesn't respond.

"What does he want?" Tom whispers. Malorie grabs his wrist to quiet him.

"So, what I do," the man says, "I go around gathering stories. I gather information. I know quite a bit about failed attempts at trying to look at the creatures. I know of successes people have had in terms of living better lives. Did you know there is a working train now?"

Malorie doesn't respond. Suddenly, Tom wants to.

"Right here in Michigan . . . a train. And did you know there are more creatures now than before? Estimates say they have tripled since first arriving. Have you noticed more activity outside your home?"

Malorie doesn't respond. But Tom really wants to. What this man is saying electrifies him. Why not exchange information? Why not learn? In the name of a better life, why not?

"There's some evidence of one having been caught," the man says. "Certainly people have tried all over."

And now Tom knows why Malorie hasn't spoken.

By her measures, this man is unsafe. Just the suggestion of capturing one must have turned her to stone. If she wasn't stone already.

"I have lists," the man says. "Patterns. A lot of information that can help you. And your stories, in turn, might help others. Please. Let's talk?"

Malorie doesn't respond.

But Tom does.

"Do you have that information written down?"

Malorie grips his wrist.

"Yes, I do." Relief in the man's voice. "I have literature on me. Right here."

Malorie grips his wrist so tight he has to grab her hand to stop it.

"Could you leave it on the front porch?"

This is Olympia speaking. Tom could kiss her.

But the man is silent for some time. Then, "That doesn't seem like an even trade. I'd be leaving everything I know, without getting anything in return."

Finally, Malorie speaks.

"Add us to the list of people who turned you away."

Tom hears a sigh through the wood.

"Are you absolutely sure?" the man asks. "It's not often I encounter a group. As you can imagine, it's not the most fruitful, nor the safest, endeavor. Are you sure you won't have me in for an hour? Maybe two? Can I at least get your names?"

"Leave us now."

"Okay," he says. "You realize I'm just a man trying to do good out here, right? I'm literally trying to give us all a better understanding of where we're at." Then, after further silence from within, "Okay. I apologize if I've scared you. I see I have."

Tom's ear is cocked to the door. He hears the man leaving the porch, shoes on the cabin stairs, breaks in the dry grass beyond, the wheelbarrow pushed once more. By the time Tom is at the door himself, his ear to the wood, he can hear the man's steps diminishing, taking the dirt road out of camp.

He turns to Malorie and Olympia. But before he can say anything, Malorie does.

"I told you not to speak," she says. "Next time, you *don't.*"

"He's gone," Olympia says.

But Tom already knows what Malorie is going to say before she says it.

"Not until we sweep the camp, he's not."

"Mom," Tom says. "He's not Gary."

Malorie doesn't hesitate with her response.

"Not another word," she says. "And wear your hood for fuck's sake, Tom."

Tom remains by the front door as Malorie readies herself to step outside, to check every cabin in the camp. The man could be staying here, Malorie will say. He could be camping out in the woods, she will say. Who knows how long he's been watching them, she will say. And the name *Gary* will come up again. As it always does in times of trouble.

But Tom isn't listening for what Malorie says or doesn't say. His ear is on the soft rustle on the other side of the cabin's front door. As what must be a welcome breeze shuffles the papers sitting out there on the porch.

The literature the man left behind after all.

TWO

Olympia sits on her bed; she reads out loud. Whoever wrote the notes, the writing is messy. Olympia thinks that's because many copies were made and who knows how deep into that chore the person was by the time they wrote this particular draft. The pile of pages is huge. Bigger than any book in the camp library. She tries to pace her reading, to slow down, but she recognizes in her own voice the excitement she's read about in numerous characters in numerous books. Authors used words like *breathless* and *eager* to describe how she feels. In part, it's the thrill of keeping a secret. Malorie doesn't know the man left the literature. And she definitely doesn't know Olympia reads it to her brother now.

"Go on," Tom says.

Tom can read on his own, of course, but he's lazy. And he can't sit still for long. Tom, Olympia knows, needs to move. He needs to be in motion. He needs to be *doing* something.

"*A man in Texas attempted to look at one under water,*" Olympia reads. "*Seventeen people were present for this. The group believed a creature to be wad-*

ing in the lake behind the campsite where they stayed. The man volunteered to go under, to look. He went mad down there and never came up again for air."

"Someone held him down," Tom says. "Nobody could just . . . stay under water till they died. Not if they could get up. Impossible."

Olympia nods. But she isn't so sure. The stories Malorie has told them, coupled with the memories of the entire school for the blind going mad at once, mean anything is possible.

"But what is madness," Olympia asks, "if not something out of the ordinary?"

"Okay," Tom says, pacing, "but this is different. The body would take over. Right? Even if you wanted to drown yourself by sitting on the bottom of a lake . . . the body would swim to the top."

"I don't know."

"I don't either. But that one feels fishy to me."

"Are you listening?"

He looks to her, gravity in his eyes.

"Of course I'm listening," he says. "Always."

Listening for Malorie. Neither wants to be caught doing this.

"A woman in Wisconsin attempted to look at one through an eclipse viewer," Olympia reads. Tom looks considerably more attentive now. *"After many discussions with her peers in which they attempted to dissuade her, she tried it alone at dawn on a clear, spring morning. She went mad immediately."*

"Okay," Tom says, "but how do we know she only looked through the viewfinder?"

"I think that's implied."

Tom laughs.

"Well, if there's one thing Mom has taught us, it's that 'implied' isn't good enough."

At the mention of Malorie: "Are you listening?"

"Olympia. Go on."

She silently reads ahead the next few handwritten lines. "This is interesting," she says. *"Sick people at a compound in Ohio, knowing they were going to die, volunteered to test out theories of how to look at the creatures."*

"Wow," Tom says. "That's brave."

"Totally. *One man went mad watching videotape of the outside world."*

"Like Mom's story."

"Yep. *One man went mad looking at photographs taken of the outside world. Another went mad looking at the negatives.* What are negatives?"

"I don't know," Tom says.

"A terminal woman went mad walking the outside world with two prisms, former paperweights, held to her eyes."

Olympia shudders. These Ohio stories describe a sad group of sick people in hospital gowns, wandering otherwise empty streets, willing to die for answers.

"Willing to die for progress," Tom says. "Terminal or not, that's noble."

Olympia agrees.

"There are fifty pages of this kind of stuff."

"And I wanna hear every one of them."

"Are you—"

But before she can finish her question, Tom points a finger at her.

"Go on," he says.

"A woman walked the streets of Branson, Missouri, wearing blinders, the type once used for horses, testing the idea that it's the peripheral vision that drives one mad."

"This isn't going to end well."

"Nope. She went mad and broke into a theater. Killed a family hiding out there."

A crack of a stick outside, and both teens close their eyes. They do not speak; they hardly breathe. Both listen as far as they can.

Olympia thinks she knows what it is, but Tom says so first.

"A deer."

They both open their eyes.

"Sane," Olympia says.

Tom shrugs. "I would have to know for certain how a sane deer behaves first."

"Could be a moose. Could be a lion."

Tom opens his mouth to refute her, but Olympia smiles as he thinks it over. She flips through the pages.

"Locations," she says. "Towns that are . . ."

But she goes quiet.

"Towns that are what?" Tom asks.

As Olympia begins to flip the page, he hurries across the cabin and sits beside her on the bed.

"Don't skip over anything," he says. "Come on."

Olympia shows him.

"The cities are arranged by how 'modern' they are."

"Modern?" Tom asks.

"I think they mean to say . . . how forward-thinking."

She sees the lights turn on in her brother's eyes, and she feels almost mean for having showed him. She suddenly wishes the man hadn't come to the door at all.

"Are these places where people have tried capturing one?"

He's excited now. Olympia makes to keep the pages from him, but to what end? She hands them over.

"Holy shit," Tom says. "Get this. *A couple in northern Illinois claimed to have trapped a creature in their toolshed. They brought me to the shed and asked that I put my ear to the door. I heard movement inside. Then I heard crying. I feigned being impressed and eventually thanked the couple and said goodbye. But later that night I returned and released their twelve-year-old son from the shed.*"

"God," Olympia says. "That's terrible!"

"Terrible. And get this: *A man in Pittsburgh claimed to have buried three creatures in his backyard. He showed me where the ground was soft. When I asked if I might dig them up, he threatened me at gunpoint, telling me that if I told anyone what he'd done to his family he'd shoot me. This is not an easy job I've taken on.*"

"Jeez," Olympia says. "And no evidence of an actual catch."

Tom sees the name of a town, *Indian River,* and a person, *Athena Hantz,* but he can't let Olympia's last statement just slip by.

"No. But that doesn't mean anything. *Someone's* got one out there, Olympia. You have to remember: there are *so many* people in the world. We just live in one little camp in one little part of Michigan. Know what I mean?" When he pauses, Olympia sees distance in his eyes, as if he's on the road to other places. "Someone's done it. And I wanna know who."

"Tom. Come on. Don't be a fool."

But Olympia understands. A list like this is all and everything Tom has ever wanted. Places where people think like he does. Places far from an abandoned camp harboring a mother with as many rules as she has blindfolds.

"Do you have a book of maps?" he asks her.

"In the library. Of course. Why? You thinking of heading somewhere more progressive?"

Tom laughs, but she hears frustration there.

She takes the pages back.

"Lists," she says, happy to move on for now. Tom, she knows, will be reading these pages for months to come. Maybe even years. "So many lists. Streets. Incidences. Temperatures. Names."

"Names?"

"I would think you would be more interested in the achievements than the actual people involved."

Tom elbows her gently.

"Let me see the names."

She shows him. Tom squints. Olympia knows this face well. Tom is connecting dots.

"Survivors," he says.

"How do you know that?"

"Look."

He points to a legend at the bottom of the first page of names. Symbols beside words like *seen* and *spotted, rumored* and . . .

"Alive . . ." Olympia says. "Oh, wow."

They both sit a little more erect on the bed.

"Check if we're in there," Tom says. "Go to Michigan."

Olympia shakes her head.

"We won't be. We *would've* been if Mom had let him in."

"Ah. Right."

But Olympia goes to Michigan anyway. There are dozens of pages for the state, as there are for most of the states in the Midwest.

"That's a lot of people," Tom says. "See? Someone's caught one."

"Well, if you consider the population seventeen years ago, this isn't that many. Remember when Mom told us about the phone book? And all the calls they made?"

"Yeah." Tom gets it. "And that was just for their immediate area."

"Exactly."

They flip through the names. Some are illegible. Others stand out.

"I got an idea," Tom says.

He hops up off Olympia's bed and goes to the dresser beside his own. From the top drawer he takes a pencil.

"Let's put our names in there anyway," he says.

Olympia is relieved. She'd been worried the list of modern cities might send her brother into weeks of self-reflection. Tom has gone quiet before. Especially when he starts thinking of the world outside the camp. Despite Malorie referring to him as "her optimist," Tom actually has long bouts of visible consternation. Olympia has read all about characters who get quiet when they get serious. But then again, she's also read of hundreds who've changed by the end of the story. And changed those around them.

Tom is beside her again. He takes the book from her and flips to the last page of Michigan names.

He writes *Camp Yadin* near the bottom of the page, where there's room. He writes his own name. He hands Olympia the pencil.

She likes this idea. She's smiling as she reads the seemingly infinite list of people. But her smile begins to sag as two names leap out at her, two that are familiar to her, though Malorie hardly ever refers to them by their actual names.

"What's up?" Tom asks.

Olympia is already flipping the page back, checking the name of the city where these two people were found.

"Olympia, what's going on? You look scared."

She doesn't even realize she's looking Tom in the eye now; all she sees are the two names written in chicken-scratch and the name *St. Ignace* like a banner, swinging weakly in a world decimated by creatures who drive you mad when you see them.

"Olympia, are you okay?"

"We have to get Mom, Tom."

"She's sweeping the camp. Besides, I don't want her to know about this—"

"We have to get Mom now."

THREE

Malorie thinks of Gary.

It makes sense. A man arrives at the camp. He knocks. He speaks from the other side of the door. All good intentions, of course. Until you let him in, of course. Then he makes friends with the others, ingratiates himself to the point where your own kids turn on you, and presto, you've welcomed an old-world madman into your life.

It's not hard to imagine Tom gravitating toward a man like Gary. A man who claims to know the truths of the new world. Nor is it difficult to imagine Olympia wooed by a stranger's tales of traveling the country, keeping notes on everything he's learned.

"Sweep the camp," she says. Tom and Olympia have assured her the man is gone, and truly, there's no better alarm system than their ears. Still, Malorie wants a look around. Did this man really just arrive, or had he been squatting in one of the other cabins for weeks? Tom was outside when he came. Does this mean something? All three of them were together when he knocked. Does this?

She gets to Cabin Eight quickly. She opens the door. Her hands are gloved, her arms and neck covered by the hoodie. She wears sweats and thick socks.

She thinks of Annette. The blind woman who went mad. Creature-mad.

How?

Before entering the cabin, she smells the air. If there's one sense that has gotten better through the years it's her sense of smell. She can tell when a storm is coming, when woods aren't far off. She can tell if something's died outside and whether a person has called a small space home.

At the threshold to Cabin Eight, she smells nothing but the empty must of wood and bunks without mattresses. Still, knife raised, she enters.

Camp Yadin has been good to her. So good. When they arrived, there were enough canned goods to last months. And seeds to begin gardens beyond that. Tools and toys. Shelter and a piano. A sailboat for the small lake. Paths to walk for exercise. Malorie knew they'd be staying for some time. But ten years have passed fast.

Tom and Olympia are not only teenagers now, they've been teenagers for a while.

She uses a thick stick to check the spaces between bunks, to poke under them. More than once she's been surprised by an animal calling a cabin home. But, in the new world, she's come to fear animals least of all. In her many interactions, she's discovered that acting angry makes them run. Even the mad ones (if she can ever be sure whether or not an animal is sane). Insects are more mysterious. Malorie doesn't know if spiders go mad. But she has found webs, here in camp, built in unsettling patterns, suggesting something was seen, something was close.

Of course, creatures have traveled the paths of the camp many times. Tom and Olympia have pointed them out from inside Cabin Three.

"Anybody here and you're gonna get stabbed," Malorie says.

She says these things to hear her own voice. She understands that, if the man who claimed to be from the census was actually in this bunk, if he was, say, crouched upon one of the beds she pokes beneath, he could easily kill her. But the kids say he left. And she has to believe that much.

Cabin Eight clean, she exits and takes the rope that leads to Cabin Nine. It's hot outside, the hottest day she can remember, but she isn't taking the hoodie off.

She thinks of Annette.

The kids don't believe you can go mad by way of touch. But the kids don't make the rules around here.

Malorie can still see the red-haired woman turning the corner of the bricked hall. The blue robe like blue wind, Annette's mouth contorted in a way only madness can shape. Malorie can still see the knife.

Her own knife touches the door to Cabin Nine before she does. She uses the tip to push it open.

She smells the air at the threshold.

All senses now, it seems. Sight, smell, touch. The creatures have rearranged how a person experiences reality. This is not new, of course, but Malorie, ever a child of the old world, will never get used to it. And if it's a matter of not being able to comprehend the creatures, as Tom the man once hypothesized, if it's a matter of going mad at the sight of something our minds simply cannot assimilate . . . why not the same fate by way of touch? Wouldn't any encounter by way of any of the senses constitute an *experience* with an impossible thing, a thing our minds cannot fathom?

She imagines wearing nose plugs, headphones to cancel sound.

She shudders as she enters the cabin. She thinks of Gary. How can she not? There was a time on the river when the fold was pulled from her eyes. And while she believed it to be a creature at the time, an unfathomable being wading in the water, what if it was Gary instead? It's not hard to imagine the man, shirtless, up to his waist, having tracked her for four years, having camped outside the home in which she raised the kids. It's not hard to imagine Gary in that river just like it's not hard to imagine him here, standing in this cabin she will not look into.

Maybe he waves.

Malorie uses the stick to poke under the bunks. The tip of it connects with something and, because she's piqued, because she's thinking of the dramatic, bearded demon from her past, she's chilled by the unknown object before realizing it's only a visor. Part of a helmet Tom had been hell-bent on making last summer.

Touching the visor with gloved fingers, she thinks of Annette again, or maybe it's that she's never stopped thinking of Annette and Gary, two horrible mysteries, as if the two had somehow raised her in the new world, the untrustworthy father and the mad mother who, together, birthed the overly protective, ever-on-edge Malorie of today.

"If anybody's in here, you're gonna get stabbed."

But nobody's in here. She can tell. And she's done a thorough sweep of the bunks, above, below, and between them.

She exits Cabin Nine and takes the rope to the lodge. There are many rooms in the lodge, including the kitchen and a basement, where much of the salvation for the past ten years has come from.

Sliding the fingers of her left hand along the rope, the knife held tight in her right, she tries to remember if she was touched when the fold was pulled an inch from her face on the river. And if she was … if something brushed against the bridge of her nose … what was it?

And who?

The walk to the lodge is uphill, but Malorie is in good shape. The best shape she's ever been in. She and her sister, Shannon, were never much for sports, despite Mom and Dad encouraging them to try. The girls would've rather walked around town than throw a ball, and neither had ever even attended so much as a high school football game. Yet here she is, able to hike for miles in a day, able to hold her own should someone be in the lodge ahead, confident with a knife and her ability to defend herself.

She doesn't want to think about Annette. She doesn't want to think about Gary. But she can't stop them from coming. As if they're constantly standing outside the cabin door of her mind. Constantly knocking.

Could you let me in for an hour or two?

Or ten years.

By the time she reaches the stone steps, she's so encumbered with thoughts of mad people and creatures, isolation and her kids, that she has to remind herself what she's doing.

She uses the knife to open the lodge door.

She steps over the threshold.

Annette stepped over the edge.

And what held her hand on the way?

Malorie smells the air. She listens. She has no doubt that, over the course of the past decade, she's stood close to many creatures. It's a fact of the new world she's had to accept. Tom and Olympia tell her there are many more now than there used to be. The man at the door said the same. But how many is that? And how much space do they now occupy?

She enters the lodge. Despite the high ceiling and open room, it's always hottest in here. Malorie thinks it's because of the tall windows, despite having painted those windows black long ago. Still, she's reminded of the saunas, so prevalent in the Upper Peninsula where she was raised, the steam boxes her mother and father insisted on each night before bed. By the time she's crossed the former common area where campers once took meals, she longs for the lake she and Shannon leaped into, following those saunas, running from the steaming rocks.

She stops. She thinks she's heard something. Movement. Something outside the lodge. But Camp Yadin plays tricks. Branches fall. Wind blows. Cabins creak.

She waits. She listens.

It is not lost on her how vulnerable she is at this moment. The man who claimed to be from the census could be standing in the corner of this room, preparing something. A creature could be inches from her face, observing, still, the effect they have on the people they should never have crossed paths with. But seventeen years into the new world, Malorie decides to treat her personal darkness differently. While she's certainly as staunch as the others at the school for the blind claimed she was, and while she may be partially *paranoid,* as her own son said while in a fit of rage, she's also able to pretend that the darkness she exists in does not include creatures and camps, life and death. Rather, she imagines she's walking through the home she grew up in. Dad is by the stove in the kitchen, listening to a game on a small radio that Mom tells him he keeps too close to the burner. Mom reads a book, sitting at the kitchen table, waiting for Shannon to take her turn at Scrabble.

This is a much nicer reality. And who's to say what's real in the dark?

As Malorie exits the common room, as she enters the hall that leads to the large kitchen in back, she can almost smell the venison Dad cooks, can hear Mom flip a page, can sense Shannon's deliberations. Nobody liked playing games with Shannon.

"If you think your mom is a perfectionist, Tom," Malorie says, "you shoulda met your aunt."

By the time she enters the kitchen, she's no longer in the home she grew up in; now she talks to Tom the man in the house she fled twelve years ago, talks about Gary.

"Stop it," she tells herself. It isn't easy. Yet years of this back-and-forth, a decade and a half of horrific memories springing like attractions in a haunted house at the Marquette County Fair, have lessened the grip these bad thoughts have on her. Despite what Tom her son might believe, Malorie does not live in fear.

She swipes the knife in front of her face as she exits the kitchen and takes the stairs to the lodge's basement. She does this because more than once she's passed through a web at the head of the steps. And more than once she's brought the brown spiders back to Cabin Three.

"If anybody is down here, they're gonna get stabbed."

Despite the fold, despite her eyes being closed, Malorie still senses that she's entered utter darkness. The unmistakable cellar smell of cold concrete and mold. It used to be she'd hurry to find the dangling cord, to bring light to a space like this. But if there's one thing the new world has incrementally destroyed, it's a fear of the dark.

She crosses the mostly open area and tells herself she's only here to grab canned goods. Could be her and Shannon retrieving cranberries for the Thanksgiving meal Mom and Dad cook together upstairs. Could be the canned goods Tom the man showed her the first morning she woke in the house on Shillingham. Or it could be what it is: Malorie searching the shelf for beans, able to pick them out among the other cans because the lids are different.

"Used to be a lot more on this shelf."

No question about that. And it feels good to assess, to do what she normally does, while listening for movement and keeping her nose open for a squatting human being who most likely pretends to be with the census.

"Who does he think he is?" she asks, unable to find the beans after all. Sometimes the gloved fingertips make this sort of task a little harder. "What did he expect me to do? Just let him in?"

As she removes the glove, as the county fair house of horrors vision of a creature reaching out and touching her exposed hand momentarily rattles her, she wonders how a man can claim to be from the census in a country where there is no organization anymore.

She finds the beans quickly and slips the glove back on.

She turns to face the basement.

Did she hear something? Something above?

The teens know the rules, but of course that doesn't mean the teens follow them. When Malorie sweeps the camp, they are to remain in Cabin Three. It's a waste of time to investigate sounds made by either Tom or Olympia while she's out making sure the three of them are still alone.

"If anybody's here," she begins. But she doesn't finish this time. Despite the fact that she's gotten very good at living with fear, she's still not immune to moments of abject horror. Like when she's standing in the basement of an abandoned camp lodge, and a man she did not see the face of was just moments ago knocking on her cabin door.

The image of a gun spins in her personal darkness. Olympia thinks they should get one. She cites the thousand books she's read and how guns have saved more than one character's life. But Malorie has been strict on this from the beginning. The last thing she wants in this camp is a tool Tom might use in the name of progress. It's not hard to imagine opening a cabin door and getting shot at by a pre-prepositioned rifle, as Tom prides himself on a triumphant invention. And, of course, it's not only Tom she doesn't trust with one. It's any of them, in the event one should see something they shouldn't.

Yet, here, now, it feels like something more than her sense of purpose and a sharp knife could be helpful.

She listens.

She smells.

She waits.

She has done these three things so often over the last ten years that she hardly remembers a time when she didn't. Sometimes, her new-world behavior seeps into her memories of the old. Didn't she sniff the air every time she entered Shannon's bedroom as a child? Didn't she ask Mom and Dad if their eyes were closed when they came home from the store?

There is no past and present behind the fold. No linear lines of any kind.

The beans in one hand, the knife in the other, and the searching stick under her arm, Malorie crosses the basement again and arrives at the stairs quicker than she thought she would.

She's scared.

It's not the nicest thing to realize. Because once it begins, once the initial, hot tendrils tickle your arms and legs, flow down your back and calves, it's hard to stop the feeling from growing to its full size: panic.

She turns to face the open basement. Did something move deeper in as she came farther out? No man is down here. She believes Tom and Olympia are right that he left, because their ears have never let her down before.

But does *something* share this space with her?

She hears Tom the man begging to be let into the attic as she gave birth to, if not his son, his namesake.

The kids know the rules, yes. They know to keep still until she returns from her sweep. Unless, of course, there's an emergency.

"Fuck you," she says to the open space. To the creatures, too.

Because sometimes it helps.

Then she's hurrying up the stairs just like she and Shannon used to do as kids. Cranberries or a book in hand, the girls would race, side by side, elbowing each other to get to the top first. Malorie remembers falling on the stairs once, scraping both elbows, seeing between the steps the face of her old stuffed Sylvester the Cat and taking the rest of the steps at a screaming run.

Now she's up in the kitchen again. She's breathing hard. She's trying to understand how a man could call himself part of any census. She's thinking about what he said about someone catching a creature.

"Why did you have to say that in front of Tom . . ."

Because Tom will not only believe something like that, he'll want to be near it.

She takes her steps slow on the way back to the common area. She pauses to listen between each. A thing she's discovered in the new world is the brief intake of breath a person takes before speaking. And the sound they make when they shift their weight from one foot to another.

Does she hear any of this now?

Malorie waits. She thinks of the man's voice and, while she doesn't want to admit it, she believes his aim was true. She'll never believe she's gotten to the point where she can judge character from behind a blindfold. And she'll never make the mistake Don made with Gary. But she's open-minded enough to think perhaps a census has to start somewhere.

As she crosses the space, she resists a sense of guilt, for having denied the man his hour or two, for not listening to what he had to say, for not telling him her own stories. Maybe she knows things others don't. Maybe she could've helped.

"No," she says, as she reaches the lodge door. No, because no matter how much the new world improves around her and her teens, she will always, *always* rely on the fold and the fold alone.

She opens the door, takes a step, and bumps into a person.

She makes to swing the knife, but Olympia speaks before she does.

"Mom! It's me and Tom!"

It takes Malorie a second before she believes it. All these thoughts of Annette and Gary, creatures and a man who says he's one thing but could be another.

"What are you doing?" Malorie asks. Her voice sounds red. "You know the rules!"

"It's an emergency," Olympia says.

"Mom," Tom says. "Seriously. You need to hear this."

"It's the man at the door," Malorie says.

"No," Olympia says. "Not exactly."

Malorie waits. She listens.

"The man left the literature," Tom says.

"What?" Malorie asks.

She imagines pictures of creatures. She imagines the teens losing their young minds by way of a photograph left on the porch.

"You didn't—" she begins. But Olympia cuts her off.

"Mom. There are pages and pages, lists of survivors."

Malorie feels something dark swirling inside her. Did they find Gary's name on that list?

"Come on!" she says. "Speak!"

When Olympia does, she's standing closer to Malorie, and

Malorie knows it's because her daughter believes she might need a stabilizing hand.

"In St. Ignace, Michigan, Mom," Olympia says.

"What? What about it?" But St. Ignace is in the Upper Peninsula. Where Malorie is from. And the city name, coming from Olympia's lips, coupled with the word *survivors,* suggests something Malorie is not prepared to hear.

"Your parents' names are on the list, Mom. Their names are on the list of survivors. Your parents are alive."

FOUR

Malorie can't sit still in what was once the lodge's main office. The desk still harbors some of the items the long-ago director used daily. A magnetized rectangle for paper clips. A yellow pad for notes. A calendar seventeen years old. There was once a two-way mirror in here, so the campers couldn't see the director observing them eating below in the common area. But that mirror has long been tucked beneath Tom's bed, materials for proposed inventions Malorie won't let him build, and a black cloth hangs in the open space instead.

She refuses to believe the news. Even the possibility of it. Then she believes it. Then she refuses. Believes it again. She's seen the names with her own eyes now. Sam and Mary Walsh. Common names, she tells herself. So many Sams. Even more Marys. And Walsh . . .

But the exact combination, and the fact that they are listed in the Upper Peninsula, is actually hurting her. It's a variety of pain, in her stomach, her bones, her heart, she's never known before.

Seventeen years ago Shannon accompanied Malorie to buy a pregnancy test. The world had already changed irrevocably by then, but the sisters didn't know it yet. The last time Malorie spoke to her parents, she told them of the baby. Then Sam and Mary Walsh stopped answering their phone.

Seventeen years.

Tom and Olympia know to leave her alone with this. They are in what used to be the secretary's office, the outer office, as Malorie sits, then stands, then sits, in here, the pages spread before her on the desk. The door is shut. She swept the room before removing her fold.

She reads the names again.

"How?"

Even this word hurts. She should be moving. North. Toward them. This is every griever's fantasy, to see Mom and Dad once more. To say the things she never said.

She should leave. *Now.*

But . . . is this real?

And how old is this list? How many years gone? The pages suggest the man who claimed to be from the census traveled most of the Midwest. And how long has that taken? Is such a thing even possible? And is this his first visit to Michigan? Or did he note these names, the names of Malorie's parents, a decade ago?

Oh, she should've let him in.

The Sam and Mary Walsh Malorie knew lived near the Wisconsin border. They'd have no reason to go to St. Ignace, to the bridge that unites Michigan's two peninsulas. Even when facing the end of the world. *Especially* then. Shannon used to joke that the Upper Peninsula *is* the end of the world. So why would Sam and Mary have migrated south?

Did they come . . . looking for their daughters?

She can't breathe. It's simply too heavy. She feels like she could faint. Or worse.

She paces the office, her eyes darting back to the names on the page. She can't calm down, can't formulate a single solid opinion. She imagines Sam and Mary Walsh surviving as long as she has, the sorrows and horrors they would have endured, the unfathomable stress of living in a world so different than the one they raised their children in.

She wants Tom the man to be here with her. She wants to hear what he would say.

Did she and Shannon give up on their parents too soon? Neither had anything to go on other than the silence from Sam and Mary's end and the thought that, perhaps, their parents were not the survivor type.

But was Malorie? When this all began . . . was *she* the survivor type?

"Fuck."

"Mom?"

It's Olympia, from the outer office.

Maybe Mom and Dad have changed, too. If there's one thing Malorie has learned while raising these kids, it's that parenthood is not static. Parenthood does not stand still. And the mother of two teens in the new world undergoes alterations, sudden instinctual thrusts, almost as powerful as the creatures she protects them from.

"No," Malorie says. Because . . . there's just no way. No way her parents are still alive in Michigan, gardening blindfolded and painting their windows black. There's no way they've endured the horrors she has and still hold hands the way they once did, always did, sitting beside each other on the couch.

She feels dizzy. Faint. She sits on the edge of the old desk and stares into the abyss of her past, her childhood, life in the old world, so long ago now and so severely, maddeningly different.

Seventeen years.

Seventeen years ago she found out she was pregnant with Tom. Only he wasn't "Tom" yet. Malorie had yet to meet her son's namesake, the man who had such a profound impact on her that she still asks him, silently, for advice on every decision she makes, sixteen years after his death. Is it possible her parents are *alive*? In a world where they didn't even meet the man she named her son after? And if so, what unspeakable occurrences have they lived through?

Who has helped them survive?

"They're not alive," she says. Because there's just no way. It's too much, too huge. Every time she hears Olympia giving her the news, the names, Malorie hears the smile that must have been present on her daughter's face. It's driving her mad. Doesn't her bright, impossibly hopeful daughter know that what she told her is actually *untrue*? They simply can't be alive. The list is wrong. There are a thousand Sam and Mary Walshes. There's no census. The man somehow got her parents' names and wrote them onto the pages, Trojan-horsing his actual intent; getting Malorie and her kids to leave the safety they've finally found.

The man is trying to destroy the peace and security of Camp Yadin.

Maybe, just maybe, the man was actually Gary.

Malorie punches the desk. Then she gets behind it, looks hard at the names on the page. It's been a long time since she rifled through Gary's briefcase and found his dangerous thoughts written down, but she doesn't think she'll ever forget the tilt of his hand, the dark electricity that was present on every page.

She studies the handwriting.

And she knows.

This is not Gary's writing. It's not even close to the same.

She looks to the office door, thinks of her teens on the other side. She knows they must be imagining a journey out, similar to their journey in, ten years gone. Tom must be excited by this. Olympia is probably already preparing.

But do they really believe this list? Has she raised them to be so naïve? This impossible, absolutely insane list of . . . of . . .

"Survivors," Malorie says.

She wants to break something. She wants to punch a hole in the office wall. She wants to kick the desk over.

So she does.

She plants a shoe against the edge of the desk and shoves as hard as she can, sending the old thing onto its side. The pages scatter like white birds leaping from a falling tree, and Olympia hollers, "Mom! Mom! Are you okay?"

She sounds scared. In the new world, when you hear someone lash out from the other side of a door, it's not hard to imagine something is in there with them.

"I'm fine," Malorie yells. "I'm fucking *fine*."

She hears the teens whispering on the other side. Tom is no doubt asking Olympia why Malorie would be upset by this news and Olympia is no doubt explaining exactly why.

Because it's been seventeen years. Because she believed they were dead. Because she grieved already and because she's felt the insatiable loss of Sam and Mary Walsh for so long that it's become part of her now.

And this? This sudden list?

This is *mean*.

Malorie cries. She doesn't want to but she can't stop it. She imagines Gary sitting across a table from a younger man, promising the man money or gold or whatever is still worth something out in the new world, if only the rube play the part of a census man. Write all these notes down for me, son, and deliver it to Cabin Three of Camp Yadin. Can you do that for me? Can you sneak these two names like worms for a fish through the front door of Cabin Three at Camp Yadin?

Big fish in there. Big to me.

"No way," Malorie says. "There's just no way. This isn't real. This isn't possible. This is not happening."

But, beyond the desk, her parents' names are still visible on the spilled pages.

Sam and Mary Walsh.

Not Gary's hand.

And something else, too. Another page, having risen to the top of the pile, as the papers went fluttering through the office. As if this particular page were trying to survive, too. A description of a mode of travel, yes, another impossibility, the proof Malorie needs to officially deny any and all of this.

The Blind Train.

Ah, yes. The man who claimed to be from the census mentioned a train.

One that heads north.

Malorie feels hot. Like someone is watching her. *Has been* watching her. Like the walls of the new world are closing in.

No to all of this. Absolutely *no*. It's too inviting, all too perfectly arranged for her to gather her teens and leave the relative tranquility of this place they call home and *have* called home for ten years. She can sense the worm lowering into the water. Can feel the hunger, wanting to taste it. It's easy to imagine Gary waiting for her on a platform in the dark.

Her parents are dead. They've been dead for seventeen years.

Malorie picks up the page that describes the train. She begins to read it, then lets it fall to the floor.

No.

No way.

She's not leaving this camp. The camp that has kept them safe. The place where Tom and Olympia have grown from children into adults, immensely intelligent teens who can hear all the way to the gates of the camp and who are happy without even knowing why. She will not jeopardize their lives for closure in her own.

She makes for the office door, momentarily assured with her decision to ignore the whole thing. The names on that page. The existence of a census at all.

She looks down once more to the pages on the floor.

The names stand out to her, even now, as she stands far from them, at the door, her hand on the knob. The names seem to be written in something like steel, impossible to remove, hardier than she is. As if the names themselves wear blindfolds and will therefore survive this new world long after Malorie succumbs to it.

She closes her eyes.

She opens the office door then closes it again without leaving the room.

She returns to the page about the train.

"Mom?" Tom calls from the outer office. "You need help in there?"

She doesn't answer. She reads:

Because of the existing tracks, a train is the safest mode of transportation in the new world. No fear of driving up onto a curve, hitting a parked car, hitting a person.

No. *No.* It's too good. Too possible. And nothing, Malorie knows, absolutely nothing is so ready-made these days.

But she reads on.

So long as the tracks are clear, and the machine travels at a slow enough speed . . .

Malorie looks away. She feels pain. Literal, physical, pain. *Are* her parents alive? Have they been alive this whole time?

She thinks of Shannon's face, telling her they weren't answering their phone anymore. She thinks of Shannon's dead body upstairs.

By her own hand.

The guilt for not having sought out Sam and Mary Walsh, to verify their deaths, is almost too rich to endure. It's been seventeen years.

The Blind Train runs on tracks between Lansing, Michigan, and Mackinaw City, Michigan.

Mackinaw City, Malorie thinks. The very tip of the Lower Peninsula. The bottom of the bridge that connects it to the Upper.

The train travels at no more than five miles an hour. It runs on coal. The windows are painted black. I know almost nothing more about it for I have yet to ride it myself.

"Nope," Malorie says.

But she's already feeling the very tips of the fingers of *yes*.

She closes her eyes and exits the inner office.

"Mom," Olympia says.

"I need to speak with Ron Handy," she says.

"The door is closed, Mom," Tom says.

She opens her eyes. She sees her two teens looking back at her with flushed faces. This must all be so incredibly exciting to them. This unreality. This lie.

"We'll walk you there," Tom says. "We can use my—"

"No," she says. "I need to speak to him alone."

She needs to speak to an adult is what she needs. Even one twice as paranoid as herself.

Ron Handy is the closest neighbor they have. At three miles, the former gas station he dwells in is far, but close enough.

She needs the self-proclaimed Humorous Hermit because

she can hardly breathe. It feels like, any second, her parents could die again. If they are alive, if they also survived these seventeen years, what's to stop them from dying right now . . . right now . . .

RIGHT NOW?

"Jesus," she says. She can't get a firm hold on any of her reactions, opinions, feelings. She imagines herself on a blind train. She imagines the people who run it. She imagines herself and her teens waiting at a train station for a month, a year, ten years, never knowing when the train is coming, not allowed to look up the tracks for a headlight in the distance.

Olympia steps to her, takes her hand.

"It's okay," she says. "It's gonna be okay."

But the words bring Malorie no comfort. It's been seventeen years.

"I need to talk to Ron Handy," she says again. Then she's tying her blindfold around her head, a motion she's done so many times that it's as natural as tucking her hair behind her ears.

"Close your eyes," she tells them. Even now. Even as the reality she's finally gotten used to has been cracked again, as she feels the physical pain of grief's reversal or perhaps grief all over again, even now she tells her teens to close their eyes.

"Okay," Olympia says.

"Closed," Tom says.

Malorie opens the office door and steps out onto a wood floor that feels too sturdy, doesn't conform to her idea of life right now, doesn't line up with the absolute darkness she falls through, a place where it's impossible to decipher the right or wrong thing to do.

FIVE

Malorie discovered Ron Handy before she found Camp Yadin. A decade ago, she'd smelled the distant odor of gasoline, walking her then six-year-olds in search of a new home. Hoping for canned goods or packaged snacks, she followed the scent to what she couldn't have known was his home, a fortified service station on the side of a Michigan country road. Ron Handy lives behind wood boards, fat mattresses, car doors, and layers of sheet metal. As far as Malorie knows, he won't even remove his blindfold inside.

Now, as she reaches the gravel shoulder of that same road, her nerves electrified, her head dizzy with too many possibilities, she realizes it's been three years since she's visited him. Ron has never come into Camp Yadin. Ron doesn't leave his place. Ever.

The old-world instinct of looking both ways before crossing the street has long been exterminated, and Malorie hurries across the gravel to the pebbled gas station lot. For all she knows, Ron

Handy is dead inside, rotting, mad flies buzzing and breeding on his remains.

She thinks of Sam and Mary Walsh rotting, too.

She reaches the fortress, shin first, banging against something hard. If Ron's alive inside, he's heard her. But she knocks on a wall of wood all the same.

"Malorie?"

It's been three years and she's still the last person he's seen. She knows this now.

"Yes, Ron. It's me."

The desperation in her voice frightens her. Did she make sure Tom and Olympia were safe and secure in Cabin Three? Did she hurry out too fast?

A series of clicks tell her that Ron is doing the equivalent of what was once simply called unlocking doors. Now it sounds more like he's moving a thousand small objects out of the way.

She hears close creaking. What feels like dark air accosts her. Stuffy. Sour. The scent of an unwashed man opening the door to his windowless home.

"Malorie!"

He sounds excited but tired. Even the one word has the aristocratic lilt Malorie encountered ten years ago. She knows that Ron is what people in the old world would have called "too smart for his own good."

"Hi, Ron," she says. "You got a minute?"

Ron laughs. Because it's funny. Because all he has is minutes, alone in his bunker of blindness.

"I was expecting a cadre of friends and family, but they seem to be running late," he says. "We've just enough time for crumpets."

Malorie wants to smile. She wants to make anxious jokes

about the horrors like Ron Handy does. But her parents' names are circling through her head like vultures, waiting for the hope to die.

"Something bothering you?" Ron asks. "Something with the kids? Who, might I add, are not kids any longer?"

"Did someone come by here, Ron? A man saying he was from the census?"

She can't see his face, but she knows this question will scare him. The mere mention of an outsider claiming to be anything is enough to send Ron Handy back inside without a word.

But he remains. And when he speaks, Malorie can hear the effort of doing so in his voice.

"No. Unless I was asleep. Or perhaps so far gone into my own head that I mistook his knocking for a thought." But the joke falls flat between them. Then, "Why not come inside? I don't much like the exterior world these days."

Blind, impatient, shell-shocked, Malorie steps inside. She waits as he slides everything back in place by the door.

"I used to live in the office," Ron says. "But there's a particular window in there that I do not like. I've covered it two dozen times over, but I just . . . do not like it."

He touches her hand, and Malorie almost cries out.

"So I moved. Now I live where they once kept the supplies. Filters and rotors. Cans of oil. Can't say I haven't considered drinking one."

"Ron . . ."

"Well, what? I don't wear the new world very well. And I'm okay with that."

He tugs on her hand, leading her deeper into his home. The moving is easier than she remembers, less junk in the way, and she understands that even a man who lives like this must make home improvements over time.

But the smell is as bad as it's ever been. Gasoline and sweat. Piss and possibly more.

She follows him through what could be a proper hallway but is probably only a path through stacks of clutter.

"Here," he says at last.

Malorie thinks of her parents.

Impossible.

"A drink?" Ron asks. "I have a little whiskey left. And I haven't found cause enough to down it."

"No," Malorie says. "But thank you."

"Well, at least take a seat. Would you believe I keep two chairs? It's probably a bad idea. There are times I believe I'm not alone."

He makes to take Malorie's other hand and feels the stack of papers instead.

"What's this?" he asks, heavy suspicion in his voice.

"The man from the census left these on our porch. It's why I'm here."

She expects Ron to ask her to leave. But he only takes her other hand and guides her to a wooden stool.

Malorie sits but it's not easy to stay still.

"Do you know anything about a train, Ron?"

Suddenly it strikes her how insane this is. How desperate she is for another opinion. Ron Handy hasn't left this space in years.

"The Blind Train," Ron says. "I've heard of it."

Malorie's voice comes out quicker than planned.

"What do you know?"

"First I'll introduce to you the medium by which I heard of it," he says. "But I warn you . . . what I'm about to play frightens me deeply. And I won't listen to it for very long. If the sight of them drives us mad . . . what might the sound of them do?"

Malorie rubs her gloved hands along the long sleeves she

wears. She thinks of redheaded Annette running mad with a knife through the school for the blind.

A radio squawks. Malorie recoils. Before she speaks, she hears a distant voice. A man says, "... *I used to enjoy that very much!*"

Then the radio goes silent again.

"So, you see," Ron says, "not as cut off as I seem to be. It was upon those very waves that I heard *mention* of a train. I can only assume your question has something to do with that stack of papers I felt in your hand."

"It does."

"And I also assume that you brought it here for me to read, which means, of course, that I would have to remove my fold to do so."

Malorie doesn't allow the moment to balloon. She senses that, if she waits another few seconds, Ron isn't going to read what the man left on her porch. He's going to find an excuse for her to leave.

"There's a list of survivors in here. By city and state."

"Really?"

"Yes. And my parents are on the list."

"Oh ... Malorie ..."

She hears the empathy in his voice. Then the long-forgotten sound of alcohol poured into an empty glass.

"Here," Ron says. "I've determined you were wrong. You *do* need a drink. And if I'm going to remove my fold ... I'm going to need one, too."

Malorie has not seen Ron Handy before. She's only heard his voice. The dozen times she's spoken with him, whether from outside his service station or in it, she's never removed her own. Ron has asked that of her. To protect himself.

She feels a glass against the back of her hand. She takes it.

"Are we ready then?" Ron asks.

But Malorie hears concern in his voice. He's nervous. She's nervous. What will she see? What will Ron Handy look like?

"You don't have to do this," she says.

"But it feels like I do," Ron says.

Malorie hears him breathe deep. Hears him stand.

"Oh, my," he says. "You're very pretty. I had no idea I was living so close to a dream." Then, "You're wearing long sleeves and a hood. On a hot day. You're worried they might touch you."

Malorie removes her fold. Ron Handy, larger than she imagined, looks like a big, scared child. They share uneasy smiles.

"Yes."

"You told me about the blind woman who went mad. Can't quit thinking of that?"

"No."

"I understand."

They stare at each other a beat. Take each other in. Malorie sees fear and exhaustion in his face. She wonders if, in the old world, Ron Handy was wealthy.

"Thank you," she says, "for calling me pretty. Living with two teens . . . I haven't had a compliment like that in a long time."

Ron reaches his glass toward her. They cheer.

"To company," he says. "And to retaining our senses, no matter how many they try to take from us."

They drink.

Malorie marvels at the amount of stuff that surrounds him. Odds and ends are piled floor to ceiling. She sees the radio. A cot. Boxes of wires and tools. Canned goods and blankets. Paint cans, magazines, and gasoline. Ron stands beside a foldout lounge chair. He wears a sport jacket and shorts.

"Not where I once imagined myself to be." Ron smiles. "But who knows . . . it might be better than where I was heading!"

He laughs. Malorie wants to, but she simply can't.

Sam and Mary Walsh.

It feels like, if she doesn't start moving now, she's going to miss the very last breath they take.

"No photos in there?" Ron asks, acknowledging the papers. She sees the paranoia in his eyes. The shiftiness. The fear.

"No. I worried about the same thing. It's all notes and diagrams."

"What else?"

"A lot."

Ron nods. He looks Malorie in the eye.

"Why do I feel afraid?"

Malorie experiences an emotion she hasn't felt in a decade or more: kinship with a fellow adult. It's large enough to bring tears to her eyes. But she doesn't allow them passage yet.

She hands Ron the stack of papers.

"The stuff about the train is on top," she says.

Ron eyes the stack. He sips from his glass.

"Well, I suppose, for me, this is a sort of reckoning."

"How?"

He smiles. "You might do all you can to avoid the new world, but it's going to come knocking, in some form or another, soon enough."

Malorie thinks of the census man. Ron squints as he reads the top page. He nods.

"On the radio, it was said the train was functioning. The host, if you could call him that, he's literally alone, so he's everything, he said he'd never take it himself."

"What did he know about it?"

"He said he didn't think it was safe."

"Why not?"

"I imagine that's because it's a blind train, Malorie."

Ron eyes her. It's supposed to be funny. Malorie doesn't know, maybe it is.

"Yes," Ron says, reading again. "Lansing. Although I actually heard it was *East* Lansing. There is a difference, you know."

"I do."

A university town. An agriculture school. Michigan State.

"How far are we from East Lansing?" she asks.

But Ron is focusing on the paper.

"It really is very interesting," he says. "Preordained paths, I mean. Train tracks. By this logic, the only other safe form of travel in the new world would be by roller coaster. Any desire to see Cedar Point, Malorie?"

Ron doesn't look at her long enough for her to have to smile.

"How far is it?" she asks again.

"It's about thirty miles. But of course that's something you'd want to be sure of before setting out on foot."

Malorie senses the world sinking. The hope she feels, the hope she cannot deny, partially turns to dust. She almost stands up. Ron sits down.

"Thirty miles," she says. "There's just . . . just no way."

Ron nods. "It's a tall order. Your stories of twenty miles on a river are mind-boggling enough."

"Fuck."

When she looks at Ron, he's staring back at her. He looks inquisitive, almost like he's observing her making a decision. Like he's wondering what it takes to do something brave.

"In the old world," Ron says, "thirty miles on foot would take about eight hours. That's at fifteen minutes a mile."

"With sight," Malorie says. "And walking a straight line."

"So double it. Triple it. Even more. I'd say it could take three days."

Malorie thinks.

"I don't mean to be the bearer of worse news," Ron says, "but there's no guarantee the train is still there. Or how often it runs. Or what the people are like, the sort of people who would consider running such a thing."

The dread he's espousing is palpable, as if Ron has just tossed her a black hole to catch.

He leans forward, causing the lounger to creak. "Imagine the type of person who feels confident enough, in this world, to engineer a train. Sound inviolable to you?"

Malorie sees madness. Annette in that engineer's seat. Gary strutting car to car, taking tickets.

"No," she says. She tries to give the word finality, but it's simply not there. Not in her voice. Not in her heart.

"But hang on," Ron says. "Let's read some more, talk some more, before we give up. Yes?"

Malorie stands. She paces as Ron continues to scan the pages. Her thoughts ping-pong, fast, images of Mom and Dad gardening under the sun. Still. Alive. No idea their daughter is breathing and sane and thinking about them right now.

Oh, what she could do for them by showing up at their home with grandkids in tow.

She sits back down. Then she stands. Then she sits again. Dad was good with chopping wood. Both were good cooks. Both could live off the land. Why would they go near the bridge?

Did someone take them there? Force them there? And even if Malorie did go, how can she be sure she'd find them?

The census man found them.

The thought is a good one. It's clear, and it means something.

"Safer Room," Ron says. When Malorie looks to him, she sees he's deeper into the stack of pages. "Did you read about these? What fancies . . ."

"Safer Room?" Malorie asks.

Ron smiles, but there's heaviness to him now. Malorie doesn't imagine he'll be joking anymore during this visit.

"His words: *Twelve-by-eight-foot holes in the ground. Bunkers for safety. If ever the creatures take over.* Well, I don't like the sound of *that*."

Malorie wants to tell Ron not to worry. He's survived ten years in this service station. He doesn't have to think about Safer Rooms. He doesn't have to think about the outside world at all. She can see the paranoia expanding in his eyes. The way he looks at her over his glass as he takes another sip. Like he's suddenly angry she's here.

"Sounds like a grave," she says. Because she knows Ron Handy is smart. He'll know it if she placates him.

"Indeed. No underground bunkers for me," he says. "I like to keep mine aloft."

So another joke after all. Good. Ron reads. Malorie, having seen some of what's in there, thinks to warn him. But she's too late.

"Oh, no," Ron says. "Oh, *no*."

He tosses the stack to the oil-stained floor. He wipes his hands on his sport coat. The look in his eyes is a fear Malorie hasn't seen in a long time. Even the housemates didn't look quite as scared as Ron does now.

"Did you *see*?" he asks her, his voice an octave higher.

"See what?" Malorie asks. She tries not to imagine a drawing. A photo. What did she miss in the stack?

But that's not what Ron means.

"Someone says they . . . *caught* one?"

"Just rumor," Malorie says quickly. "That's impossible."

"But to even think to *try*?"

Ron sets his drink on a stack of paint cans. He wipes his hands on his coat again, as if, by doing so, he might erase the fact that he's touched papers suggesting a creature could be caught.

"Oh, Malorie," Ron says. "It's too much. All of this. It's *overwhelming me.*"

"I'm sorry, Ron," Malorie says. She should go. She should get up and leave this place. Why did she come here?

"My sister's name is in there, too," Ron suddenly says.

"What?"

He rises and turns his back to her.

"My sister's *name,* Malorie." He's almost shouting now.

"On the survivor list?" Malorie asks. She looks to the pages he's discarded.

"*Yes.* My sister is on the list, too. What don't you understand about that? *My sister is on the list!*"

Malorie doesn't know what to say. Here she hasn't processed her own news yet.

She bends and takes up the papers.

"My God," Ron says. "My God, my God, my *God.*"

Malorie doesn't read the words in her lap. She only feels the presence of Ron's emotions. The sadness, the futility, the fact that he's just learned of his sister having survived at least the arrival of the creatures. Here, a paranoid hermit has gotten word of something worth venturing into the new world for.

Ron sits again. He's smiling, but his expression scares her. As if his eyes are made of black cloth. As if he isn't capable of seeing her at all.

His hand slides to the chair's armrest. He lifts the blindfold and, smiling yet, secures it around his head.

Malorie doesn't know what to say. She shouldn't say anything at all. She should go.

"Thank you for letting me in, Ron," she says. Then she asks it because she feels as though she must. "Would you take that train to see your sister again?"

"Hmm?" Like he doesn't know what she's talking about. Like she's brought up a subject from some hours ago, a trifle in the course of more important matters. "Oh, that? I wouldn't have to. She was listed as a survivor in Saugatuck. South of us."

Malorie waits. But she can't stop herself.

"Maybe . . ." she begins. "Maybe it'd be good for you . . . to . . ."

Ron's hand darts out and blasts the volume on the ham radio. He moves fast and the sound is loud and Malorie's already setting the rest of her drink on the floor and rising to leave.

Ron twists the dial. He's speaking to her, Malorie can see his mouth move, but the radio inhales the words.

She wants to thank him. Wants to tell him he doesn't have to go looking for his sister today. He could go tomorrow. He can do whatever he wants whenever he wants to. He's earned that.

He doesn't have to seek her out at all.

But . . .

But he should.

It strikes her then, a truth erupting from nothingness. Yes, Ron Handy should search for his sister. Otherwise he will die, as he is now, living in this squalor and confinement, no sense of purpose, no purpose at all.

Suddenly, with violent clarity, Malorie knows she's going to search for her parents.

The physical rush following this decision steals her breath.

She secures her fold. A voice comes through the radio, a woman.

"They're not necessarily taller than they were before . . . but wider. They take up more space . . ."

Ron kicks the radio.

"Oh, just go away!" he yells. But does he speak to the creatures . . . or Malorie? "Take the train," he says then, turning the radio down. "Oh, please, Malorie, for both of us. *Take the train.*"

She doesn't have to see his eyes to know that he's crying.

"I'm going to," she says. And her eyes don't have to be open for her to cry, either. "Ron, I'm sorry I upset you. You didn't do anything to deserve this today. I'm so sorry."

"Take the train, Malorie."

Then, as if it's the only way for him to survive, as if it's what's kept him alive this long, Ron laughs.

"Now, shoo, you!" Levity again. "I'm expecting a murder of friends to arrive any minute and I have sprucing to do."

"Thank you, Ron."

She's thinking of a blind train. And the distance between here and there. Thirty miles roll out before her like a fallen spool, thread unraveling from her once stable fingers, never to be wound perfect again.

Get to the train.

Take it.

To her parents.

"Malorie?" Ron asks. As if he isn't sure she's still here.

"Yes?"

"Take those filthy pages with you, if you don't mind. I don't want anybody thinking I read that sort of stuff. I'm a respected man, after all. A scholar. And it's important for us thinkers to keep doing what we do best. Waiting for that inevitable death. At peace. And alone."

SIX

Tom packs his one bag. But he wants to bring two. He wants to bring a lot. What better place to experiment with his inventions than in the real world? He considers hiding some from Malorie. And if he can't fit them in, maybe he doesn't need a change of pants, a change of shoes, or even food after all.

Malorie is up at the lodge, hurriedly gathering canned goods for what she told him and Olympia is going to be "a long trip." Neither of the teens has traveled very far from Camp Yadin since they arrived ten years ago. Tom remembers the river well. The school for the blind. The long, winding journey that delivered them here. And here is home. Has *been* home. He knows every sound in this place, every creak, the wind through the trees, the wind across the lake. Malorie didn't have to tell him she was going to the lodge; she could've just gone, and Tom would've heard it all play out, just as he has, just as he heard the lodge door open and close upon her entrance.

"Are you scared?" Olympia asks.

Tom looks to her across the cabin. Olympia's bed is on the opposite side of the space, a distance they agreed upon two years ago.

"Of what?" he asks. But he can't hide it. His voice trembles. And besides, Olympia seems to see things nobody else does.

She doesn't respond with words. Only a serious look that's meant to underscore the horrors of the world they are about to enter. In this moment, she looks like Malorie to Tom, despite not being related by blood.

"I'm sufficiently scared," Tom says. He's on his knees by his bunk, eyeing the many inventions he's kept under his bed. One is something close to the viewfinders people once viewed eclipses through. It's not lost on him that the census papers listed a similar method as being an eventual cause of madness. He can't help but wonder what else he's been proud of that won't work. But he doesn't let these thoughts linger. He moves what's left of the office's two-way mirror out of the way and reaches for more.

"She's going to need our ears in a big way," Olympia says.

"I know."

"And she's gonna need us in other ways, too."

Tom doesn't look at her when he responds.

"What does that mean?" he asks.

"It means she's gotta be feeling a lot."

"Maybe you read too many books, Olympia."

"Hey, I'm serious."

"Feelings? You really think Mom has those kinds of feelings? All she cares about is the blindfold."

He lifts a helmet from the floor. The visor is supposed to close over the eyes when he presses the line switch. But it doesn't work right now.

"Are you kidding me?" Olympia asks. "Tell me you're kidding."

"She lives entirely by rules," Tom says. "There's not much room for invention in there."

"She lives by the blindfold, yes," Olympia says. "And so do we."

"Do we?" Now he does turn to face her. "We've *grown up* in this world, Olympia. Don't you think we know it better than she does?"

Olympia's cheeks redden the way they do when he exacerbates her.

"Tom. Listen to me. Today isn't the day to make a stand. She's scared to death as it is. We've got thirty miles to walk. Do you have any idea how far that is?"

"We're more than that from the school for the blind. We've done it before. We were fine."

"And blindfolded."

Tom looks back to his inventions. A Hula-Hoop that is to be worn like a belt so that the hoop touches anything before the body does. The plastic tubes he'd fashioned to it hang loosely.

"Right," Tom says, because it's best not to argue with Olympia for too long. When she gets going, she's hard to stop. "What are you bringing?"

"Clothes. Tools. Exactly what Mom told us to bring."

Tom smiles.

"But not *only* what Mom said. What else?"

"Nothing."

But she is. He can tell. Olympia keeps secrets, too.

"You're bringing books, aren't you?"

"Am not."

"Olympia . . ."

Tom gets up and crosses the cabin. He catches her just as she tries to slide a handful of books beneath her bunk.

"You are!" he says. "And so what's the difference between you bringing something of your own and me doing the same?"

"Stop it, Tom."

"Well?"

"Because the things I like don't put us in danger. Okay?"

This hurts. This belittles everything Tom is passionate about.

"Okay," he says. "Fuck you."

"Tom!"

He crosses the cabin again and gets on his knees by his bed. He reaches under.

"If you can bring books you've already read, if you can spend your precious space on *that*, then I can bring what I want, too."

"I didn't exactly say you couldn't."

"You thought it."

Then he finds it. Deep under his bed. His handmade glasses.

Malorie won't know they're in his bag unless she checks. And if she does, he'll fight for them.

"I'm scared," Olympia says.

Tom, feeling emboldened, turns to her again.

"We've lived with them our whole lives."

"Maybe," she says. "But they've gotten worse."

"Have they?" But Tom knows this, too.

"A lot more of them now," Olympia says.

"Well, stop it. And don't say that kind of thing in front of Mom. If you do she's gonna get even harder on us."

"We've never ridden a train," Olympia says.

"No. So?"

"I've read about them. They're huge. They carry a lot of people. A lot could go wrong."

"Mom wouldn't even consider it if it was dangerous."

"She might," Olympia says. "For her parents."

In the distance, the lodge door opens and closes again.

"Do you think they're alive?" Tom asks.

They search each other's faces for answers. Malorie's boots flatten distant grass, loud enough for the two to hear, them alone.

"I want them to be," Olympia says, "but I don't think they are."

"Olympia . . ."

"Whether that list is old or not, I don't think they're alive."

"Why not?"

"I mean . . . I mean Mom *wants* them to be alive. You know? And I've read about characters who want something so bad they believe it's actually happening."

"But the names . . ."

"I know," Olympia says. "Like I said, I want them to be. I just—"

A hard knocking at the door interrupts her.

"Guys? Eyes closed?"

"Yes," Tom says. He does it.

"Yes," Olympia says.

The door creaks open, and Malorie steps inside. Right away Tom can hear the energy in her breathing. When she speaks, it's with more urgency than he's heard in a long time.

"How close are we?" she asks.

"I'm packed," Tom says.

"I'm right there," Olympia says.

Malorie closes the door. She takes the broom from beside it and begins to sweep the cabin. The door was open, after all, even if only momentarily.

"In the old world," she says, "we had weather forecasters. People to tell us what we might expect."

"I brought my rain stuff," Olympia says.

"You should have packed everything I told you to pack and nothing more."

Tom hears her close to him. She sweeps around him, then under his bed.

"Did either of you take anything else?"

The teens know better than to hesitate when answering. They might be able to hear to the gates of camp, but Malorie can hear a lie like no one else.

"Nope," Tom says.

"Just what you said," Olympia says.

"Okay." Malorie stops sweeping. "You can open your eyes."

They do.

Tom is stricken by how alive Malorie looks. Her eyes appear bright with memories, realizations, decisions. The bag beside her is full. She wears a hoodie and long pants, gloves and boots. In one hand is the blindfold she just removed.

"Listen to me," she says. "We've never done what we're about to do. We've never been where we're about to go. We're really, *really* going to need each other."

It strikes Tom, suddenly, that the only thing that could trump Malorie's safety measures, the only thing that could possibly eclipse her way of life and the life she has insisted upon for these seventeen years, is family.

"I want you both to know I'm prepared for the fact that we may not find them. That we probably won't. Do you understand?"

"Yes," Tom says.

"Yes," Olympia says.

"I'm ready for this to end in failure. But not in our failure. Do you understand?"

"Yes."

"Yes."

"I don't know if you do." She breathes in, she holds it, she breathes out. She almost looks like a warrior to Tom. He lightly fingers the outside of his bag. The glasses are within. Malorie continues, "Whether we find them or not, the fact that we're going means something. A great deal. There are people out there too afraid to attempt what we're about to try."

"The train," Olympia says.

Malorie looks to her quickly.

"Are you worried about the train?" she asks. "Oh, Olympia. I am, too." Then, "Are either of you against doing this?"

Tom can tell she hasn't taken this into account until now. It's all over her face.

"I'm not against it," he says. "I'm excited."

He looks to her bag, sees the census pages jutting out the top. Malorie shakes her head no.

"Don't be excited, Tom. Please. Just be alert." She turns to Olympia. "And you?"

"I want them to be alive," she says.

Malorie nods. Then she motions for the two of them to come to her, and they do. In the center of the cabin she grips each of their wrists.

"This *is* the right thing to do," she says. "Imagine you two found out I was living alone, someplace else. You'd do the same, right?"

"Yes," Olympia says.

"We wouldn't let you go," Tom says.

Malorie breathes deep again.

"Okay," she says. "Let's go. Get the last of your things."

She looks to Tom's bag.

"You're set?" she asks. "Nothing extra in there?"

Tom shakes his head no. Malorie nods.

"Okay. How many are out there?"

"Right now?" he asks.

Olympia cocks an ear to the cabin wall. Tom stands still. After a minute of silence, of listening, both teens respond with the same number at the same time.

"One."

"Jesus Christ," Malorie says. "There's even one for our very first step. Let's hope that ratio doesn't last."

Tom zips his bag and puts on his hoodie. By the time his head comes through the top, Olympia's bag is beside her, too.

"Gloves," Malorie says.

But both teens are already putting them on.

"I love you guys," she says.

And Tom feels it.

He looks to her bag again and sees the tops of the white pages. He thinks of the story the man at the door alluded to. Tales of a creature caught.

Could it be?

"Okay," Malorie says. "Blindfolds."

They put them on. As Tom closes his eyes and secures the fabric to his face, he imagines himself on a mountaintop with a box, as people all over the world line up to see what's inside.

Yes, *see*, as Tom will allow them a look with his glasses, the very glasses he built himself.

"Now," Malorie says, a touch of hysteria in her voice. "*Now*, let's go."

As they cross the threshold of Cabin Three, as they take that first step toward a train none of them can know for sure will be there, it strikes Tom that he's hearing something in Malorie's voice that he hasn't heard in a long time.

Risk.

It scares him. Because risk implies doubt. And if there's one thing Malorie never expresses, it's doubt in her decisions regarding the outside world.

Stepping out, Tom feels young, much younger than Malorie. As if all her stories about the old world suddenly carry more weight. Now, here, they make up the history of someone who's lived a life more like the worldly characters in Olympia's books. Now, here, Malorie seems like she knows more than he does. This after years of Tom believing the opposite.

"Come on," Malorie says.

And Tom knows she says it to herself.

He listens. He moves. And no matter how hard he tries to shove this feeling away, this sense of being green, he can't shake the doubt that rattles in Malorie's voice.

"Come on."

Risk.

They're taking one.

A big one.

Big enough to change how he sees the world.

Already. One step from home.

SEVEN

Malorie feels the darkness. It doesn't press in on her but rather slides across her arms and legs, her neck, her nose, her eyes. Yes, even her eyes feel exposed to the new world, her eyes that are not only closed but protected by the blindfold. It feels like the darkness, her personal darkness, the one she travels through, has gotten into her sleeves and boots, gloves and pants.

Sam and Mary Walsh. St. Ignace.

Unbelievable.

"Do not remove your hoods."

She can't count how many times she's said this to the teens already. She does not hold their hands like she did the last time they took to these woods, heading the opposite way a decade ago. Tom and Olympia are sixteen years old now. At times one or the other walks ahead, at times they both take the lead, leaving Malorie in the back like the frightened friend traveling through those darkened halls of the county fair's house of horrors. She and Shannon did that. Every year, if Malorie remembers right. She can still hear Shannon laughing, now, even as she listens for Tom's footsteps, for Olympia's directions, for the sounds of what exists beyond the small space the three of them make. She remembers reaching out to Shannon on those rides, at those booths, in that haunted house, looking for her sister at age sixteen, feeling a bond she knows Tom and Olympia feel now.

"Guys?"

"Yes," Olympia says. "Right here, Mom. We're still on the path."

The path, yes. One Malorie has never seen, of course. A path that school buses no doubt once used to deliver campers for the summer. It's not hard to imagine a bus appearing, suddenly, now, ahead, taking a turn too tightly, barreling down upon them.

But old-world fears are silly out here. Malorie's ear is on the creature the kids said was outside the cabin.

"The road isn't far," Tom says.

Malorie is past asking how they can hear these things. She'll never rid herself of the image of them as babies, sleeping, blindfolded, under chicken-wire cribs covered in black cloth. She'll never forget the two of them seated at the kitchen table, age three, their tiny heads cocked toward the amplifiers that delivered sounds from outside the house.

They haven't used amplifiers in years.

"Hang on," Tom says.

"No," Olympia says. "It's nothing."

"Hang on," Tom repeats.

Malorie remains still. The bag is tight to her back. It feels light enough to carry thirty miles. She can do it. And she'll need all the energy she can get. She doesn't want to begin to guess what shelters, what abandoned edifices, what people they will encounter on their way.

"Cover your faces," she says.

She covers her own with gloved hands. The black leather presses against the black fabric of the fold, layering the darkness.

"Don't let it touch you," she says.

She doesn't know what it means for one to touch a person any more than she knows if one can be touched at all. But the image of Annette turning the corner in the hall at the school for the blind is as present as the images of her and Shannon at the county fair.

"There's nothing," Olympia says.

"There's *something*," Tom says. "Whether it's a creature or not, I don't know."

"You don't know?" Malorie asks. This scares her. Do they move differently now? Do they move at all?

Something crashes through the bushes, and Malorie cries out. She reaches for the teens, instinctively, before covering her chin and mouth with the black gloves.

"A deer," Tom says. Malorie hears defeat in his voice. His sister was right. "If I was allowed to build my sound meter, we would've known that right away."

The "sound meter" is a failed invention of Tom's, an idea he had for verifying what moved in the woods around camp. He believes it could've worked with minor tweaks, but Malorie destroyed it before he could try.

"No talk like that now," Malorie says, lowering the gloves at last. "Was the deer sane?"

She thinks of Victor the dog, chewing his own legs.

"Yes," Olympia says.

Still, ten years deep, and no complete knowledge of which animals go mad, which don't, and why.

Malorie wonders if there's more information about this in the census pages she carries in her bag.

They reach the road a minute later, sooner than Malorie

thought they would. The service station that houses Ron Handy is two miles to their left. But they need to go right. The many roads they will take are east of here.

Still, Malorie turns a blind eye Ron's way. She imagines him in his own darkness there. Does he think of his sister just as she thinks of hers? Is he steeling himself for a run, south, of his own?

She wants so badly for this to be the case. But she knows it's not.

"Good luck," she says quietly, as if this is goodbye. Forever.

As she turns to face the road again, her shoulder strikes something.

She freezes.

Whatever it was, it's taller than the teens. She swipes at her arm, as if able to remove the touch of a creature.

"Guys!" she says.

But Olympia is beside her, guiding her, suddenly, around a tree.

"We have to move slow," Olympia says. "Really slow. Lots of trees this way. Remember?"

Yes. And perhaps Malorie needed the reminder.

"You don't hear anything else?" she asks.

"No," Tom says. But Olympia remains silent a beat. Is it the hesitation of a lie? Is Olympia only being careful?

"Nothing," she finally says.

"Did you lose track of the one you heard outside the cabin?"

Hesitation again.

"No."

"Where did it go?"

"To the lake," Olympia says.

Despite not being able to hear the water from this distance, Malorie listens.

"Tom?" she asks. "Did you hear the same thing?"

"I lost track of it," Tom says.

"You what? You can't do that out here. You cannot lose track of anything out here. Do you understand?"

"Mom . . ."

"Tom. Do you understand or not?"

"Yeah. Sure."

"No yeah, no sure. This isn't the time to daydream. I need you. Olympia needs you."

"Okay. I'm sorry. Olympia said it's in the lake. Then it's in the lake."

Malorie listens. She thinks she can hear the open road going in either direction.

"Fine," she says. "Let's go."

She feels the road beneath her boots but she knows they won't be on solid footing for long. The map in her bag includes paths through woods, over farmland, across rivers.

Sam and Mary Walsh.

It's impossible not to imagine them on the couch in the home she grew up in. But now, rather than a view of the garden and the street, there are blankets over the windows.

And if they're not at home, not in the only place Malorie can imagine them to be, what roads have they taken, and what did they hear along the way?

"Quiet," Malorie says, though the teens aren't talking. *"Listen."*

And she thinks of the train. And she hopes the stop they just made, the few minutes they took to talk about the whereabouts of the creature, hasn't made it so they miss it. Because if they do, if they miss the train by an hour, by a day . . . how can they be sure they'll learn its schedule, if it has a schedule at all?

Malorie walks. She wants to move faster than they are, faster than they can. She wants to make up the time they just took to talk. She wants to make up the ten years they spent at Camp

Yadin. And the six years before that. She wants to return to the moment when her parents stopped answering their phones, when she and Shannon shared a silent look in which both agreed Sam and Mary Walsh had died.

Malorie wants it all back. Now.

"Mom," Olympia says. "Be careful."

Her daughter's hand comes to her wrist, guides her across a dip in the road.

"Thank you," she says. She wants to believe in Fate, wants to believe there is a reason for everything. That they were supposed to leave now. That no time has been lost. That a bigger purpose will be revealed in the end.

But Malorie doesn't think this way.

"Hey," Tom says. "There's something ahead in the road."

Malorie opens her mouth to tell the teens to stop. But she doesn't want to stop. And if the world is teeming with creatures now, and if they're present with every step she takes toward her parents, then she's going to have to live with walking among them.

She thinks of something else she read in the census papers. Something about a town called Indian River. And the woman who runs it.

Athena Hantz.

She simply cannot let Tom read about that place. The descriptions, the dangers, were enough to blanch Malorie white. But Athena Hantz's philosophy is what sticks with Malorie now. The woman claimed to live freely among creatures. No different than she lived before their arrival. And the way the census man put it, his exact words, were chilling:

Miss Hantz claims she has "wholly accepted the creatures." She insists they no longer drive people mad and have no intention of doing so. She believes, fiercely, they have changed over time. Her words: "They don't punish us anymore."

What he wrote next was worse:

This philosophy, scant as it is, has garnered followers.

And his summation was perhaps most troubling of all:

Without being able to verify if she lives the way she claims, I only have our brief encounter to judge her by. And by my own estimation, Athena Hantz is sane.

"Should we stop?" Tom asks. Malorie knows where this question is coming from. Has she ever not told them to stop in the presence of a creature?

Malorie thinks of the people like the woman from Indian River. The people who populate the papers in her bag.

Those people are unsafe. For that, every decision they make is coming from an unsafe place.

But Malorie, now, out in the world again, must trust herself. She must believe in her own rules and the lifestyle she has forged for her teens.

"Hoods up, cover your faces," she says. "And keep walking."

EIGHT

The teens sleep, but Malorie can't do it.

They walked thirteen hours today, and the map tells her they've only gone nine miles. It's daunting. It's overwhelming.

Malorie doubts herself.

They're in what was once a bait and tackle shop. The map tells her the names of the nearby lakes. And the old smell of worms and water remain. The teens sleep by what was once the front register. Malorie is near them. She's under a blanket, the cloth edges secured to the ground by her own boots. She's on her knees, her legs sore from the walking, her nose close to the map on the ground. The flashlight shows her the legend, the mileage, and how unfathomably far they have to go. A little math helps. It's close to an hour and a half per mile, walking blind along existing roads, through former crop fields, woods, even some swamp. Because the distance to East Lansing (if Ron is right that it's East Lansing and not Lansing) is almost exactly twenty-one miles, this means they could have thirty walking hours to go. That would be two more days' worth, if they put in the work they did today. In the old world, these figures aren't much. A long weekend. But now, under the blanket, Malorie feels an urgency she hasn't experienced before. Even leaving the house by way of the river required four years of gathering the courage to do so. Right now, she would run if she could.

"Dammit," she says.

She thinks of her parents, difficult not to refer to them as Sam and Mary Walsh, the written names like a fire in her head.

She pulls the papers closer and flips past the scant information about the train. As she does, she recalls Ron's fear of "the people who run it." Tom said anyone who could get a train running would have to be very smart, but Malorie doesn't agree. The whole world, it seems, is crazy. And everybody within it is only a gradation.

She stops at a page titled: *WHAT WE KNOW ABOUT THEM*.

She almost laughs, exhausted, at this headline. The page ought to be blank, for all people have learned about the creatures. But Malorie quickly sees it isn't.

The list immediately makes her uneasy.

They make noise, though not traditional sound. There is no flat-footed creak upon floorboards. Rather, it's as if the floorboards themselves momentarily morph before returning to their natural state.

Malorie doesn't like this. She doesn't want to read this at all. She imagines even the floor going mad.

Some claim their shadows travel without them. Others claim there's only one creature, in all the world, and that its many shadows stretch across the planet like dark fingers.

She doesn't need this folklore. She doesn't need rumors and theories. She needs facts.

There are stories of intentional attacks in what was once New York City. Rumors of aggression in Des Moines, Iowa. NOTE: Only people who live in areas where people-on-people crime was once common seem to suggest these things. There is no verifiable account of a creature forcing a person to look at it.

Tom snores, and Malorie clicks off the light. Her heart is hammering. Even reading about the creatures tends to send fog to the mind, a cloud to reason.

Olympia snores. Two teens vying for space, even in sleep.

In the dark, she remembers a time at home, after school, when she and Shannon fought over who would get to pick what board game the family would play in the living room. Dad, exasperated, told them they could both choose and play their own games. Malorie can see him, his hair as dark as her own, his eyes set deep in his face. She thought of Mom and Dad as law back then. A law to be broken of course, but law nonetheless. And when Shannon got bored with her own game and joined Malorie with hers, Malorie understood that their father had somehow, invisibly, made that happen.

She hopes she's done things like this for her kids. She thinks she has.

She feels a tap on her back.

She falls flat to the floor, heart thudding.

"Mom."

It's Olympia, whispering, her lips pressed to Malorie's ear through the fabric of the blanket.

"What?" Malorie whispers back.

"We're not alone in here."

Malorie goes cold.

"Someone is standing in the doorway," Olympia says. *"I can hear them breathing."*

Malorie's mind seems to stop. For a second. She thinks nothing. Only feels. Then, an image of Gary. As if he's been waiting to reveal himself all this time and chose now to do so. She has to decide something, fast.

"Is the door closed?" she whispers.

But she's already got her eyes closed, and she's already getting up, slow, quiet, from under the blanket.

Standing, she turns to the door. No time to listen.

"Get out," she says. "Whoever you are, get out. I'm armed. All five of us are armed."

No response. But she can feel the person, can feel the presence some twenty feet away.

"Get *out,*" she says.

She hears the familiar sound of Tom waking. Olympia whispers something to him.

"Eyes *closed,*" Malorie tells him. Then, "You're leaving us no choice."

"Do it then," a voice says, a man, from across the shop. "If you're armed, shoot me."

At the sound of his voice, Malorie's mind goes cold. She's not looking, but is he?

"I'll shoot you," Tom says.

"Tom . . ." Malorie starts, but she stops herself.

"I mean it," the man says. "Do it. I'm a day away from opening my eyes outside anyway. You'd save me the complications of suicide."

Malorie believes she recognizes sanity in his voice. But she can't be sure. And she won't let herself decide.

"Get out," she repeats.

"I've been living by the side of this road for two years," he says. "I heard you enter Dabney's."

"Tom," Malorie says, "Olympia, do not speak to this man. Do not open your eyes."

"I'm not crazy," the man says. He sounds young, younger than Malorie, older than the teens. "I'm just really not well. But I've survived. Like you have."

"Get out."

Silence. A scoff? A smile? She doesn't ask.

"But I don't want to," the man says. "I want to make contact. Don't you?"

"We have enough," Olympia says.

"Olympia . . ."

"Do you?" the man asks. "I have nobody. I heard you guys, I came in."

"While we were sleeping," Malorie says. "Get out now."

"Yeah, I waited for you to fall asleep because I didn't know if you were any more dangerous than you think I am."

"We're dangerous," Malorie says. *"Get out."*

Silence. Malorie makes fists of her hands.

"All right," the man says.

"Now."

But Malorie knows they won't be spending the night here now. No matter what this man does, she's going to instruct the teens to gather their things and they're going to leave this place. They'll walk, paranoid, through the dark of night. And even in the new world, a walk at night feels less safe than one during the day.

"Let me leave you with something," the young man says.

"Don't open your eyes," Malorie tells the teens.

"Just some words, okay? I want you three to know that the world isn't gonna get any better. We gotta start over."

"You said 'three,'" Malorie says. "Your eyes are open."

"Yeah? Well, I'm not the only one."

"Close your eyes," she hisses at the teens.

Her hands in fists, she steels herself. Her parents flash like fire in her mind, names in St. Ignace, taken by the winds of the Straits of Mackinac, blown across Lake Michigan. Lost to her.

Again.

"GET OUT!"

Her voice is almost unrecognizable to herself. She sounds like a woman who has endured years of tension, paranoia, and loss.

And so she is.

The man doesn't answer. But the door opens and closes.

"Tom?" Malorie asks.

"He's walking away," Tom says.

"Olympia?"

"Yes, he's leaving."

"He's walking up the road," Tom says. Malorie hears disappointment in his voice.

"Which way?"

"The way we came."

"Get your things," Malorie says. "We're continuing. Now."

She hears the teens packing their things back into their bags. She does the same.

"Tom," Malorie says, "I know what you're thinking."

"Just like you know that guy was unsafe? Just like you knew the census guy couldn't help us?"

"Tom . . ."

"Mom," Tom says, and his voice is closer than she expects it to be. "The census man gave us the names of your parents. You were wrong. That's all there is to it. You were wrong."

But Tom is shaken, too. Malorie can hear it. A stranger in the same space as them. A man speaking of suicide and the end of the world.

Malorie waits by the door, her fists gloved now. The teens are ready before she expects them to be.

"Listen," she says, tightening the fold around her face.

"He went the way we came," Olympia says.

Malorie breathes in, she holds it, she breathes out.

She opens the door.

"Go. Now."

Then they're walking again, too fast, through the dark, hardly any sleep between them. Malorie looks blind over her shoulder, back to where the teens said the man went.

She feels for him. Just like she feels for Ron Handy. Just like she feels for every person involved in all the horrid experiments documented in the papers left by the census man.

Isn't everybody just doing the best they can?

Isn't she?

"It's cold," Olympia says.

It is hours before the sun will rise. The sky and the road are as dark as the world behind their folds.

"We'll warm up," Malorie says.

But she can't stop thinking of the young man. He talked of ending his own life without needing a creature to make him do it.

Malorie allows herself to imagine what he might have been like in the old world and what he might've been doing now if the creatures never came.

Would he have been a good friend? A thoughtful person? A father?

Her heart burns for him. For all of them. Ron Handy. The census man. The people described in the census papers.

But the empathy is short-lived as something howls in the dark distance. Malorie thinks it's a dog. A wolf. A man.

"We'll find somewhere else to sleep," she says. "I promise. Just a little farther."

But whatever the distance is to peace of mind feels more than just a little farther. It feels like it's beyond the state of Michigan. Beyond the world. New or old.

And absolutely beyond the last stop of any train, real or imagined.

NINE

Nineteen miles along old country highways, not maintained, overgrown, cracked, no longer used.

Malorie feels insane. The old way. Exhausted, sore, and like she's chosen to put her teens in danger, hastily, without enough of a plan.

The hood covers her head and neck and the blindfold her eyes. She wears sleeves and gloves despite the heat and also despite the lack of any concrete proof that the creatures have ever destroyed someone's mind through touch. She drinks from the water bottles they've refilled numerous times on their journey (using filters from the camp kitchen rather than the ones Tom invented himself, a thing Tom argued against). She reminds them they need to eat, and she continually asks the teens what they hear. More than once they've come to a complete stop and waited upwards of a half hour, as Olympia seemed certain one was near, even when Tom didn't agree.

And no matter what they are enduring or when, Malorie thinks of Mom and Dad.

It's not hard to pluck a good memory of the two of them, the way they were. Both effusive, both smart as hell. They were what her friends called "hippies," though neither lived that exact life-style. It was their positivity her peers made light of, the way her parents had of constantly talking about expanding the mind.

Intelligence, Dad told the sisters, *is being able to talk your way out of a fight.*

This after Malorie had fought with them about bedtime. Oh, how she wishes she had those fights, those words, that time back.

And here . . . she might.

The thought is almost too big to acknowledge. Nobody is granted a reversal of grief.

Nobody.

They would love the teens, Malorie thinks. But she wonders if Tom's progressive nature would frighten them. It's an odd, sudden thought to have, and it feels wholly out of place. As if, for a moment, Malorie was nervous to introduce her son to her parents. She has nobody to tell her if this feeling is natural. No book to reference. No friends to ask. Sam and Mary Walsh would love both kids. She knows this. Yet thoughts of Tom are becoming cloudier by the hour.

She walks. She listens. She thinks.

It hurts, as if the creatures and the new world they've created are present in her memories of the old. She remembers sneaking into a movie with Shannon, a movie rated R for nudity, and how, despite the images, hard kissing they'd never witnessed before in any way, Shannon fell asleep. Malorie sees her sister's eyes are closed and wonders, now, was there something Shannon was hiding from? A thing that could've driven her mad? How about when

Mom and Dad lowered the blinds at night, as Mom (*Mary, Mary Walsh, Sam and Mary Walsh*) told the girls that moonlight induced nightmares, and oh how the sisters giggled at the idea. Was Mom actually taking the same precautions Malorie takes now?

Close the blinds. Close your eyes.

Memory and the now, melded.

Her childhood bedroom has blankets over the windows. The bus ride to school is terrifying, as the driver can't look.

The train the train the TRAIN you're heading toward is a blind train, Malorie, what are you doing what are you doing what?

Sam and Mary sit in the front seat of the family car. Shannon and Malorie play games in the back. Dad turns the wheel suddenly, and the girls cry out and Mom says that was close, and Malorie, now, here, Malorie remembers it as if there was something in the road Dad wasn't supposed to see, something that drove him mad.

But Mom and Dad might not be mad.

And somehow that's the craziest part of all.

"A car," Tom says.

For a second Malorie imagines he's read her mind, as if her son, who has performed so many incredible auditory feats, heard all the way into her head.

"A car?" she echoes.

"Something," Olympia says.

"Not something," Tom says. "A car."

"Stop," Malorie says. "Side of the road. Now."

She doesn't want to step off the road. She doesn't want the straight line made between herself and her parents to be compromised. She wants to go to them, go to them, go to them now.

"Car," Olympia says.

"Told you," Tom says.

"Now," Malorie says.

She feels grass beneath her boots but it's not far enough. In the new world, someone driving could be driving blind. Malorie's done it herself.

"Farther," she says.

But she hears the engine pick up speed. As if the driver saw them. As if the driver is looking for people just like them.

"Down," Malorie says. But she can hear it's too late for that. The car is closer, closer, and slowing to a halt.

It's level with them now.

It stops.

The engine idles. It revs. It idles. It revs.

Malorie imagines a gun pointing out an open window. A face behind it, shaped by madness.

But nobody speaks. And no sudden sound breaks the sky above the open country road.

Malorie faces the car.

The car idles.

She thinks of Camp Yadin and how safe they were. She can almost feel the texture of the rope in her gloved hands, rope connecting each building, one of which housed canned goods, another with a garden beside it. She sees herself, waking there, walking there, living there, safe. She hears herself asking the teens what might be outside. She hears their answers. They lived alone. They lived safe.

They lived by the blindfold.

The grass beside her crunches fast, too fast. Malorie cries out.

It sounds like an animal.

Something slams into the side of the car.

"Don't move!" she yells to the teens, but her voice is lost in the noise of repeated blows to the side of the car. She hears a man yelling, someone who sounds dangerously angry, possibly mad.

Then she recognizes the voice as Tom's.

Tom is screaming at the driver to leave.

"Go! GO! GO!"

Malorie rushes to the sound of him, to grab him, to get him away from the car. But the engine is revving so hard that dust rises like a curtain, and Malorie coughs.

The engine revs again, and Malorie holds a hand over her mouth and reaches for Tom with the other. She finds his shoulder.

Or does she?

Is this the shoulder of the driver?

A hand falls upon hers.

"GO!" Tom yells. And Malorie pulls back. Despite the chaos, despite the fear, it strikes her, suddenly, that Tom is a man now.

Another blow to the car. Then Malorie has him by the waist. She's pulling him back. Olympia says something, words lost in the din of the engine.

The car moves, and Malorie bumps hard against Tom as he's flung back into her.

"Go, you stupid assholes!" Tom yells. "Just go!"

Tears in his voice. Malorie doesn't understand. His emotions sound wider, more powerful, than they ever did in the cabin.

"Tom," she says. "Calm down!"

But Tom is far from that. And the car is driving away.

"Why, Mom? Why? Weren't you gonna tell them to go? Weren't you gonna tell them to leave? *That's what you do!*"

Malorie wasn't expecting this. He's not mad at the car, he's mad at her. As if she were somehow the danger and not the stranger idling without speaking.

"Tom, we've survived this long—"

"That's all we do!"

"Tom—"

"That's all we do is survive!"

This steals her breath. She doesn't know what to say.

The car grows quiet in the distance, and Malorie knows she'll never know what the driver had in mind.

In the old world, he or she could've given them a ride to the train.

"Come on," Olympia says. The mediator.

The teens return to the road, their shoes crunching the gravel on the shoulder. But Malorie can't stop thinking of what Tom just said.

All we do is survive!

Not a boast. A gripe.

Malorie walks. Again the faces of her parents return to her mind's eye. Their jokes. Their advice. The way they parented, too.

She hopes they've lived by the same rules she has.

"Ready, Mom?" Olympia says. Still mediating. Still attempting to sidestep the fact that Tom just blew up at Malorie.

Malorie doesn't respond. She only walks, knowing the teens can hear her, can pinpoint her exact location with their ears.

And as she walks, she hopes her parents have done exactly what Tom has suddenly accused her of.

She hopes they live by the fold.

She hopes all they do is survive.

TEN

Tom waits for Malorie to fall asleep. Even in the dark, it's not hard for him to determine. Malorie and Olympia don't always snore, but both breathe differently when they go under. Tom believes he can hear it when they dream. Often, back in Camp Yadin, this idea comforted him and eased him into his own deep slumber.

They're in a barn. Olympia found it a mile and a half after Malorie asked that they abandon the road and walk "in tandem" until they found a place for the night. Tandem, for these three, means Malorie sticks to the road, Tom walks some forty feet into the grass, Olympia forty feet beyond him. The teens can hear how close each are to one another, and the sound of Malorie's shoes makes it so they don't go too far to get back. When Olympia called out what she'd found, a dirt drive first, then the barn itself, Tom began planning.

It's all driving him a bit mad.

He understands Malorie grew up in a world where it was normal to look outside, to *see* the barn, and therefore to detect any sign of danger. But he doesn't think she *really* understands that he and Olympia can do the same thing with their ears. She's praised them for it through the years, but her bottomless precautions reveal what she really thinks: they're vulnerable children without her. Tom's out in the world, for the first time since he was six years old, and the last thing he wants more of is Malorie. He can hear if something is near a barn. It's more than sound. It's *instinct*. One Tom and Olympia trust like Malorie once trusted her eyes.

Now, he hears the deep, elongated breathing of his mom and sister. Both are exhausted, as well both should be. They've come twenty-four miles over varied terrain, the sun beating down upon their long sleeves, hoods, blindfolds, and gloves. They've eaten what rations Malorie collected from camp and drank filtered water from ravines, rivers, and cricks. And while all three were active around Yadin, none of them have walked this much in a decade.

Tom, who has been lying on a floor of harsh, wilted hay, gets up. He moves quiet as he can, aware that, while Malorie won't wake to the noise, Olympia easily could. Despite planning to do the very thing Olympia loves doing, he doesn't want his sister to know what he has in mind.

Reading.

He takes crouched steps, one at a time, his arms extended, his fingers searching in the darkness for Malorie's bag. He knows where it is. He's kept his ear on the spot, the exact spot, since she set it there twenty-five minutes ago.

A flutter from the loft, and Tom cocks his ear toward it. He already knows it's only a bird. But will it flap its wings? Will it wake Malorie?

He finds the straps that have kept the bag tight to Malorie's back for the duration of their walk. He lifts it from the hay with care.

He pauses. He listens. He hears nobody outside the barn.

The door does not creak when he opens it. He slips outside, already removing the flashlight from his pocket, already pulling out the rolled blanket.

Eyes closed, he moves swiftly to the side of the barn, covers himself and the bag with the blanket, secures it to the ground with his knees and elbows, and turns on the light.

He opens his eyes.

It strikes him that, even if something had gotten under the blanket with him, he wouldn't care. He believes he'd have heard it before seeing it, would've had time to close his eyes.

He's so sick of being afraid of the creatures.

Sick of living by the fold.

The white tips of the pages appeal to him like so many invitations, asking him to read, read on, read on till morning.

He knows exactly where he wants to begin. Back in Cabin Three he caught a glimpse of a section, words that jumped out at him, before he was distracted by Olympia. Those words have whispered to him since.

He removes the stack from the bag and flips through until he reaches the page headed: INDIAN RIVER.

It's a city in northern Michigan. And the description of it is everywhere Tom wants to be.

He reads:

Indian River, Michigan, has become one of the most progressive communities I've yet to encounter. Their citizenry numbers three hundred. Most sleep in tents and what was once a plain, two-story brick office building. But none spend their days indoors.

Tom's heart picks up speed. Already he can tell these are his kind of people. The kind that push back against the creatures.

A town of many inventions, Indian River is not for the faint of heart. One man claims to have caught a creature, but this was not corroborated by anyone else I spoke to. NOTE: Almost everyone I asked told me they hoped he had.

"Yes!" Tom half cries out, half whispers. He can't help it. A whole town of people who *want* to hear a creature was caught?

And maybe, just maybe, one was.

The de facto leader of the town is a woman named Athena Hantz. It was difficult for me to gauge her age as she has the passion of the young and the fortitude of someone much older. Miss Hantz claims she has "wholly accepted the creatures." She insists they no longer drive people mad and have no intention of doing so. She believes, fiercely, they have changed over time. Her words: "They don't punish us anymore."

Tom's eyes widen. This is heavy stuff. The idea that the creatures have changed . . .

He thinks of the man from the bait shop. He didn't die when he left. This after saying he was close to looking.

Did he look?

Tom reads:

Without being able to verify if she lives the way she claims, I only have our brief encounter to judge her by. And by my own estimation, Athena Hantz is sane.

Tom nods along with the words. He's impressed the census man felt compelled to include this. He wants to wake his mom, to show her, to say, see, *see*? Not everybody who thinks differently than Malorie is mad!

Athena Hantz.

Without any idea what she looks or sounds like, Tom imagines Athena Hantz is his mother instead. What would it mean for him to have been raised by a person like this in a place like that?

Indian River already feels more like home than Camp Yadin ever did.

He reads on:

In every corner of this community, somebody is attempting something new. For this, they've had their share of tragedies.

Tom nods. Of course they have. They had to have. That's how invention works. Failures are guaranteed.

Doesn't Malorie understand that? Doesn't she get that you can wear a blindfold your entire life, but all you're doing is perpetuating the lie that you cannot see?

One such instance occurred while attempting to "slow down" the process of insanity by securing a volunteer to a tree and leaving her outside to "watch all night." The thinking here was that, if the person who has gone mad does not receive immediate gratification, perhaps the initial urge will subside, and the feelings of wanting to hurt herself or another would eventually go away. The community of Indian River fed soup to a madwoman this way, a woman tied to the tree, who did not, it turns out, avoid the known demise. Rather, she pretended to, ten days tied to the tree, and when the others cut her loose, finally, she lashed out. NOTE: While this sounds foolish and is something most survivors would never consider, the people of Indian River did learn from this experience. The initial, manic urge did indeed subside. But, unfortunately for those involved, it was replaced with cunning. This begs the question: who else out there has seen a creature but was incapable of carrying out their immediate fantasies? Who else out there is feigning sanity? I do not know if Athena Hantz was present for this experiment.

Tom has to stop to consider this one. It's all so amazing. While he's factored in ways of viewing the creatures, he's never considered altering the actual effect they have on people. As if madness were a malleable thing, a thing to be tamed.

He remembers the time he opened his eyes outside, a time Malorie doesn't know about, but Olympia does. A creature had passed through camp and Tom, angry, restless, inspired, got close to the ground where it had just stood. There, he cupped his hands over his eyes and looked to the grass. He needed to know if the imprint of a creature, the effect of the creature on its immediate environment, would have the same effect as seeing one outright. He rationalized the danger away by telling himself Malorie and Olympia needed to know. The whole world needed to know. Because if an imprint left behind could drive one mad, perhaps there weren't as many creatures in the vicinity, or on the planet, to begin with. Maybe their absence, but recent presence, could be just as bad.

He feels some embarrassment for the experiment now. While the census pages describe incredible feats, he knows in his heart his own precarious moment wouldn't have helped anyone, because nobody knew he was experimenting.

This is one of the many trials of living with Malorie Walsh. Not being permitted to speak of such things.

He reads on:

The people of Indian River do not drink. It's a community ordinance. But they do smoke marijuana. I've yet to come upon a community who values the elasticity of the human imagination quite like this one. It's a difficult town to describe, in ordinary terms, as they do things here that are not done anywhere else. Depending on one's personal stance, Athena Hantz's description of her own town is either spot on or chilling: "We're allowed," she told me. When I asked her what she meant by that, she only smiled.

"Hell yeah," Tom says. "Hell. Yes."

They do things here that are not done anywhere else.

It's invigorating. Electrifying.

We're allowed . . .

Indian River is north of Lansing. Tom checked Malorie's map twice before they left Yadin. It's on the way to Mackinaw City.

Could he . . . might he . . . will he get to experience this city, these people, in person?

He wants to cry out. He wants to throw the blanket aside and run, loud, through the fields that no doubt lie beyond the barn. He wants to feel the night upon him. The open air. The freedom of the people who live in Indian River.

And he wants to see it. The world. The stars, the sky, the moon, the darkness.

He wants to *see* the night. This night. Every night. The night he learned about Indian River and the people who live there. The night he discovered others *do* think like he does. What's the word Olympia uses for this kind of thing?

Relate.

Yes. Tom relates. It's enough to make him want to climb to the top of the barn and scream hallelujah. The world isn't made up of people who only think like Malorie. The world isn't made up of people who only live by the fold. Not everybody will remind you, over and over, to wear your blindfold and your hoodie and your gloves when *you're* the one who ought to be reminding *them* since *you* were the one born into this world in the first place.

"YES!"

He's said it too loud. He doesn't care. Let Mom come blindly flailing, feeling for the outer walls of the barn. Let her come shuddering into the night, this night, *his* night. There are people out there who think the way he does! There are people who understand that sixteen years could easily become thirty-two, then sixty-four, and . . . and . . . and an entire lifetime gone, sucked up into the paranoid *rules* of the Goddamn creatures.

He wishes Athena Hantz was his mom.

He flips the pages, wants to keep reading, doesn't need to sleep. He's sixteen years old, he's hungry for a new life, he's wide awake under a night's sky that's no different than day's to him. He thinks of the train, wants it to exist as badly as Malorie does. He imagines people like the people of Indian River riding that very machine. He imagines like-minded strangers discussing more than just black fabric.

He brings the pages closer to his nose.

He hears footsteps coming around the side of the barn.

He turns off the light.

Huddled beneath the blanket, his first instinct is to keep the papers close to his chest. He realizes, with sudden clarity, that it's more important to him to hold on to these pages than it is to warn Malorie and Olympia that something is near.

He closes his eyes.

He listens.

Whatever it is, it's close. It moves slow. He doesn't think it's an animal, but it's hard to tell in all this open space. Inside a house there's an echo, dimensions, a blueprint.

Outside it's different.

Whatever it is, it steps closer. Tom doesn't want to feel afraid, but that's what he is. He wants the fear within him to pour out, to leave him, to flow back toward the road, back to Camp Yadin, back to the school for the blind, back to the house he was born in.

Another step in the grass. It's a creature. He knows this now.

The sky is silent; his mom and sister breathe steady on the other side of the wood wall. He slowly removes the blanket from his head. The cool night air chills him, and he doesn't want to tremble in the presence of a creature.

We're allowed, he thinks.

Yet he shudders.

He stands. He rolls up the sleeves of his hoodie.

"Touch me," he says. "I dare you."

His own voice frightens him. The audacity to dare a creature.

Whatever it is, it's stopped. It's near the wall. Just as Tom is.

"Touch me," he says again. "Prove Mom wrong."

He raises his bare arms to it.

All he has to do is open his eyes. All he has to do is look. Once. See what it does to you. Then he'd really be able to invent something, to make real change. Because if he doesn't know what they do, how can he stop them from doing it?

He knows all the theories. Most people, like Mom, believe the creatures are beyond human comprehension. That seeing one is like glimpsing the void, infinity, or the face of God.

But Tom wonders . . . what if they've changed? And what if it's just a matter of accepting them?

He thinks of his glasses in his bag in the barn. He thinks of Athena Hantz.

The creature isn't moving. Dark wind blows, and Tom imagines it blowing his eyes wide open. Blame it on the night. The night came and lifted his eyelids the way people once raised the blinds in their homes in the morning. Malorie's told him and Olympia about those days, when her own parents would fill the house with light, how it felt so much bigger because you could see, see, *SEE* the world outside. And how you felt like that was yours, too, the world outside your home.

Tom begins to open his lids. He's actually doing it. His eyes roll back in his head so that only the whites are showing. He hasn't looked yet. But he's standing before a creature with his lids parted.

The feeling is incredible.

He doesn't speak. And the creature doesn't move. Arms extended, eyes rolled back, Tom feels invincible, like he's going to be the first person on the planet to capture a creature.

Something brushes his arm.

Tom closes his eyes. The bird in the barn loft takes flight. Tom ducks at the sound. He swipes at his arm. Swipes again. Malorie's words, Malorie's worst fears, come rushing at him in the darkness of his own imagination. The flapping wings echo in the barn, loud. For a moment he mistakes it for the creature rising into the sky.

Neither Malorie nor Olympia speak from within.

Is the creature still in front of him?

Was he touched? Is he going mad?

"Where are you?"

Tom isn't able to articulate how he knows this, but it doesn't feel like the creature is standing where it was. Is it closer now? Farther? Did it flutter away, after all?

Or did it step right to him and . . . touch . . .

He goes cold. All over.

What was he just doing, standing before a creature with his eyes partially open? What if he'd seen one? What would he have done to his mom, his sister, himself?

He swipes at his arm again, then bends quick and picks up the blanket.

Grass flattens behind him. To his left, more. Two places now. Three. Something in the distance. Something coming around the side of the barn.

Something on top of the barn.

"Oh, shit," Tom says.

He's not shuddering any longer. Now he's full shaking.

He hears more of them, more steps deep in the fields. A second on the barn. Is one above him on the wall? Literally, on the wall of the barn?

"Oh, shit," he says again because it's all he can think to say. He moves fast, grabbing Malorie's bag, remembering to grab it despite the dread spreading within.

Dread . . . or madness?

Another behind him. How many?

He moves quick to the barn door. He enters.

"Mom," Tom says. "Olympia. Get up!"

Olympia doesn't stir. She's already awake.

"I hear them," she says.

Tom, eyes closed, slides the barn door shut behind him.

Malorie is awake now.

"How many?" she says. And her voice is a solid straight line in the darkness.

"A lot," Olympia says.

Malorie doesn't tell them to keep their eyes closed. She doesn't tell them to put on their hoods.

"Come here," she says. "Both of you."

Tom goes to her in the darkness. He sets her bag close to where he believes it was. Will she notice if it's not in the exact place? Does it matter? He's counted ten of them outside. Three on the barn. Seven in the grass. Does it matter if Malorie discovers he was reading?

That he was touched?

Almost to her, he realizes he's still holding the pages. He can't slide them back into the bag now without her hearing.

Does it matter?

Movement outside. He can hear Olympia has already joined Malorie in the center of the barn. No sudden noises out there, no banging, no knocking. All quiet, deliberate steps. The creatures closing in.

He brushes frantically at his arm. He rolls his sleeves down.

His mind is whirling, too fast to hold. Malorie believes you can go mad by touch.

Is it true?

Is it?

"Mom," he says, horror in his voice. But he doesn't care about hiding it. He needs her. Wants her near. Wants her to say he's fine.

He believes, with complete certainty, that if he wasn't fine, if he did start losing his mind, Malorie would remain hidden from him just like she hides from the creatures.

"MOM!"

Her hand is on his wrist. She pulls him to her. He feels Olympia there, the three of them, crowded together.

"Gloves," Malorie says.

Tom puts on his gloves.

He listens. He can't tell. He listens. He doesn't know.

He listens.

Malorie grips his wrist harder, and he thinks it's because he's breathing heavy. He imagines a woman tied to a tree in Indian River. He imagines her pretending not to be mad. He can see the town feeding her soup as she feigns sanity, as she waits for the day when they will inevitably cut the ropes that bind her.

"There's nothing in here," Olympia says.

As if she knows. As if she could see Tom's head, turning this way and that, trying so hard to get a lock on a sound, anything, here in the barn.

Malorie doesn't ask her if they're still outside because, Tom knows, even his mom can hear that much.

The grass flattens. The barn creaks.

"Just wait," Malorie says.

And her voice is a solid object in Tom's dismay.

It's not hard to imagine himself choking her, cracking Olympia's skull, had he opened his eyes another sliver when facing the one by the side of the barn.

What was he thinking? What was he *doing*?

Olympia said there isn't one in the barn, Olympia said there isn't one in the barn, Olympia said—

"They're not moving," Olympia says.

"They're not trying to get in?" Malorie asks.

"No. But they're not leaving, either."

Tom can't stop thinking about his arm. He brushes at it again. He imagines something traveling into him, into his blood, pumping toward his mind. Something strong enough to make him want to hurt the two people he loves. Strong enough to drive him mad.

Yet nothing is happening.

Is it?

Malorie has scared the teens deeply with her descriptions of what real madness could be. Like how the madman doesn't know his mind is cracked, how that's what makes him mad. And how, maybe, just maybe, when they touch you, you go mad slowly instead.

Did he see one outside? Were his eyes open wider than he thought they were?

Is he mad without knowing he's mad?

Tom is having trouble breathing. He has to stop feeling this way. This scared. He's so tired of being told he's *supposed* to be scared. He thinks of the people of Indian River. Are they afraid? Do they live in fear? When they hear quiet steps in the dark, when they hear something on the roof of the barn . . . do they fall to pieces the way Tom does now?

He digs deep, into himself, searching for strength. He's looking for the part that was thrilled by the pages he read outside. He tries to relate to the teen he just was, standing near the barn, eyes partially open, a creature so close. Where has that teen gone? And how did he vanish so fast?

"I count thirteen," Olympia says.

But Malorie is doing what she's always done in moments like this. She's starting to list off the reasons they'll be fine, the reasons they'll make it through this night. Even as Tom hears his own fears echoing in her voice.

"There's no record of one ever attacking."

But what does this mean? How would the person who was "attacked" live to tell about it? And all those who have gone mad . . . who would believe them if, just before burying their heads in the garden they once tended, they say it was their own fault, no creature made them look?

"They're not interested in us."

But it sounds to Tom like they are. Like they're really very interested in them after all. There's another on the roof now. More in the fields.

"They don't mean us any harm."

Yet they haven't left, have they? Malorie's told Tom about his namesake's theory that the creatures only observe what they do to people. That they have no agenda. Yet at some point they would have to see the damage they cause. Right? At some point it *would* become a choice.

"They don't know what they do."

Maybe, Tom thinks. Maybe. But mindless or not, without morality or with, there're more of them now than there used to be. And nobody has any proof of them attempting to get back to where they came from.

Even now, in the throes of horror, trembling at his mother's and sister's sides, swiping at his arm where he felt something touch him, Tom can't stop himself from trying to solve them.

"What are they doing?" Malorie asks. Tom is so busy thinking that he's forgotten the role he normally plays. He listens. Hard. He hears movement in the fields. A rustling more corporeal than wind.

"Tom, what are they doing?"

He listens through the barn's wood walls, to places where the wind doesn't blow unobstructed. Places occupied by something other than open air.

"Tom?"

Mom sounds scared. She always does. Despite the list of reasons not to worry, Malorie sounds like she knows this could be the one. The time when even the blindfold doesn't protect them. The time the creatures finally get to her, get to her children, drive them insane.

Tom cocks an ear to the roof.

How many are up there? And why? If they mean no harm . . . if they've never attacked . . . why are they on the roof of the barn?

"I'm not sure," Olympia says.

This is supposed to be Tom's department. Always has been. Olympia possesses a preternatural ability to sense a creature's exact location, but it's Tom who can hear what they do and, sometimes, what they are about to do next.

His ear is on the loft.

He wonders, distantly, if Olympia hears it, too.

Something is in the loft.

The bird suddenly explodes into flight, squawking, crying, singing a song that makes no sense, has no rhyme, has no end. Malorie grips Tom's wrist harder as the bird flails through the barn and strikes a wood wall. It falls to the hay, rises, and flies madly into the wall again.

It falls. Again. Rises. Again.

Flies madly into the wall.

"There's one in the loft," Tom says.

Malorie stands up.

"Now," she says. *"Now."*

The teens rise without argument. Tom finds his bag quick in the darkness, but the few seconds he's away from Malorie are bad ones. Like the thing from the loft could come down.

Like it wants to touch him.

Malorie says, "Why are the pages out of my bag?"

As he moves, Tom imagines himself living in Indian River. He imagines waking in a town with other people, people ready to invent.

"Tom?" Malorie says.

"Mom," Olympia says. "It's moving."

It is. Tom hears it, too.

"Go," Malorie says.

Then Tom asks it. Because he can't not.

"Are you bringing the pages with you?"

He has to know. He can't leave them here.

But Malorie doesn't respond. Instead, Tom feels a hand on his wrist. Her hand. Her fingers ride up his arm, to make sure he's rolled down his sleeves. He has.

But it reminds him of being touched.

He shudders.

This time, though, he forces the feeling, the fear, out. And, for a moment, it works. For a hideously unfamiliar moment, Tom feels fearless in the face of so many creatures, as his mom pulls him toward the barn door, as Olympia breathes steadily beside him.

Malorie slides the door open. Tom feels the cold night, colder yet, rush into the barn, touching his nose, his mouth, his chin.

"Olympia," Malorie says.

It's obvious that she isn't looking to Tom for help. Why not? Can she tell he was touched by something? Does she think he's going mad?

"There's one blocking the door," Olympia says.

The loft behind them creaks.

"Back up," Malorie says.

"Wait," Tom says. "It's moving."

He hears it stepping out of the way.

"Go," Olympia says. "Now."

Malorie moves first, Olympia right behind her. But before leaving the barn, Tom turns his blindfolded face to the loft.

The ladder creaks.

Footsteps in the hay.

He thinks of Athena Hantz just as a hand, Olympia's, reaches into the barn and pulls him outside.

"Cover your faces," Malorie says. And her voice is unabridged hysteria.

As he listens to her, as he moves, fleeing the barn, he tries hard to hang on to the feeling he had, the fearlessness, that moment, just now, inside the barn when he felt brave.

It was extraordinary.

And now it's gone.

But he believes he can feel it again.

Indian River.

The community's name sparkles in his personal darkness. As if the letters that make up the words are forged in fire, enormous bright squares beckoning him, telling him, hey, hey, we're scared, too, but either you live a partial life or you experiment.

You test.

You invent.

Indian River.

We're allowed.

Come on.

Come on.

"Tom!" Malorie calls. "Come on!"

Then he's moving, the stealthy sounds of what swarms the barn receding. He catches up to his mom and his sister as their shoes crush the gravel of the shoulder before leveling out on the old unused country road.

They walk. They don't speak. They listen. They move fast.

And when enough space has gotten between them and the place they hoped might provide a night of sanctuary, Malorie's voice cracks the silence.

"No," she says.

Tom knows what she means. He knows she's answering what he asked before they left the barn. She's saying she didn't take the pages.

But Tom hears something in Malorie's voice that she claims to hear so often in theirs.

A lie.

He hears the crinkle of paper in her bag, too.

And as the three continue toward a place that may or may not harbor a mode of transport large enough to carry them north, Tom feels gratitude, to the pages, for teaching him, already, that while it's okay to be scared, you've got to push back while you tremble.

He's in the big world now. This isn't Camp Yadin.

In the distance, behind them, he hears the creaking of the barn, as if more creatures now walk on its roof.

Do they look to the fleeing trio? Do they know what they do?

It doesn't matter to Tom. Not right now. As he walks, in step with Malorie and Olympia, it doesn't matter what the creatures mean to do.

All that matters is what he means to do.

From here on out. In the big world.

He's not mad.

He's fearless. He's fighting back.

He's allowed.

ELEVEN

Olympia is keeping secrets.

She's done it for years now, almost as long as she can remember. She was doing it at the Jane Tucker School for the Blind, and she thinks it's possible it was even before then. In the house she was born. Maybe even the minute she was born. She's read enough books to know that it's not totally shameful to keep secrets and that some secrets are better kept in the interest of maintaining balance with the other people around you.

Yet, every day, it feels worse.

She knows Tom was outside the barn, reading, when the creatures came last night. She doesn't think they were drawn to him just because they saw him; she believes they can sense the fact that her brother wants to figure out how to beat them.

Maybe they can tell Tom wants to make contact, of any sort?

She knows Tom brought the glasses from under his bed. She doesn't know if they'll work, but she definitely doesn't think he should try.

Secrets. Tom doesn't know she knows. And Malorie doesn't know he has them.

But Olympia knows. Lots of things.

Sometimes this infuses her with a sense of great importance. Other times it makes her feel like she's a liar. Like she hasn't been truthful with Malorie and Tom over time.

She hasn't.

It's impossible to lie to herself, though she's read of characters who benefit from doing it. Like how they understand the people they care about are complex, and so they ignore some of the bad stuff about each other. And why not? Does it matter that Tom resents Malorie? Does it matter that Malorie is growing distant from Tom? The old world is wholly different than the new, yes, but Olympia's discovered that people mostly remain the same. The characters in her books aren't so different from those in her life.

Today, they walked until the sun came up, and now it's begun its long descent.

But they're close.

They walk slow because they're tired and they're hot and at turns it all feels like a fool's errand. There are no road signs telling them the train is close. No billboards like in the books.

But they walk. And they hope. And Olympia does all she can to make her mom feel at peace with her decision to do this.

She wants so badly for Malorie's parents to be alive. They are, she supposes, her grandparents, whether by blood or not, and she's read enough about grandparents to know the impact they can have on a teenager's life.

Oh, how she wants them to be alive. In St. Ignace. Or closer. Waiting on the platform for their family. Like grandparents used to do.

"Only two miles to go," Tom says.

They're walking as fast as they safely can.

Olympia hears the pep in her brother's voice. He's been mostly quiet today. She wonders if he assumes they take his silence to mean he's listening. But Olympia knows better. Tom goes quiet when he's planning. Back in Camp Yadin that usually meant he was coming up with the materials he'd need for a new helmet, protective body armor, heavier gloves. But out here, she wonders.

Does it have to do with what he was reading outside the barn last night?

Malorie doesn't speak much either, but it's not hard to guess at what she's thinking. Malorie believed her parents dead for seventeen years. This means, of course, that she's already grieved. It's hard for Olympia to imagine a world where blindfolds weren't central to a person's wardrobe, but if she opens her mind, if she really puts herself in Malorie's place, she can do it. She thinks: what if the world was turned so upside down that she, Olympia, didn't think Malorie could've survived? After seventeen years, weren't Malorie's parents dead anyway?

Dead to Malorie?

"How are we going to find it once we get there?" Olympia asks. Something to say. Then she wishes she didn't. She knows this answer. Malorie will say they'll listen, of course. And if they encounter any people, they'll have to ask what they know.

"We'll listen," Malorie says. And, on cue, "We'll talk to people."

Olympia senses Tom's reaction, knows it's coming before it does.

"Maybe," he says. As in, *maybe you'll let us talk to people.*

Malorie stops walking. Olympia wants to shuffle her along, tell her not to worry about Tom. Now's not the time. We're so close.

"I'll say who we talk to," Malorie says. "And you'll listen when I do."

Tom stops, too.

"Sure, Mom. Okay." Anger in his voice.

"Yes, completely fucking okay."

"You act like I don't listen," Tom says. "You act like we don't do every single crazy thing you tell us to!"

"*Listening* isn't good enough," Malorie says. "Believing that what I'm saying is right, *that's* what matters."

Olympia steps from them to the side of the road. Maybe they just need to have it out finally.

"We have minds of our own!" Tom yells.

"Jesus Christ, Tom," Malorie says. "You have no idea what you're talking about."

"Yes I do!"

"No. You don't. You've lived a completely sheltered life."

"Well, whose fault is that?"

"*Not mine!*" Malorie screams. They're screaming now.

Olympia steps farther, onto neglected grass tall enough to touch her gloved hand.

Her heel connects with something soft.

"It's one hundred percent your fault," Tom says. "We live by your rules."

"That's right. You *live*. You're *alive*. Thanks to my rules."

"Mom! You won't let us talk to anybody but you!"

"What's somebody else gonna do for you, Tom? Teach you how to tie a better blindfold?"

Olympia kneels in the tall grass, to feel for what she nearly stepped on.

"That's so close-minded, Mom!" Tom says. "It's just . . . it's insane!"

"Tom, you will listen to me . . ."

"Maybe I won't!"

Olympia touches it then withdraws her gloved hand.

"I'm sick of it!" Tom says.

"You?" Malorie yells. "You aren't *allowed* to be sick of anything!"

It's a woman at Olympia's knees. A knife in her heart. Her own fingers on the handle.

"We don't even know if they still drive people mad," Tom says. But there is less force behind this.

"We what?" Malorie asks. "What does that even mean?"

Olympia removes her glove. The blood is caked, hardened by the sun. The way it climbs up the woman's neck it feels like fingers.

"Olympia!" Malorie yells.

Olympia stands up.

"Right here, Mom."

Silence then. As if, by mentioning Olympia's name, Malorie has added some element of balance.

"No more," Malorie says. Olympia knows she doesn't only say it to Tom. She says it to everything. To the creatures. To the fact that she's searching for people she's already grieved.

Olympia cocks an ear ahead.

"Guys," she says. "I hear an engine."

She doesn't think it's a car. It sounds more like a generator, the steady hum of an amplifier. A big one.

"Ahead?" Malorie asks.

"Yes."

"It's not a car," Tom says.

"No," Olympia says.

"Tell me more," Malorie says.

"It's . . . wider than a car . . ." Tom says.

"It's the train," Malorie says.

Olympia blanches. Is Mom right? Is this what a train sounds like?

It sounds huge.

"We gotta move fast," Malorie says. "Two miles?"

"A little less," Tom says.

"Now," Malorie says. Tendrils of hysteria present. *"Now."*

The train.

Is it, though? Or is that, as Olympia has read in so many books, only what they want it to be?

Malorie and Tom are gaining distance on her. Olympia turns once, back to the dead woman in the tall grass on the side of the country road.

"I'm sorry," she says. "Sorry I didn't acknowledge you at all."

But she knows this was the right thing to do. Her mom and her brother are working together, ahead, neither any darker for a dead body.

An omen.

A portent.

Not now.

And sometimes, again, keeping secrets is the right thing to do.

She hurries to catch up with them. The unfamiliar engine hums steady in the distance, and she imagines a machine bigger than the house she was born in.

She moves.

She catches up.

She keeps secrets.

TWELVE

Malorie's mind is ablaze.

She thinks it's a train. She wants it to be. She can't tell. She's never focused so hard on a sound, any sound. What does a train actually sound like, from this distance, from this state of mind?

She moves fast. Too fast. Yet Olympia is a step ahead. Her daughter calls out when there are dips in the road, and more than once she's reached back to take Malorie by the arm.

It doesn't matter that she fought with Tom. Nothing matters right now but the incredible hum in the distance. Every few feet the source sounds like it's coming from a different place. To her right; no, left. It's got to be less than a mile now, no, more like three. At times, the sound vanishes altogether, and Malorie imagines a train vanishing, like a trick on television, the whole giant thing fading until, just when she thinks it's gone, it appears again, over a horizon that could be near or far.

"Tom?" she asks.

"Yes. I'm fine."

She doesn't need to ask after Olympia. Her daughter is leading the rush, like she's done so many times before. Malorie remembers the trip from the school for the blind to Camp Yadin. Even then, little Olympia took charge.

"Watch out," Olympia calls. "Big turn in the road."

Malorie moves toward her, her daughter, while thinking of herself as a daughter, daughter to Sam and Mary Walsh. She suddenly can't tell the difference between who's who here, and then Olympia's hand is at her elbow, guiding her.

Olympia says something about the train, how it might not be leaving, might not be there at all. But Malorie's mind is so gorged with the possibility of seeing her parents that she's mistaking the train for them, as if it's Mom and Dad idling in the distance.

"I can run ahead," Tom says. Because he doesn't worry about falling. Because he'd bounce back up. Because he's sixteen.

"No," Malorie says. But maybe this is one time she should say yes. "You can't get hurt. Not now."

Her voice is breathless, the syllables broken by heaves. Is she panicking?

It strikes her that Sam and Mary Walsh *could* be standing by the monster that idles. If the train goes to Mackinaw City, and if her parents had, at one point, worked their way downstate, doesn't it stand to reason they could've taken the train south? Even as Malorie runs to take it up to them?

Reason.

The word sounds wholly out of place here. *Reason* in a world gone mad. A world gone dark. A world where she could conceivably be passing her mom and dad *right now,* the two of them quiet for the sound of three people running toward them, the two of them still working their way downstate, the two of them looking for her.

It's not a train, Malorie thinks. Because it can't be. Because the idling engine of a train doesn't go quiet, then rise again. It doesn't sound exactly like this. And because it would be too unfathomably good for her if it *is* there.

If there's one thing Malorie hasn't had, it's breaks.

Has anyone?

But she moves toward it still. Nearly running now.

Both teens are ahead; Olympia calls out the dips in the road, Tom says they have less than a mile to go. Malorie's legs scream. Her chest is too hot. Her head is swelling with memories. Mom and Dad taking her and Shannon to the zoo. How the sisters followed the painted elephant prints to where the brilliant leviathan stood in a large enclosure, but nowhere near big enough. How Dad picked Malorie up and told her he wished he could sneak the animal out of the park, put it under his coat, walk it all the way back to Africa. Malorie remembers laughing at this, then understanding what he meant, then understanding that her dad was a nice man. She remembers Mom, at a store, standing in line to buy the sisters jeans. How the woman in front of them was two dollars short. How Mom gave her those two dollars.

Oh, how Malorie wants to see these two people again. The yearning has conquered her body. The hope, the rush, the possibility . . .

But she won't let herself do this, won't let herself commit. It might not be a train at all.

And even if it is . . . who drives it?

"Come on!" Tom calls excitedly. Malorie hears him nearly fall over and regain his balance. She feels Olympia's hand at her elbow.

"Come on!" Tom yells again. And he sounds sixteen. So does Olympia. Two teenagers living, right now, a memory, a thing they will never forget, Malorie knows; she has memories of her own. Mom and Dad laughing with the neighbors at the kitchen table.

Dad wearing a funny wig on Halloween. Mom stringing lights up on the roof in December.

She thinks, suddenly, of Ron Handy. How the man must be thinking of his sister, now, pining to touch her hand again, hurting to hear her voice.

"It might not—" Malorie starts, short of breath. "It might not even be—" She can hardly get the words out. "It might not even be a train!"

On cue, a whistle blows.

It shatters Malorie's personal darkness, the black sky split up the middle by a cloud of white metallic steam, billowing with the force of a bona fide train.

Oh my God, she thinks. *Oh my God oh my God oh my God.*

And she's running, her mind wild, fresh colors in the dark, one the color of belief.

It's a train after all. There's no doubting that now.

"COME ON!"

Did she yell it? Was it Tom? No, Olympia. Olympia is leading again. She's calling out what to watch for. Like she's a cat, able to react faster to the drops and curves than Malorie ever will be able to again. And it's working. Branches strike her arm, and her knees almost give out as the road begins to unspool downhill, but Malorie is running, no longer simply moving, running to a blind train, a train that heads north, to where her parents have been listed as *survivors*.

The sun is hot and still high and because the road is downhill, she can hear the engine idling, much louder than it was before. She can see the image, as if the whole insane scenario is a Norman Rockwell painting; creamy white steam rising from the head of a black train, its wheels shimmering in the summer sun. She imagines men and women with parasols on the platform, engineers and ushers taking tickets, children afraid to board, pets tight on leashes, bags and cases, shoes on creaking boards, the tracks leading off into the future, north, like a secret door to Mom and Dad.

Sam and Mary Walsh.

Malorie falls.

She bangs her knee hard on the road and realizes it's not soft dirt anymore, it's packed, possibly pavement. She's hot beneath the hoodie and gloves, sweating behind the blindfold. And it strikes her, as she's getting back up, as Olympia's hands settle on her shoulders, that the reality of the moment is nothing like a fabled painting of the old world. The train doesn't glisten, it sits, most likely rusted out in parts, probably dangerously wired for electricity. There's no way the machine has passed any safety codes, this much she knows. The windows must be painted black, and it's easy to imagine that paint dripping down the sides of the train's body, reaching the giant wheels. She would bet money there are boards missing, spaces along the twin tracks that lead north, yes, but not the north it used to be. Here, the train will ride into blackness, all its passengers blindfolded, even the engineer unable to look outside. And what would he see if he did? There are no families saying goodbye, no pets to be sure. And the luggage the passengers take with them are only bags stuffed with canned goods and batteries, extra shoes and black cloth.

Who else would ride a train like this? And why?

Malorie is up, moving again, her knee be damned. The idea of the train leaving now, before they get there, is almost too cruel to comprehend. How long would they have to call this area home, waiting for it to return?

"We're so close," Tom says.

And Malorie knows they are. Her son's voice is nearly inaudible among the roar of the big engine. She imagines Tom sucked up into a new world, where industry reigns once again, where jobs are wanted, workers needed, professions opening onto infinite paths, journeys her teens might've taken two decades ago.

"Stay close," Malorie calls.

She can't be sure where Tom and Olympia are. How far ahead? Olympia's voice emerges from the noise, a semblance of assurance, but only near for long as a bat might have been, flying low over the blindfolded woman attempting to run this last bit of road.

Will Malorie and her teens be protected, safe from whoever else is on board? Is there food? Water? Bathrooms? Beds?

And what does it cost to ride?

"Guys!" Malorie calls. A hand is at her elbow, then gone.

The whistle shrieks again.

They're so close.

"Tom!" she yells. "Olympia!"

But it's the voice of a man that answers.

"You've got seconds," the man says. "You better hurry!"

It feels, momentarily, horribly, like the man means she has seconds to live. And maybe that is what he means. And maybe she does.

But she rushes, arms up. Hands take her own, smaller hands, Olympia.

The sound of the train changes, and Malorie knows it's starting to move. The deep exhale of machinery waking up.

"Oh, no," she says, breathless.

"It's still here," Tom says.

Tom! Tom is here, too.

But the train is moving. Malorie is sure of this now.

And other people are yelling, calling out, something about clearing the way, clearing the tracks.

The engine roars. The whistle blows.

Steam. A train. So close.

But it's moving.

"Come on!" Olympia says.

"It's leaving!" Tom yells.

But they do not stop. They move. Upon creaking boards now. The platform? The station? Malorie cracks shoulders with someone else, someone who shouts out at her to be careful. The old-world phrase sounds like a harbinger of things to come.

"We gotta leap onto the back," Olympia says. Malorie imagines her daughter read that in a book. Characters, train hoppers, hoboes. She can't believe she's agreeing to this. There's no way she can justify this idea. It's not the mother she's been for sixteen years.

"Mom!" Olympia calls.

Malorie reaches for her, doesn't find her. The train sounds like it's moving faster, too fast, the engine no longer exhaling but breathing, steady, rising to face the north.

"We can't do it," Malorie says. She sees Ron Handy in his service station, a dirty glass of old whiskey in hand. She sees him crying, now, grappling with the horror of choosing not to go to his sister.

Malorie tries to close her mind's eye, the eye behind the eyes that are already closed, all of it behind the blindfold she lives by. She doesn't want to think of Ron Handy or Camp Yadin, Tom the man or Olympia the woman, the Jane Tucker School for the Blind, Annette or Gary. She wants to focus on the sound of the train, moving, the rolling wheels, the squealing of metal, the pumping, the steam, the machine. Yet her mom and dad appear, standing as they were at the end of the dock on Twin Lakes, deep in the Upper Peninsula. They're smiling her way, encouraging, you can make it, swim, come on, you're so close. Dad's hair is still brown and Mom doesn't yet wear glasses, and they're the people they were when Malorie was a child, swimming for the first time.

Only they're wearing blindfolds suddenly, their hands extended. They can't see Malorie, and it feels like nobody knows how to connect. They call to her, just as voices call to her as she runs, and Malorie flails, hot from the sun, unsure she's going to make it, sensing something huge in the water with her, sensing something huge (and moving) in the darkness with her now, as she runs, as the toes of her boots connect with the tracks.

Tracks!

Malorie is running for a train!

Come on, Malorie!

Shannon. Even her sister is encouraging her from the dock. The same sister who expressed jealousy and said but the lake was hers to swim in and had to be consoled by (*Sam and Mary Walsh*) Mom and Dad. Now Shannon calls to her, her voice high and energized. She's rooting for Malorie to make it just as Malorie once rooted for Shannon to make it in the new world, just as that new world was replacing the old one, even as Shannon believed in the creatures before Malorie did.

Come on, Malorie!

And Malorie reaches for the dock, blindly, the water and the darkness above her head it seems, so that she might be running sideways now, might be running toward the earth or even away from the train.

Mom and Dad are laughing, and Malorie knows it's because she's going to make it.

A hand grips her own.

The train isn't moving fast. Can't move fast. Blind.

She's pulled forward, and a second hand takes her second hand, and Malorie's feet are suddenly dragging. Her shin connects with something metal and the sound of the machine is so loud, so terribly loud, that she feels like it's falling from the sky, falling directly above her.

"Step up," Tom says.

It's Tom who has her. Tom holds her, guides her to a set of metal steps.

Malorie raises a leg, puts it down, but her boot connects with nothing and she's dragged again.

The teens are talking fast, yelling at each other, trying to pull Malorie to safety.

Malorie lifts her leg again and this time, when she lunges, the tip of her boot is supported by the first metal step.

"You can do it," Olympia says.

Malorie pulls herself up, all the way, onto solid footing. She's standing—standing!—gripping metal bannisters, already thinking that, however long this trip takes, she will not take off her fold for the duration.

They are moving without walking. In the new world.

A man's voice breaks her reverie.

"You got her?"

"Yes," Olympia says. She sounds like Shannon did on the dock.

"Who is that?" Malorie asks. But the thunder that usually accompanies these inquiries from her is absent.

They just made a moving train.

The man is talking again, but his voice grows distant. Malorie understands he's heading deeper into the train. She hears a door slide closed.

She climbs the remaining steps.

Olympia and Tom are there. She hugs them in turn, as the three exclaim brief hollows of relief. Then she turns to face the darkness she just ran through, wondering if this was the right decision, if this isn't the most dangerous thing she's ever done.

She has put her teens' lives in danger. There is no rationalizing this. No pretending she hasn't.

"We did it," Olympia says. She sounds ecstatic. Alive. Like a teen who has begun the biggest adventure of her life.

Malorie faces the train's back door, the world of dirt roads and Camp Yadin fading out behind her.

She breathes in, she holds it, she breathes out.

Who knows what kind of people are inside this train.

Or how many.

She thinks, *If it gets bad, we can leap.*

"Okay," she says, flecks of mania in her voice. "Keep your folds and hoodies on. Gloves, too. We're going in."

She feels a pat against her bag. Is it Tom trying to hug her again?

Malorie steps between her teens and finds the handle for the sliding door. She thinks of her mom and dad because she can't not think of them. Their names, emblazoned on the pages in her bag, their names that got her on this train.

"You do exactly what I say," she says. "And you only talk to who I say you can talk to. You tell *nobody* where we are going or why. We are not here to make friends. We are here to get from one place to another. That is all. Do you understand?"

"Yes," Olympia says.

"Yes," Tom says.

"Okay," Malorie says. "I love you guys."

All images, memories, and fantasies leave Malorie's mind at once, leaving only the infinite black of what's to come before her.

She slides the door open.

She breathes in, she holds it, she breathes out.

And the trio enters the blind train.

THE BLIND TRAIN

THIRTEEN

This will end in madness.

Because it always does. When Malorie is around other people, someone makes a mistake. Someone tries something they shouldn't. Someone believes something they shouldn't. No two minds are alike, she knows. Not even her teens, raised as they have been in the same exact manner, having experienced the same exact series of events from when they were born to now, this minute, running for, and making, a train. Even someone who appears kindhearted might glance out a window. Even someone abrasive might never. The old constructs of good and bad have long been replaced with safe and unsafe. Are you a safe person? She thinks she is. She knows she is. At the school for the blind she was ridiculed for it. Others thought her precautions meant she thought they weren't doing it right. Insecurities, here, even in the face of madness, the sight of a creature, not of this world, not of the old world, anyway. Long dead is the idea of the enthusiast, the go-getter, the happy man, woman, or child. Now, you either look or you do not. You either live by the fold or you do not. You either dedicate your life to the darkness, shared, at times, by rope, by hands, by voice, with those closest to you. Or you do not.

And this, this place that smells of people, where bodies can be heard shifting in the darkness, where conversations mingle with the throbbing of the engine and the rolling of the wheels on the pre-existing tracks, this place will end in madness, too.

Malorie only hopes they get to Mackinaw City first.

Someone walks toward them; Malorie hears heavy steps in what feels like a hall. The teens behind her, she stops and puts her arms out, acting the part of a shield. She thinks she hears movement behind a door to her left. Sleeping cars, then. A house moving at five miles per hour on a track. This is good. Or can be. Personal space. And if they get that space and someone invades it?

Jump.

"Latecomers," a man's voice. Sounds about Malorie's age. "But comers all the same. David told me you just made it. Welcome. Isn't it fantastic?"

Malorie feels the swaying of the car. Movement without moving her own legs. The first since taking a rowboat twelve years ago.

She doesn't speak. She isn't sure what to say, how to respond. This isn't the same as encountering someone in Camp Yadin, a place she called home. This also isn't like meeting someone in the woods, with no semblance of society at hand.

"I have a feeling you're not going to want to do this," the man begins. Malorie leans back, into her teens. "But you don't have to wear your folds on the train."

"Don't listen to him," Malorie says.

"No, no. I get it," the man says. "I didn't mean to get us started on the wrong foot. Honestly. Don't worry. Some people prefer to wear them the whole time. But the truth is—"

"Who are you?"

The man laughs. It sounds like an old-world laugh. The kind she might've heard at a party.

"Dean Watts," the man says. "The owner of this train. Though that word doesn't have the same panache it once did, does it? How about . . . I'm the one who thought we ought to try using the big dead train after all."

Malorie imagines a person as optimistic as Tom the man once was. Would he have done something like this? Had he lived to try?

"You've gotta be overwhelmed," Dean says. "Everybody is the first time."

"Have you had repeat riders?"

"Some. There's a man who rode back and forth a dozen times. He—"

"How many times has this train run?"

"I've got an idea," Dean says. "How about you follow me to the dining car. We sit down. I answer all your questions. Believe me, during the blind restoration of this thing, I spent enough time standing in the halls."

"We'd like a private car if one is available."

She hears Tom huff behind her. She knows he wants to meet people. She can only imagine how unfathomably cosmopolitan this man Dean's voice and life must sound to her son.

"We do have one," Dean says. "Several, actually. The train is ten cars long. There's a dining car, two storage cars, six passenger cars, and two that are more or less delivery spaces. We get almost all our orders and requests via telegram." He goes silent a second. "Did you know the world is using telegrams again?"

She can tell by the way he asked he knows she didn't. Can he tell she wants to know what he's delivering?

"And before you ask," he says, "we deliver all sorts of things.

Furniture. Blankets. Canned goods. Even the dead. To loved ones who have gotten word of their location."

Malorie can't process everything the man says. She has ten questions for each unfathomable statement he makes.

She thought she had some grasp on the new world. Then . . . a knock on a cabin door has delivered her a train, a telegram, and the names of her parents.

"Here's the thing," Dean says. "I want everyone who rides to be as comfortable as possible. It's not like we're making money here. There's no such thing anymore. But I do care. You'll just have to trust me that much."

But Malorie doesn't want anybody telling her who she'll have to trust.

"A private car," she says. "That's all."

"Might I ask what you're on board for?"

The train rocks. It's not going anywhere near as fast as the trains Malorie took in the old world. It feels more like she's riding a bike. Yet, for someone who hasn't even ridden a bike in sixteen years, the motion is alarming. She has questions. Should she ask them? It's dangerous enough that she's brought the teens this far. In fact, it's downright insane. Now that's she's here, on board, swaying with the motion, listening to the whining wheels, facing a stranger in a hall she cannot see, a stranger who, she assumes, does not wear a fold, who looks directly at her, it's not hard to count this as the single most unsafe thing she's ever done.

There is no good or bad anymore.

Only safe or—

"Just a car," she says again. "That's all."

Dean claps his hands together.

"Okay. I get it. Follow me and I'll show you the first available one."

"Is there one right here in this car?"

"No," Dean says. "We're standing in one of the storage cars. As glamorous as you can imagine. Come this way."

He moves and she follows. She can feel the energy of the teens behind her as if they are bridled horses, waiting to be freed. Both, she knows, must be out of their heads with curiosity. Tom has tried, over time, to invent other modes of travel. At Camp Yadin he fashioned a wheelbarrow into something of a padded rolling chair. It strikes Malorie now that Tom's silly invention feels safer to her than this giant, swaying machine.

Yet Dean does sound smart. This means something to her. And while smart does not beget safe, it's better than the alternative.

"How can you be sure the tracks are clear?" she asks.

She thinks she can hear Dean smile.

Is she really on a train? Can this be?

"I'm telling you, let's sit down in the dining car. There are *so* many exciting answers for all the questions you're asking. I mean, think about it . . ." He stops walking, and Malorie nearly bumps into him when he speaks again. "Wait. I didn't even ask your names yet."

Malorie can almost feel the words crawling up the throats of her teens.

"I'm Jill," she says first. "And this is John and Jamie."

"How old are you, John?"

"He's twenty."

She thinks she hears something like a smile on Dean's face again. He knows she's lying. But she doesn't care. She wants to get to a car. Close the door. Lock it.

Sam and Mary Walsh.

"And you, Jamie?" Dean asks.

"She's twenty-one," Malorie says.

"A great age. Any age is a good one in this world. It means you've survived."

They walk. The train sways. Malorie imagines a black landscape passing, gradations of darkness, a world she and her teens will never see.

"Is that music?" Tom suddenly asks.

Dean stops again.

"You can hear that?" He goes quiet, and Malorie listens for what Tom heard. "There are three musicians on board. Playing guitars in the dining car. They do it often. I can't believe you can hear them, John."

Malorie finds Tom's wrist in the darkness and grips it. They are in the new world now, but that does not mean they are of it.

Don't get lazy.

The three-word mantra has kept her and these teens alive for so long. The small but powerful phrase that separates her and has always separated her from the people who think they can defeat indefatigable circumstance.

But despite his mom's hand, Tom still responds.

"It sounds good."

Dean laughs again. Malorie wonders if she turns red in front of him.

"It definitely does," Dean says. "But it's not as cool as the fact that your ears work like they do. *That,* John, is phenomenal."

"Who keeps the tracks clear?" Malorie asks again. Her own voice sounds petty. Like she's looking for control. "How can you be sure we aren't going to crash?"

Dean stops walking again, and this time Malorie does bump into him. She can tell he's taller than she is, wider. She backs up.

"Do you remember Buster Keaton?" he asks her. She thinks of her dad. Dad liked Buster Keaton.

"Please, just tell me how—"

"He made a movie called *The General*. Brilliant sequence where he's clearing the tracks of falling logs. It's so well orchestrated that you almost think it's magic. Well, this isn't anywhere near as funny as that, but at the head of the train, there's a smaller, metal cart. And upon that cart is a man named Michael. And Michael makes sure nothing enormous has fallen across the tracks."

"Isn't that dangerous?" Malorie asks. "What he's doing?"

"Of course it is. But Michael wants to do it."

"But he could die out there and we wouldn't know."

"Jill," Dean says. "I have answers for all these questions. Good ones. If you'd—"

"Please. Answer them now."

She feels something she hasn't felt in ages. Something like overstepping. For the first time since leaving the school for the blind, Malorie is demanding answers from someone who is helping her.

Isn't Dean helping her? Isn't this train helping her reach her parents?

"So Michael has a switchbox with him out there. The engineer—"

"There's an engineer?"

"There has to be. Her name is Tanya. She's incredible. If Tanya doesn't receive a transmission from Michael's box for more than ten minutes, for whatever reason, even if we discover later he only dropped it, she stops the train."

"Has this happened before?"

"No."

"And has Michael ever found objects on the tracks? Ones you had to make stops for? To clear?"

"Yes. Fallen trees. And once, a dead herd of elk. We think they went mad."

"Mad . . ."

"There are stretches this train passes in which hundreds of creatures roam."

Malorie thinks to turn around. She thinks to take the teens and walk straight out the back of the train and leap back to the tracks. They could brave the walk again. They could be back in Yadin in a few days.

But she doesn't want to leave. Not yet. She trusts just enough of what she hears in Dean's voice to make her stay. So instead, she asks more questions. And it feels a little like she's dipping a toe in the new world after all.

"How do you know that?"

Dean breathes deep, and Malorie braces herself for something she doesn't want to hear.

"Well, two ways," he says.

"Yeah?" Pressing.

"Yes. One is similar to what I'm understanding about John here. We've had young riders who can hear much better than you or I ever will."

"And the other?"

Dean spills it.

"Passengers have gone mad. Riders who perhaps took the train for an opportunity to watch the world pass."

"But how?" Panic rising in her voice. "The windows are blackened, right?"

"Of course. But—"

"Then how?"

"Between cars. If one really wanted to look . . . they could."

Malorie steels herself.

"How many passengers have gone mad on this train?" she asks.

Dean doesn't hesitate.

"Seven."

The shape of panic now. In the vicinity. So close to her.

"And what happened to those people?"

Dean doesn't hesitate again.

"Myself and David escorted them off."

"You tossed them off the train?" Olympia asks.

"Yes. Without a bit of debate, I'm sorry to say."

Malorie likes this answer. But she's far from feeling safe.

"They didn't ask to go mad," she says.

"I know that," Dean says. "Believe me. I'm haunted by every one of them."

Malorie tries not to think of Gary. She tries to shove him as far from her mind's eye as she can. But there he is. In a distant corner. At the far right side of the darkness.

He waves.

"There're two open cars this way," Dean says. "Come on."

Malorie decides, here, now, to continue. Dean didn't try to hide the past from her. This means something.

She can tell he walks slowly for them. She reaches both arms out, feeling the walls of the hall as it sways with the motion of the train.

"So, like I said, this is a storage car," he says. "This and the next. There's a bathroom here, too."

Malorie thinks of what he said about transporting dead bodies. Are there caskets on the other side of this wall? Dead people swaying even as she does?

"All sorts of stuff in there," Dean says. "Survival stuff."

Malorie wants to feel good about this. Two cars full of supplies. As if they dragged the basement of the lodge at Camp Yadin with them.

"And this," Dean says, "is the door to the next car."

She hears it slide open.

"You're already blindfolded so I won't tell you to close your eyes. We've tried dozens of ways to block off the view between cars, but either the wind takes them, the motion breaks them, or those who've wanted to look do so anyway. Come on."

Malorie feels a hand in hers. It's not Tom. Not Olympia. She pulls back.

"Sorry," Dean says. "I just thought—"

"We can manage."

"All right. Follow me."

She reaches behind her and takes Olympia's hand. The air is cold between cars. Powerful.

Inside the second car, Dean closes the door behind them.

"More storage. Clothes for the needy, though we're all needy now, aren't we?"

Malorie imagines an alternate reality with this man, one in which she would say yes, we're all needy, and winters in Michigan are brutal, and how kind to deliver clothes, what an incredible thing you've started here.

But she doesn't want to talk any more than she has to. She wants that private room, that space. No more.

They walk.

"Another door," Dean says. "Ahead is the first of the passenger cars."

Someone opens the door before Dean does. The person comes fast, and Dean is shoved back into Malorie.

Malorie grips Olympia's wrist. This is it. The moment they're going to have to leap from the train. It's not hard to imagine the gravel cutting into her elbows and knees just like it did when she fell off her bike, riding it for the first time. She can still see Mom crouched beside her, placing a Band-Aid on a cut.

"Sorry," a man says. "Bathroom."

He gets by Malorie and the teens clumsily, apologizing as he goes, his words breathless the way words are when someone hurries.

"You see?" Dean says. "A bit like the old world after all."

He laughs, and Malorie wants to laugh, too. But she was prepared to leap from a moving train, mistaking a man in a hurry for a man gone mad.

"Door," Dean reminds her.

They step through. Between cars, the motion is stronger, the wind stronger, the feeling that she's doing something she shouldn't be doing stronger, too.

"Here," Dean says once they're through. "This room is open."

She hears a door slide. The sound of the wheels gets louder. A distant grating comes into focus. The outside world that much closer. As if Dean has let some of it in.

But this is what she's asked for. This is what she wants. The safety of privacy. Where Tom and Olympia will not be tempted to discuss anything with anybody lurking deeper on this train.

She steps into the room.

"It's actually quite nice," Dean says. "If you decide to remove your fold, you'll find red cushions on a bench. Two twin beds. A mirror. And I've learned that, at this slow speed, it can sometimes feel like what a hotel once did. Do you remember those, Jill?"

"Of course."

But Malorie is feeling around the room, learning the dimensions. Her fingers alight upon a broom handle.

"For the more anxious set," Dean says. "You can sweep the room to your heart's delight every time you return to it." Then, as if needing to explain the possibility of her leaving the car in the first place, he says, "There's a second bathroom in the next car up. Just knock is all we ask."

"This is amazing," Malorie says because she has to. Because

she can't keep it in anymore. Of course tracks are the answer. In a world gone blind, the only safe roads are the ones that grip the vehicle and tell it where to go.

She thinks of the man Michael, alone out front, searching for debris in whatever way he does it.

"Thanks," Dean says. "We're extremely proud of it. And like I said . . . no money. But what are you gonna do? Sit in the dark your whole life? Not me. Not us. We gotta try *something*, don't we? And I have an idea or two."

"Yes," Tom says.

Malorie is so swept up in the moment that she doesn't allow herself to get angry at Tom for speaking. It strikes her that she's already trusting Dean after all.

She remembers, briefly, feeling this way all the time.

"I have a feeling you have more than an idea or two," Malorie says.

This is good, talking like she used to, back when every word wasn't tethered to survival.

"I admit it," Dean says. "I do. But for me, and I'm not just saying this to placate you, for me the absolute key is safety. There's simply no way around that. A train, today, has to be much safer than it was seventeen years ago. It simply has to be, or there'd be no reason for it to exist. It's ironic, no? That in a world with no litigation, we've become even more careful?"

"Thank you, Dean," Malorie says. Because that's enough for now. That's enough loosening up.

Dean's eyes are open. Dean could see something. It feels like she's standing near a bomb. Something could go wrong. Everything could explode. Any second. Other people have their eyes open on this train. She has so many questions. Has a creature ever made it on board? Into one of the rooms?

"You're welcome," Dean says. "And so you know, this car is

already stocked with cans and water. It's all in the cupboard beside the mirror. The windows are indeed blacked out. In fact, there is technically no window at all in this car, as all the glass on the sides of the train has been replaced with sheet metal, painted black. I've never seen this train from the outside, for reasons you can easily guess. But I assume it's a bit like Frankenstein. Pieces, brought together, brought to life. I'm so glad you guys made it."

"Thank you," Malorie says again. There is a finality in her tone. But she's not the last one to speak to Dean.

"Thank you," Olympia says. "This is all . . . overwhelming."

"It's so great," Tom says.

Malorie wonders if Dean is judging her. Does he look from her blindfolded teens to her, covered in cloth? Does a sympathetic expression adorn his face? Does he think he knows what's right and what isn't? Even for her?

She sets her bag down. It doesn't matter. That's enough loosening up for one day. For one lifetime.

"The trip to Mackinaw City is about two days, barring any delays," Dean says. "To some that sounds like nothing, to others an eternity. If you need me for any reason, I'm usually in the dining car. And while that sounds like I'm living it up, it really means David and I are working on new ideas or talking to Tanya, checking on Michael. But," he pauses, "at least there's some music." Then, "I hope to see you in there, Jill."

Malorie breathes in, holds it, breathes out.

"You won't," she says.

Is it Dean who sighs? Or Tom?

"Okay," Dean says. "Please, enjoy."

He steps into the hall, and Malorie slides the door closed behind him.

Then, for the first time since making the train, she allows the swaying to take her. As if she's on a singular wave, traversing the entire distance between herself and her parents.

Mom and Dad might be at the end of this line. They might be anywhere in the world. They might also be buried. She imagines stepping off the train, crossing a bridge, searching St. Ignace for Sam and Mary Walsh.

It feels good, necessary, to let herself be taken. For someone else to be in charge of the events to follow. It's a feeling she hasn't experienced in seventeen years.

She's so briefly relieved to be alone in this room, the door closed behind her, that it doesn't quite bother her when Tom speaks. When he says, "I like him, Mom. I like that man."

FOURTEEN

They spend the night in their private car. The hours pass, and with each one Malorie feels closer. Safer. The reality of this experience becomes palatable, a thing she wouldn't have dreamed possible in Camp Yadin. When she visited Ron Handy, the idea of a train felt more akin to a giant spider, something that could leap at her, attack her, kill her. But now the details of the train are filling in. The sounds and the smells. The feel of the cushions beneath the bench she sits on. The sense of being taken. And within this new reality (they're on a *train*), she finds her own strength, her own rules to live by, a way to convince herself she has not put her teens in danger. They could leap. They could fight. They could stay in this car until the train stops.

But Malorie knows that isn't how this is going to go. She hasn't fully admitted it, but the tendrils of acquiescence have arrived. And they only get stronger as the hours pass.

Yes, she is going to visit that dining car. She is going to talk with Dean Watts about his train. If she's honest with herself, she'll admit it's not only because the teens have a safe place to stay. It's not only because an old-world mode of travel that she believed long dead has risen. Yes, she is awed by the machine that carries her. Yes, the romanticized past is present in this way.

But none of that is why she wants to speak with Dean.

The reason is, she *likes* him.

It's a feeling she hasn't felt in years. A decade or more. A thing she also thought long buried, yet now, opening its eyes.

"Sleep," she tells her teens. But they already do. She hears them both breathing heavy, the light snoring of two young people who deserve rest after the few days they've had.

Malorie deserves rest, too.

And so she allows herself some. She closes her eyes, behind the blindfold. She allows the train to take her north, closer to the place where her parents were listed as having survived. How long ago was that list made? Right now it doesn't matter. Right now she needs sleep. And for the hours to move. So that two days pass as quickly as they can. As the machine that takes them cuts through an entire world she is no longer allowed to look at. Where creatures no doubt outnumber the people. Where the reason for all these precautions, all this fear, roams freer than the people who have survived them.

Malorie sleeps.

Rocked to sleep.

And the hours pass.

And the dreams that come include Sam and Mary Walsh. At turns they stand before her, living, before becoming dust, sand blown away by a moving train, two tiny points in infinity that no sane woman can be expected to find.

And in the dreams there are creatures.

Everywhere.

FIFTEEN

Despite the setting, the voices of other people, the sound of guitars being played, the motion of the train, and the man Dean himself sitting across a table she has not and will not see, Malorie still thinks of her parents. And how can she not? The last time she rode a train, it was with them, the Wolverine Line, from Detroit to Chicago, as Dad spent the beginning of his vacation in the bar car and his two daughters stared out the train windows, watching a wholly new landscape pass with more precision than it ever did in a minivan. It was exhilarating then, two Upper Peninsula teens heading to the big city for the first time in their lives. They only saw a sliver of Detroit, their drive down taking them over the bridge, through Mackinaw City, Gaylord, Bay City, Flint, and Saginaw before reaching the bustle of the suburbs of Detroit, the very area Shannon and Malorie would eventually move to, shortly before Shannon looked out a window and took her own life. Back then, on the Wolverine Line, the car full to capacity, Dad laughing with strangers in the bar car, Mom reading a book across the aisle, the idea of Chicago might as well have been Oz. Glittering constructs and shimmering suits, magic in every brick and bone.

"Here," Dean says. He guides Malorie's hand to a plate. "Fruit if you want it."

Malorie, blindfolded, wonders if it's possible that somehow the very train they took to Chicago, the cars themselves, made their way through some sort of boxcar arc, orphans moved from one location to another, so that here she sits in the very same rectangle that she and her sister once rode, feeling then the electricity of infinity ahead.

"Shoot," Dean says. "Hit me with all you want to know."

But before she does, a woman's voice comes close.

"Dean," the woman says. "There's a man in car six who thinks a spider or some bug is crawling on him. I keep telling him I don't see anything, but he insists."

"And he wants us to get rid of it?"

"I guess so."

Dean laughs. It sounds genuine to Malorie.

"Some people do expect old-world luxuries when they board, Jill."

Malorie momentarily thinks that he's talking to the woman. She's forgotten she is "Jill."

"Car six?" he asks the woman.

"Yeah."

"I'll take care of it. Thanks."

Then, the two are alone again. Only they're not. Malorie hears the quiet conversation of other people. Hears them discussing cities in Michigan, the telegram, the fact that they're on a train and if a train again, why not everything again, why not the entire old world again, sooner than later?

Malorie imagines Tom the man sitting across from her, sitting everywhere in here. It's been sixteen years. In a way, she attributes this progress to him. This is what he's accomplished. He's brought back the train.

Just like he once brought back a phone book that led Malorie to the school for the blind, then to Camp Yadin, where a man delivered a pile of papers with her parents' names on them.

"All right," Dean says. "Hit me."

"How many times has a creature got on board?"

"None."

"How do you know?"

"Well, I suppose I don't. But the people who went mad on this train saw something outside."

"How do you know?"

"Again, maybe I don't. But myself and the other staff walk around without folds. So, I suppose something would've happened to one of us by now had there been one on board. Again, the people who went—"

"You said people transport dead bodies."

"We deliver them, yes."

"Are there any on board right now?"

"Yes."

"Where?"

"Two caskets in storage car one. About exactly where we first met. By the back door. I would recommend not sleeping in there. Smells a bit of the grave."

"Thank you for the honesty."

"Any sunnier questions? Like, how many people died putting the train back together?"

"I'm sorry," Malorie says. "But right now all I care about is those two teens. All I care about is getting them where we're going safely."

"Well, where are you going?"

"I don't feel like telling you that."

"But I'm someone who might be able to give you the most direct route."

"I don't feel like saying."

"Fair enough."

"Are there any passengers on this train that worry you?"

"Worry me? No. There is a blind woman, but she's better off than any of us. Why do you wear the hoodie and gloves?"

The question catches Malorie off guard. It's the first time she's felt anything close to being socially self-conscious in a long time. It's an old-world state of mind she has not missed.

"You think they can drive us mad by touching us," Dean says.

Hearing him say it makes it more real. And less.

"And I'm sure you have reason to believe this," he says.

"I do."

"Jesus," he says. "Here I invited you to the dining car to assuage your nerves and you've gone and rattled mine."

"I'm good at that."

Dean laughs. But not without weight.

"Tell me, Jill," he says, "how have you been able to keep it up for this long?"

"Safety?"

"Not just that. You act like we all did when it first happened, when they first arrived. Do you have any idea how many people weren't able to stay focused like you have? I'll guess we'll never know that exact number. But you still live by the blindfold and the blindfold alone."

The guitars in the room go slightly out of tune before one of the players finds his or her place again.

"Do you know anything about a census?" she asks, avoiding his question.

"I've heard they're out there, but I haven't met anybody yet. Why?"

"I'm just curious. The numbers of the world. Statistics."

"And? Would you take more risks, depending on those numbers? Or would you still do things the way we did them when the world first changed?"

If anybody else had asked her this question, she would've left the table, the car, and possibly the train. She doesn't want to talk about taking more risks. But the man reminds her so much of Tom the man that she can't bring herself to turn from him.

When's the last time Malorie heard an optimistic voice her own age? When's the last time she could swap ideas, theories, even just moods with someone who understands the world as she does for having witnessed its change? Tom, her son, speaks like this. But he's only sixteen. And her job, as she sees it, is to make sure he remains smart about whatever he wants to do. That means telling him no. That means discouraging him. That means . . .

Take note, she thinks. *Your son talks a lot like the one man whose advice you've leaned on for the past seventeen years. And all you do is tell him no.*

"I wouldn't change a thing," she says. But it feels wrong to say it, like she means it in a different way than she feels it. Malorie understands that Tom and Olympia were born into this world. She understands that they hear better than she does, that their instincts are naturally stronger than hers will ever be. She gets that Tom and Olympia could be reading a book, completely distracted, and still close their eyes before something rushed into view, as if they can sense an intake of air when anything, man, woman, creature, is near. But she also knows that she herself is the sole survivor of two major incidents—unfathomable tragedies where everyone else went mad and hurt one another, hurt themselves. Forget the countless harrowing events—Shannon's death, Ron Handy in the service station, the trip on the river—Malorie has actually walked from the new world equivalent of two train wrecks. The house on Shillingham and the school for the blind. In the old world she would've been on the news for this. And when the reporter asked her how she did it, she would've held up a black piece of cloth and said no more.

While Dean doesn't know any of this yet, does he sense she's been through more than most?

"Do you have kids?" she asks him.

"I had two. Both went mad."

"I'm—"

"So we were at home, a ranch, no second floor, windows boarded up, blankets over the boards. I'd sealed every door in the house. We had a lot of food. Dry goods. Canned goods. Enough to last months. In my infinite wisdom, my plan was to simply wait. In the dark. Macy was nine and Eric seven, and I couldn't risk one or the two of them getting into something, getting into anything, while I was, say, asleep. So the whole place was boarded, sealed, safe. No light. We used buckets in the basement and covered the buckets with stone slabs. Honestly, I can't imagine living any safer than we did."

Dean pauses. Malorie wants to see his face. She thinks of Tom the man telling her of his daughter's death in the cellar of the house Malorie gave birth in. She knows the bad part of Dean's story is eventually coming. She readies herself for it.

"After a while, I didn't know what was day or night. You know? We really were living in darkness. Some options had crossed my mind. Just as I imagine they crossed everybody's. Maybe we could view the things through cameras. Maybe we could blind ourselves and carry on without the constant horror of going mad. But I didn't take any action on any of these ideas. We felt for one another in the dark, we called out each other's names, we slept in the same bed. All in the dark. As if the house itself was one giant blindfold. I was waiting for a literal message, I think. Waiting for a knock at the door, someone to come tell us it was over.

It's the ultimate fantasy for those of us from the old world, isn't it? Word that the whole nightmare has come to an end? Well, no magical word came. And then it still didn't come. And then it still didn't come all over again. I think we lived that way for seven months, Jill. Macy and Eric growing up in the dark. As if we lived in a cave. And all the while I kept thinking how unfair it was that I, a capable father, had somehow been rendered a useless man. All I did was wait. I made no moves to better our situation. I did nothing but hold their hands down the basement steps and open their cans of food for them. And when they heard sounds outside, when they got scared, I told them they should be. I told them there were things outside that could destroy their minds."

He pauses again. The train seems to glide. The musicians play soft, simple chords, back and forth, back and forth.

When Dean talks again, she hears tears in his voice.

"One day or night, who can tell, I woke to the sound of the kids laughing. You'd think this is a good thing, right? Any time two kids can laugh after months of living in complete darkness, shitting and pissing in buckets, you'd think that's a good thing. But it didn't sound right to me. Didn't sound happy. I sat up quick and stared long into the darkness, thinking maybe I'd dreamt the sound of them. But I heard them again. Wide awake. They were somewhere deeper in the house. I called out and they just . . . laughed some more. I got up and left the bedroom, feeling my way along the walls, thinking I was going to find them in the living room. Macy would tell me what she was laughing at and what was making her little brother laugh so hard, and that would be that. Right? Well, when I got to the living room, they sounded deeper in the house still. Way into the house, way back by the laundry room. I passed through the living room, blind, arms out, calling for them, and when I got to the laundry room, I heard them laughing behind me. Way back into the house. As if they were back by the bedroom I'd woke in."

The train shakes, a single bump. Dean goes on.

"So I headed back through the living room, into the hall again, into the bedroom. I'm calling, 'Macy! Eric! You're scaring Daddy! Where are you guys?' And the laughter came again, back behind me. As if . . . as if I kept passing through the place they actually were, if that makes sense. As if they were laughing in the living room and I simply couldn't find them there.

"So I went to the basement. Even though that's not where the sound was coming from. I took the steps, calling out to them, sweating by now, thinking, over and over, *They're playing a game, they're playing a game.* Because that's what I wanted, isn't it? Didn't I want to discover that, despite the sealed windows and doors, despite the plain food, the lack of light and exercise, despite the fact that Daddy was obviously scared, despite the perpetual darkness, didn't I want to think my kids were having *fun?* When I got to the basement, I heard them laughing upstairs. So I went right back up. By now I was yelling. 'Macy! Eric! This isn't funny, dammit! You're scaring Daddy!' Then I heard them whispering. And I knew what this type of whispering meant. I guess you could call it conspiring, though usually when parents put it that way they're trying to be funny about it. This wasn't funny. I couldn't find my own kids in the darkness of our own home and they'd gone from laughing to whispering. And I recognized the type of whispering, too. I'm sure you've experienced it with your own kids. The sound of little ones daring one another to do something. Something they hadn't ever done before.

"So I ran. All through the house. Most of the furniture was out of the way because we'd set it up like that, because we lived in darkness. But I clipped my hip on the fireplace pretty bad and I bashed the side of my head against a wall. None of that mattered at the time except that it slowed me down. I got across the house again and heard them whispering behind me. So I turned and went back, and there it was again, the two of them, whispering behind me again. I was screaming by then. Howling their names, demanding they tell me where they were hiding and now. And they did tell me. But not with words. The next thing I heard was a dull . . . hitting sound. Sounded like it does when you drive a knife into a melon. I just . . . I . . ."

Malorie doesn't know what to say, doesn't know how to express what she feels.

"I found them then," Dean says. "Beside the very bed I woke up in. The two of them dead from having stabbed one another with knives from the kitchen drawer. The knives I'd used a thousand times to cut up their canned meat and fruit. They didn't cry out when they did it. They didn't make any sound at all. They laughed and laughed and then dared one another to do it. I'll never know exactly how it was done. But the day my two little ones went mad and killed each other, that's the day I unsealed the back door. To carry them outside. To bury them. And even then, racked with despair, completely fucking destroyed, I kept thinking, *They saw one, despite everything you did, Dean, they saw one anyway.* And you know what, Jill?"

"What?"

"I never found the sliver."

Malorie doesn't ask him what he means. She knows what he means.

"I never found the hole in the wall, the space between boards, the infinitesimal spot they must've looked through, looked outside, to have seen what did that to them. Oh, I tried. You can trust me on that. I looked everywhere with a flashlight, no longer caring if I saw one myself or not. Just moved through the darkness of that house for six weeks, searching. Mostly on my knees.

Looking for that sliver of light, that Goddamn little space, over-looked, that they, as children, who saw the world different than I did, must've found."

"My name is Malorie," she says. Because she doesn't know what else to say.

Dean laughs. It's strained, and it's loaded with tears.

Malorie reaches across the table but doesn't find his hand right away. For a second it feels as if she's on her knees, aping the walk of children, looking for light in a house of darkness.

Then she finds it. Or he finds hers. Either way, she grips his hand.

"I'm so sorry."

"Yeah," Dean says. "Yep. But hey, it's the day I decided to start looking again. And that means something." Then, "Thank you, Malorie. For trusting me with your real name. And for listening to the worst thing that could've happened to a man. Shit. And look at me now. I'm the guy who got a train running again. In the new world. No small feat. But I'll tell you what . . . every run we make, day or night, it still feels like I'm searching for that sliver of open space, that tiny hole, that speck in the universe I didn't cover up. The point in space and time that my kids found. The one that drove them mad."

SIXTEEN

"Mom's gonna kill you if she catches you," Olympia says.

"How's she gonna catch me? She'll be blindfolded."

Olympia knows this is true. And Tom's not the only one with his eyes open.

She watches her brother pore over the pages he's taken from Malorie's bag, the census papers that excite him more than any other written word she's ever seen him hold.

"Indian River," he says. "Did you read about that place? Did you read about Athena Hantz? These people are unreal."

Olympia doesn't answer. She's looking in the mirror. The man Dean was right; this is a nice space. The bench, the bed, a high ceiling even. But the sensation of moving without using her own two feet is so foreign that she places her fingers on the counter, for balance.

It almost feels like she's holding on to the only life she's known. Because Olympia has no doubt things have changed. Whether Tom knows it or not, they're never going back to Camp Yadin.

"Listen to this," her brother says, crouched over the papers right beside Malorie's open bag so he can shove them back in the second they hear her coming. "Athena Hantz claims to have lived with one for two years. You hear that, Olympia? Two years! She told the census man that the thing never bothered her. It just 'stood in the corner of the kitchen for a while, then did the same in the living room.' Unreal!"

Olympia doesn't like when Tom talks like this. It's not just that Malorie would freak out if she heard it. It has something more to do with herself. The way she sees the world. On her own. She likes that he's excited by something, anything. She's read about enough characters who need moments like these in their lives. Yet, hearing Tom, it feels like she's not only on a train, but that there's a second one, barreling toward her, an incident on its way.

"Why not go through the papers with Mom?" she asks.

"Are you kidding? She'd be afraid the letters are shaped like a creature. She wouldn't get this at all."

"But she brought the pages. Did you think of that? Her parents' names are in there."

"I hear you, but no. Ha. Not a chance. She doesn't get it like I do. That's just so not . . . Mom."

Olympia doesn't argue this. But she wants to. There's a part of her that just wants the two of them to sit still until the end of this experience, all the way to Mackinaw City. There, Tom can say all the crazy stuff he wants to, and Malorie can either get upset with it or not. But if anything jeopardizes Malorie's chances of seeing her parents, finding out if they really are alive, Olympia might go mad herself.

She gets it. She isn't sure Tom does. The magnitude of this moment. The fact that Malorie has raised them for sixteen years, believing herself to be alone in the world, no family or friends to help. It's harrowing. At turns, it sounds almost worse to discover they are alive, as if Malorie was not only robbed of the life she thought she was living but had been fooled into sorrow as well.

"What's wrong?" Tom asks.

Olympia looks to him in the glass. Did her face reveal heavy thoughts? Jesus, sometimes it feels like Tom can hear her thoughts.

"Nothing."

"Okay," he says. But it's the mocking way he has of saying certain things. She sees him reach to his bag, his eyes still on the pages. He fumbles inside until he removes what she knew he would.

His glasses.

His special glasses.

Tom explained them to her in great detail a month after he made them. And while Olympia was frightened by the philosophy he espoused, she was much more scared of him using them.

He wears them now, as he reads.

"Get this," he says. "A family in Pennsylvania built helmets the size of 'wardrobe boxes' so there was room for food and water *inside* the helmet. I mean, this stuff is unbelievable!"

Olympia eyes herself. She wants to feel the excitement Tom feels. She wants to give in to the rush of being on this train, of moving, of heading north without being forced to lead her mom through woods, along empty roads, in a boat. She wants so badly to be sixteen like sixteen used to be. It sounds like it was once an incredible thing, a magical thing, being a kid. Hanging out with other teens your age. Learning how to drive a car. Sneaking out of the house. Going, walking, *looking* anywhere you wanted to.

Did people realize how good they had it back then? It wasn't just a matter of being able to see or not. She's read of plenty of blind characters who lived brilliant lives. But it's the fear—of what's out there. And the constant ringing of a mother's voice, reminding her and Tom, demanding, commanding, *Do you understand? Do you understand? DO YOU UNDERSTAND?*

"What's wrong?" Tom asks again.

When Olympia looks to him in the glass she sees herself, reflected in the lenses of the glasses he's built. For this, two mirrors face each other, and her own form is repeated, over and over, into infinity.

"Athena Hantz says we're allowed to look," Tom says. "She says it's all a matter of us accepting them. Living *with* them."

Olympia thinks of the predominant theory that a creature drives you mad because people can't fathom what they are. Malorie's told her about the man Tom was named after, and how he was sure that the entities outside their house, the house Olympia and Tom were born in, simply couldn't be understood.

But what does this mean for those who can look? For those who are immune? Does it mean those people are smarter? Does it mean they look at the world in a different way, just different enough to save themselves without realizing they're doing it? Does it mean those people are already mad, and no amount of unfathomable information can change that, speed it up, bring it to a bloody end?

"Indian River," Tom says again. He shakes his head, flipping through the pages.

Her brother is enamored with making progress. For as long as she can remember, he's proffered ideas, theories, inventions.

She wishes he would stop thinking this way.

But is that just Malorie talking? Is Olympia's worldview only Malorie's and nothing of her own? What if she'd been raised by her blood-mother? What if she and Tom had been raised by their namesakes instead?

Where would they be right now? What would they know? What would they believe?

And if people are right, that the creatures cause harm because they are beyond human comprehension . . . then what would someone like Tom the man make of people who were raised with the knowledge of the creatures' existence? What about the people who do fathom them because they've lived with them their entire lives?

Olympia looks to Tom just as he looks up, quick, to the door, a half second before a knock rattles her reverie.

Tom quickly shoves the papers back into Malorie's bag. He removes his glasses and hides them in his lap.

"Hello?" a man says. "Anybody home?"

Tom looks to Olympia. Do they speak? They know they shouldn't. They know Malorie would kill them if they do.

But Tom does. And Olympia knew he would.

"Yes," Tom says. "Who's there?"

"Ah!" the man says. "My name is Henry. We are neighbors. Insomuch as everyone on board lives in the same traveling neighborhood."

He sounds older than Mom, Olympia thinks. Maybe as old as Sam and Mary Walsh. Did somebody think this man was dead for years, too? Has he survived the new world in anonymity like Olympia and Tom's grandparents might have?

"Nice to meet you," Tom says. He smiles Olympia's way. This is all so incredible. First, leaving home. Then, making the train. Now, *on* the train and here a man, a stranger comes to say hello.

"If you don't mind," the man says, "I'd like to slide your door open. I'm old-fashioned in that I like to look at the people I speak to. And here, on this train, we're allowed to."

"Allowed to what?" Tom asks.

"Allowed to look!" The man laughs.

Tom and Olympia exchange a glance. Olympia's excitement is tempered. Was the man listening to them? Or is the word "allowed" fashionable in the real world?

"I don't know," Olympia says to Tom.

She's worried about Malorie discovering they're talking to a stranger. She's scared to open the door for him.

And is she really considering doing that? Opening the door? Is entering the real world such a slippery slope?

It doesn't matter if she's considering it or not. Tom is already up, crossing the cabin, sliding the door open.

Olympia thinks to close her eyes. Because that's what she's been told to do her entire life. Despite what the man Dean says about this being a safe place.

The school for the blind was considered safe. The home they were born in was considered safe. Why should this train be any different?

But it *is* different. She can't deny this. And, again, she feels a sense of having shed her skin, of having stepped, clearly, into a new phase, a second life.

"Hi," Tom says. "I'm Tom."

And now, giving out their actual names.

"Tom." The man smiles. "What a wonderful appellation."

The man, Olympia sees, is much older than Malorie. He has gray hair and white stubble on his chin and face. Olympia hasn't seen someone this man's age in ten years, not since the school for the blind.

"And you?" Henry says, raising his eyebrows her way.

It chills her that they're doing this. And more. Something more. Something similar to leaving Camp Yadin behind. That feeling of never getting something back again.

"I'm Jamie," Olympia says.

Henry smiles. He wears a sweater, despite the heat, and sweat drips down his cheeks.

Does he know she's lying about her name? He looks like he does.

"Well," he says. "I just wanted to introduce myself and to let you know . . . if you want to learn anything about this train, anything at all, feel free to knock on my door. I'm what people used to call a regular. My good friend Nathan and I are just a couple cars that way. Cabin Sixteen, I believe."

He points up the hall as the train shakes, and for a second he looks blurry to Olympia. Out of focus.

Then he bows. He holds one hand to his belly and extends the other arm out, as if he's just wrapped a performance.

Olympia knows the word: *theatrical.*

"Thank you," Tom says.

Henry winks.

Then he steps out of sight, and Olympia hurries to the door and slides it closed.

"What's wrong with you?" she says. "Giving him your real name."

"Oh, stop it," Tom says. "Mom doesn't have the same hold on us out here."

"What does that mean?"

But she doesn't feel like arguing. Instead, she looks to the closed door.

Her stomach swirls uneasily.

"There are bad people out here," she says.

"Come on."

"I mean it, Tom. And that one . . ."

"That one what?"

"That one acted just like the kind of person Mom says we need to watch out for."

"Oh, really? You think so?"

"Yes, I do. She's told us a million times to watch out for theatrical people. Mom says those people wear masks."

Tom scoffs. "Now you sound like her."

"Oh? And what's so bad about that? You really need to think about what you're saying before you say it."

But Olympia's eye is on the closed, sliding door. Her ear, too, listening. Is the man Henry still on the other side? Did he go back to his own room yet? Can she hear him moving up the hall?

"Hey," Tom says. "I'm not gonna freak Mom out. Don't worry about it. Okay? I just . . . there's a lot more to the world than Camp Yadin. And we're seeing that for ourselves. Right now."

It doesn't matter what Tom's saying. Olympia's listening to the hall.

Does he move out there?

She hears nothing. She steps to the door.

"The only way we're gonna get anywhere," Tom says, "is if we—"

"Close your eyes, Tom."

"What?"

"Do it."

He does.

Olympia slides the door open, quickly. She expects to see the silver-haired man standing, staring back.

But the hall is empty. She closes the door.

"What's going on?" Tom asks.

"Nothing. Sorry."

Tom scoffs again. "And you don't think you're starting to act like Mom? Jeez. The only difference is you don't always wear your fold! Even when we're outside!"

Olympia feels exposed. How does he know this?

"How would you know?"

"Are you kidding? I can hear the cloth against your skin when you wear it," he says. He gets up and stands behind her. Both of them are reflected in the glass now. "And I know when there's no cloth on that face of yours. So don't get all dramatic on me. You break rules, too."

She's trying not to look him in the eye.

Don't get all dramatic on me.

Dramatic.

Malorie has used the word a thousand times. Always a warning.

Is there a type? Are the ones who perform on this stage, the new world, the maddest?

"Anyway," Tom says. "Get ready to close your eyes. To pretend to go along with the rules. Mom just left the dining car."

SEVENTEEN

As the door to the dining car closes behind her, Malorie walks with her arms outstretched.

She brushes shoulders with someone.

"Excuse me," she says.

She hears a woman whisper to someone else, "Why is she still wearing her fold?"

She hears fear in the question and knows the woman wonders if she should be doing the same. But there's mockery, too. The same tone she heard so often at the school for the blind. She feels it. With each person she passes, with each conversation she momentarily halts, she knows the people on this train are wondering about her.

Paranoid.

But this train is set up to be wrecked. She knows this. Just like the house where she gave birth to Tom was set up to be wrecked. And the school for the blind. And, possibly, Camp Yadin, had they stayed there any longer.

This train will go mad.

There are more people here than lived in the house. But fewer than the school.

"Excuse me," she says, as her gloved fingers nick what is probably the top of somebody's head.

The first car is like the one she rode in with Shannon a lifetime ago, with people seated like they used to be.

She moves fast.

Tom and Olympia have been alone too long.

This train will go mad. She knows this. Eventually, the metal sheets Dean secured to the train's side will come loose. Eventually someone crazy in an old-world way will lower something onto the tracks, too late for the man Michael to clear them. Eventually *someone* will see something and someone will go mad. A crazy person will be allowed onto the train. Someone who doesn't believe in the creatures. Someone who will want everyone else to think the same way he does.

She reaches the end of the car. She opens the door.

In the moment between cars, she thinks of a blink. Perhaps, the inverse of one. Darkness, darkness, darkness, a blink of the world, darkness, darkness, darkness. She thinks of Shannon pointing out the dilapidated buildings and weird city names. Malorie laughed at her sister's jokes, and soon they were making up stories, giving names to the people they saw out in the fields on the horizon. Giving them lives and interests, relationships and problems. Malorie remembers their mother, across the aisle, smiling at them. She wanted to impress Mom in that moment, wanted Mary Walsh to think her daughters funny. There was a boy at school, a writer already, whom everybody called imaginative, and Malorie wanted Mom and Dad (*Sam and Mary Walsh*) to say the same about her.

And Mom did.

On cue, she nodded Malorie's way and said, *Those are better stories than the one I'm reading.*

Now, it's impossible not to see Mom as she might look today. Older, whiter, meeker. She must be wearing a blindfold because, even in Malorie's imagination, she can't have anybody *look* in a public place. Certainly no one she cares about.

She sees Mom, blind, reaching out across the aisle. Her fingers are white and wrinkled and she says, *Do you hear that? People are talking in the cabins you pass. And when people talk, they reveal themselves. And when they reveal themselves, you need to be listening.*

Malorie almost starts at the sound of voices coming from her right. Her gloved hand on the wall, she understands she has come to the series of cars with rooms, like the one Tom and Olympia are in. Here people have spaces of their own. Here people have two beds, red cushions on a bench, a mirror.

Here, too, people talk.

Malorie stops. She listens.

She hears:

"... *a new start. And that means everything. Not just where we live, Judy, but* how *we live. And how we treat each other, too* ..."

Malorie asks herself if she, too, is starting over. But she knows this isn't the case. What she's doing is justifying all the living she's already done.

She continues, up the hall, gloved hands sliding along both walls. The fingers of her right hand intermittently touch doors. She hears voices. A new set. She pauses. She listens.

She hears:

"... *have to find a bath sooner than later* ..."

"... *longest we've ever gone* ..."

She continues. She thinks of the dead bodies in storage. The safest two passengers on board.

Her gloved fingers touch the walls. Another door.

She hears:

"*. . . never again in my life. I mean it. No more big houses. I want us to find the smallest shack in the state to call home . . .*"

She continues. She bumps into someone.

"Excuse me," she says.

She has no doubt this person is eyeing her the way they did at the school for the blind. Here she stands, hoodie and gloves, blindfolded in a place where they've been told they don't need to be. Long sleeves and long pants. Her hair covers her neck.

She makes to pass the person and bumps into him again.

It's a him. She can tell. He's soft in the middle and taller than her and he smells like a man.

"Excuse me," she says again.

Maybe the man is old. Like Dad must be now. She recalls the first time she saw her father had aged. It was during a soccer game of Shannon's. Malorie was in the stands with Mom and Dad, and Shannon's team was up by five goals, and another man asked Dad if he wanted to shoot baskets on the small court beside the soccer field. Dad said sure and joined him, and Malorie watched as the two started to play one-on-one. Then the other soccer team scored, and Malorie got swept up in Shannon's game again. When she looked back to the half-court, she saw Dad, the strongest man in the world, lean and fit, a full head of dark hair like her own, she saw Sam Walsh on the ground, one hand on his shoulder, grimacing.

She went to tell Mom, but by then Dad was already getting up. And when the other man tossed Dad the ball again, Dad made to shoot, then stopped himself. He passed the ball back and made his way to the bleachers. When he sat down beside Malorie, he said, *Guess I can't do that anymore.*

Now, Malorie reaches out, and the tips of her gloved fingers touch the body before her.

"Please," she says. But she says no more. What is this man doing? And what is she doing? Has she forgotten that, just because she's taken every precaution to avoid the creatures, actual people have always been and will always be just as bad?

"Move," she says.

But the man doesn't move.

Malorie breathes in, she holds it, she breathes out. She thinks of redheaded Annette going mad, because how can she not? A blind woman gone mad. And maybe it wasn't from the touch of a creature after all but the touch of a man.

"Please, if you would," she says. "Move."

Maybe the man is old. Maybe the man is asleep. Maybe his back is to her and she's got it all wrong. Maybe he's blindfolded, too. Maybe he's deaf.

Maybe.

She hears no movement. She doesn't know what else to say. She could knock on the nearest door. Call out for assistance. She could stand still until someone else enters the hall and asks the man to move for her.

The train shakes. It makes her think how feeble this all is, how everybody in the world is only on somebody else's train, somebody else's big idea, and how safe that person thinks is how safe it is for all.

Tom and Olympia are on the other side of this man. This man who will not move.

"Please," she says.

She has to decide. She can't sit still. She didn't take her kids and leave her home and make it here just to be frightened into standing still by someone she doesn't know. Someone she's never seen. Someone she will never see again.

So she moves. She walks as if the man was never here. She

passes where he must be. She doesn't feel him. Doesn't hit him. Doesn't bump into anything at all.

She stops, reaches out behind her, feels both walls. The train rattles as she takes another step forward. She reaches out. Feels nobody. She goes the length of the hall, then back. All the way. She feels to know the doors to each cabin are closed and have been closed, since she did not hear them move. She smells the air. It still smells of a person, of a man. She can easily recall the touch of him. A bigger body. Like Dad's was.

She looks up, blind, as if the man could somehow be hiding on the ceiling.

She makes it to the end of the hall again. She must pass through another set of doors to get to the next car. Then another at the end of that one. And so on.

She listens. Voices within the cabin beside her.

She hears:

". . . *someone on board claims to have caught one.*"

"*What do you mean?*"

"*I met him between cars.*"

"*Who?*"

"*He says it's stowed in one of the caskets in storage.*"

Malorie moves before she decides to. She's through the doors and into the next hall, and her hands are extended, and her mind's eye is cluttered with so many memories, so much fear, that it becomes even darker, as if, this whole time, all these years, she's actually had the lights on, and the words she's just heard through the closed door of a stranger's cabin on a stranger's train have flipped the switch off for good.

He claims to have caught one.

On board.

Stowed in one of the caskets in storage.

"Tom," she says, "Olympia."

Breathless, but breathing. Moving on her own but ultimately carried by the train.

By somebody else's big idea.

Someone else's idea of safe.

EIGHTEEN

"We're not leaving this cabin until we get there," she says. She's still wearing her fold, her hoodie, her gloves. She's made sure her teens are doing the same.

She doesn't ask that they repeat what she's said. She believes the ferocity of her tone is enough.

But is it?

"What happened?" Tom asks.

Of course *Tom* asks this. And of course Tom is going to resist. She crosses the cabin so that she's closer to him. So that there's no question as to how serious she is.

"It doesn't matter," she says, tremors in her voice. "I said we're staying. That means we are."

"But, Mom . . ."

"Tom."

. . . claims to have caught one.

The phrase is a horror. The census man spoke about somebody who asserted the same thing. Malorie read of other claims in the pages he left behind. Indian River, right here in Michigan. Close. In its way, the new world is the wild west: lawless and boastful. She understands the chances of any of this being verified are slim to none. But what kind of person would brag of such a thing in the first place?

And in a public place . . .

That person worries her as much as what might be in a coffin in storage.

"Mom," Olympia starts, like she's about to tell her something she's been meaning to say. But Malorie doesn't want to hear any more. She doesn't think she can take any more. They're out in the world. They're on a train with people they do not know. In the hands of others now.

"Not now," she says.

And she asks herself: is it true that she fears men more than she does the creatures? Is she being honest with herself when she says the person who claims to have caught one is worse than the lauded catch could ever be?

Her personal darkness turns green, then sickly, as if the entire world is wrinkled and decaying. As if every memory and every thought is filtered through black fabric, all the hopes and reverse-grieving stolen, only cold wind remaining.

It's something she hasn't considered in a long time. Something she hasn't quite told herself before.

It's not people who have driven her to the brink of paranoia.

It's the creatures.

They stole her life. They destroyed the world she loved. They took her sister and, she once believed, her parents. They took Tom the man and Olympia the woman, and Rick and Annette from the school for the blind. Even the census man doesn't know how many lives were taken by the unfathomable entities because even the ones tallying the numbers aren't allowed to look at them.

She feels chilled, sickly, and so she steps to where she thinks the mirror is and feels the counter for a sink. There isn't one. She gets to her knees and feels for a container, anything to—

She finds one. A small metal garbage can. She brings it to her face just in time as the sickness comes out of her, splashes her chin but only her chin as almost every other part of her is covered in cloth and clothes.

Olympia is by her side.

"You need to lie down," she says.

But the advice is so jarring, so entirely not what she thinks she should do, that it almost comes to Malorie as a memory. She hears her mom saying the same thing after she'd picked her up from school for being sick in the bathroom. She remembers the sights on the drive home. It was autumn. Mom pointed out the colors, told Malorie a lot of people get sick when the seasons change, told her don't worry.

How about when the world changes, Mom? she thinks. *And how about seventeen years after the world changes? Do they get sick then? And do they ever get better if they do?*

Yet, still, the images comfort her. Even now, harried and afraid. The sights and smells of autumn. How it once was. How it must still be, though Malorie doesn't have proof of that anymore.

"No," she says. "I'll be okay."

But the silence from her teens following this statement tells her they don't believe it. That's fine. Somebody on this train spoke of a man who claims to have caught one. Says the thing lies in a box in storage.

Now isn't the time to lie down.

She breathes in. She holds it. She breathes out.

Then she's up again. Can this be happening? It's bad enough that they can touch you now (can they?), it's bad enough that there are more of them now than there used to be (are there?), it's bad enough that this very train will pass through what Dean described as a concentrated area, a place where, for whatever unholy reason (and Malorie doesn't want to know what that reason is) they congregate alongside the tracks, but now this? That one might actually be with them *on the train*?

"We have to tell everyone to close their eyes," she says. Because now she's thinking of the other people on board. Not because she worries for their happiness. But because of what they might do to her and her kids if that thing in the box (is it really there?) were to get out and walk the same halls Malorie just took herself. Out there where men don't feel they have to respond to the smaller, blindfolded woman who keeps her entire body covered for fear of contact of any kind.

Jesus, she thinks. *You gotta slow down.*

"Well, we can't tell everyone if we can't leave the cabin," Tom says.

And Malorie slaps him.

It's sudden and it's unplanned, and it feels like the only thing to do.

Because Tom has been looking for a reason to leave this cabin since the moment she said they wouldn't be leaving it anymore. Because Tom is at that damnable age where he believes he must resist *every fucking thing his mother tells him.*

He's walking away from her now, no doubt a hand to his face. She can't help but feel pride for having touched what she believes to be the cloth of his fold at the tips of her gloved fingers when she slapped him. Even now, having done something she would never have dreamed herself capable of doing seventeen years ago, even now she thinks, *Good. He's wearing his fold.*

"Wow," Tom says. And he's about to say a lot more. She can tell. She can hear it in the three letters, as if they comprise a picked lock, the door now open to everything.

"Wait," Olympia says. "Hang on. This is crazy. Mom, you need to calm down. We're okay. This is good. We're on a train. We're heading to see your parents. We're—"

Then it comes, Tom's rage, but in an unexpected form. Malorie anticipates a rash of words. She even braces herself for a return strike. But no, the door to their cabin slides open, then closes, and Tom's angry steps thunder up the hall.

"No," she says, imagining a box in storage opened, the lid slid aside, something terrible sitting up. She makes for the door, and Olympia holds her and talks to her, says things like *Mom come on, he needs a minute, Mom it's okay, Mom don't go out there angry, Mom let him be, Mom it's Tom, remember Tom? Your own son?*

Remember Tom?

Mom?

And Malorie does. Or close. She remembers Tom the man, her son's namesake, instead.

The incredible man enters her mind's eye with startling detail, and she's momentarily embarrassed he witnessed her striking her son.

Tom, she thinks, *I'm sorry.*

But does she say it to the man or to the son? She's crying now, in Olympia's arms, behind her fold, crying at the echo of Tom the man's scream to be let into the attic where Malorie is in labor. As the creatures Gary convinced Don to let inside walk the house below.

"It's okay," Olympia says. "We're gonna get there safe. We're gonna—"

"No," Malorie says. "We're not. Not this time. We pushed our luck. We shouldn't have left. We had it good. We survived the house. The school. We had it good and *I got greedy*. I saw the names of my parents and I lost my mind. I got lazy, Olympia. *I got lazy.*"

Her voice cracks with the last of these words. Olympia makes to say something, but Malorie is already removing her daughter's hands from her shoulders.

She feels pride for the gloves Olympia wears.

Even now.

Then she's out the door, too. Off to find him. Tom, who, of all the people on this train, would be most excited about a caught creature in a box.

And the proof of progress such a horror would be.

NINETEEN

Tom's eyes are open. Because damn it all. Why not? The man who runs the train walks with eyes open. And he's ridden it every single time it's gone! Malorie's crossed a line. That's all there is to it. Maybe it all made sense when they were little kids, when they were going to take the rowboat to the school. Maybe *then* Mom had reason to be the way she is. But today? Here? They're out in the world now. Tom has never felt, heard, smelled, or *seen* anything like this. He's walking the hall. Doors to his left. A black wall to his right. It all shakes. It rattles. Why? Because they're on a train. A thing he and Olympia have never done before. Christ, they haven't done anything before!

Malorie has gone too far.

It's the first time she's struck him since using a flyswatter when he and Olympia were babies, teaching them to wake with their eyes closed. And this wasn't a lesson. This was anger. Darkness, darkness, darkness. Doesn't Malorie get it? Whether you were born into this world or not, you're *told* how it used to be. And then? Then, you want to know that world for yourself.

You want to see it.

The door opens at the end of the hall, and a woman steps through. Her eyes are closed until the door shuts behind her. Then she opens her eyes. She sees Tom and smiles nervously. He wonders if she thought, for a second, that he was a creature. He doesn't know what to make of her. How many women has he seen in his life? How many men? Back at the school for the blind there were lots of people. But Tom was six years old. He's sixteen now.

Doesn't Malorie get it?

Tom waves. He didn't mean to do it. It just happened. The woman, older than him but not quite as old as Malorie, nods back. She's walking toward him. He's walking toward her.

He thinks he's got to say something, because he's electrified by this moment. His face is still red from being hit and yet he's as excited as he's ever been.

He realizes, suddenly, ecstatically, how true this is.

This really is the most liberated he's ever felt in his life.

And all he had to do was walk out on Malorie to find it.

He makes to speak, he opens his mouth, but the woman slides open the door to her right and slips into the cabin.

She closes the door.

He wonders if there's someone in there who makes endless rules, too. He wonders if she closes her eyes in there, pretends she didn't just have them open in the hall.

Tom smiles. Wow. It feels good.

He removes his gloves and hoodie. He doesn't want them anymore. He lets them fall to the floor of the hall just as he would let his clothes fall to the side of his bunk back in Cabin Three of Camp Yadin.

It feels great.

He slides the door open at the end of the car. He closes his eyes.

Doesn't Malorie get it? The man told them what to do. What was safe. And Tom is doing it. That's all there is to it. That's all there's ever been to it. They don't have to stay in their room the whole trip. They don't have to wear their folds and their gloves. They don't have to be so scared.

But Malorie has no sense of this. No instincts at all.

The thought of it makes him mad again. Madder. But he doesn't want to be angry. He wants to be free.

He passes between cars. Opens the next door. Lets it slide closed behind him.

He opens his eyes.

Another hall. Doors to his left. People hiding like Malorie hides. Tom isn't going to hide anymore. Tom isn't going to live by Malorie's rules anymore. Tom isn't ever going back to Camp Yadin again.

He pauses. His heart beats powerfully with the realization that he really isn't ever going back again.

Back to the only place they've ever really called home.

Never going.

Back.

Again.

"Good," he says.

A door opens to his left. A man steps out. He closes the door behind him.

"Hello," he says.

Tom can hardly believe it. It's what the world is like in his sister's books. People step out their front doors and wave to one another and ask how their days have been.

"How's your day been?" Tom asks.

The man, much older, eyes him suspiciously. Is it because he wonders what a sixteen-year-old is doing walking the train alone? Does the man think Tom is being unsafe? Can he tell Tom was just slapped?

Tom brings a hand to his face.

"Good," the man says. He doesn't move. Just stands in front of the closed door to his room as if Tom might slip inside and take something.

Tom passes him. He reaches the end of the car, looks back, sees the man still standing there, still facing him. Only now his eyes are closed.

Tom closes his own. Opens the door. Steps between the cars.

And stops.

He pulls his glasses from his pocket and places them on his face.

The air swirls here. A small cyclone between cars. Windy enough to blow a blindfold from a face if you don't have it tied tight enough.

The wind goes up the short sleeves of his shirt, down the neck.

It feels incredible. Standing outside as the world whips by. He's not walking. He's not rowing. He's not being told what to do.

He opens his eyes. He turns his head to the left.

Through the glasses, *his* glasses, he sees the world passing.

Trees. Signs. They don't stay in sight quite long enough for him to read. But he sees letters. Outside. In the real world.

He smiles.

This is incredible.

He looks right.

More of it, only the horizon seems to stretch into forever in this direction.

Are there any creatures out there? Is he looking at one now? Through the glasses he made? The exact kind of glasses that could be written about in the census man's book of discoveries?

The feeling is overwhelming. Who cares if he got slapped? He almost wants to thank Malorie for doing it. He wants to thank her for giving him reason to leave her side.

Indian River.

The city name comes to him in giant letters, surrounded by trees and street signs. He imagines Indian River has horizons like the one he's looking at now. Endless sights and a lot of people who want to see them.

Athena Hantz.

A woman who doesn't think like Malorie. A woman who thinks like *him.*

The world passes. Greens and browns. Signs. Homes. A fence. It's *wonderful.*

Tom feels like he could do anything. Absolutely anything he's ever wanted to.

The door opens in front of him. He looks to see a man coming toward him, a man with his eyes closed. But this isn't just any man. This is Dean Watts.

Tom steps aside, *watches* as Dean Watts, the owner and creator of this very train, passes him, opens the next door, steps through, and slides it closed again.

The feeling is unbelievable. Like he's fooled even the smartest man on the train. The man who brought the train back from the dead.

He doesn't want this moment to end. He wants it to last another sixteen years. Outside, eyes open, free.

He steps to the end of the platform between cars. This is where someone would jump if they wanted to. This is where Dean might've thrown someone off, too.

Tom sits, cross-legged, glasses on. The wind comes at him, and he raises his arms.

He feels it. All of it. Every bit of this moment in time.

Nobody is out here with him. Nobody passes between the cars.

And nobody, absolutely nobody, tells him what to do.

TWENTY

Malorie knows it's Dean before she runs into him, before he speaks. She's not convinced her other senses have gotten stronger in the new world, but she can smell certain people and places seconds before reaching them.

"Malorie," Dean says. "Are you well?"

She doesn't want to tell him what she heard. The casket in storage. She doesn't want a panic. She only cares about finding Tom and getting out of here before it all goes mad.

"No," she says. She hates that there's fear in her voice. She hates that she's speaking to what would have once been considered an intelligent, interesting person, and all she can do about is be afraid.

"What's wrong?"

"This whole thing is wrong," she says. "The train. Thinking we can push back. All of this is insane."

"Hey, Malorie. Wait . . ."

"I'm finding my son and we're getting off. We're walking home because back there, when my teenager storms off angry, I know where he's going and who he's with."

She makes to pass him. Dean doesn't reach out to stop her, but his voice does.

"Don't you think that, now that they've seen the train, now that they've ridden it, it won't be the same back home?"

Malorie doesn't have time to do this right now. She needs to keep moving, needs to make sure her son, who she's protected for *sixteen years,* doesn't do something dangerous.

Oh, my God, she thinks. *You hit Tom.*

It's like she just hit him again. And again now. The memory of it feels more like a realization every time it returns. And the only color she can see is the color of a face that has been slapped.

"Are you sure he went this way?" Dean asks.

"Yes. No. I don't know."

"I just came from the dining car," he says. "And I didn't see him."

This is somehow worse. Like the train itself swallowed him. As if, by severing the umbilical cord (because that's what it felt like, even to Malorie), Tom stepped into Malorie's personal darkness and was pulled so deep she'll never see him again.

"He's here somewhere," Dean says. "We'll find him. So don't worry. I'll help."

Malorie doesn't want help. She doesn't want to be here at all. It's because of men like Dean Watts that everyone goes mad in the end. It's the people who think beyond the fold.

Tom the man appears then, in the dark. He stands before the couch in the living room of the house where Malorie met him. At his feet are the pieces of a helmet he's failed to keep together.

"I'm not gonna be able to get anything done until you find him anyway," Dean says.

"Okay," Malorie says. "Help me then."

Because Tom the man wasn't the reason that house went mad. That outcome, that blood, stains the hands of Gary. Gary, who convinced Don to tear the drapes down. Gary, who entered the house like a little, lethal spider in thespian's clothing. It's been sixteen years and she still shudders at the thought of him. Of his voice. His face. His beard. His jacket. His notebook. His words. His chalky white hands upon Don's shoulder. Whispering in Don's ear like a demon. Telling him the creatures aren't real, mankind has lost their collective mind. Man is the creature he fears.

Malorie walks up the hall, fast. Dean is close behind.

"You two had a fight?" he asks.

"Something like that."

"Well," Dean says. "My eyes are open. And I can tell you he isn't in this hall."

"How about the cabins? Is he in someone else's room?"

"Whose would he be in?"

They've reached the end of the hall. Dean opens the door.

The air comes at her, fresh and cool, and Malorie, blind, turns her head left, imagining Tom leaping from the moving train, stepping off between cars.

She hears the sound of the slap, her hand against Tom's face.

"He's not in this hall, either," Dean says as they enter the next car. "But there's something ahead you're not going to like."

"What?" Malorie freezes. She thinks of the casket in storage.

"Sorry," Dean says. "It's just clothing. But . . . a hoodie and some gloves. And, yes, a blindfold, too."

"Oh, God."

Because now Tom didn't just storm off. Now he's discarded the armor.

Malorie can't think straight. She needs to find him. She needs to get off this train.

And she can't keep what she heard to herself anymore.

"I overheard someone talking about a creature on board," she says, her voice rattled, nearly hoarse. "Someone in one of the cabins said something about a creature in one of the caskets in storage."

Dean is quiet. Is he studying her? Is he weighing how paranoid she really is? And the next words he speaks . . . Will they placate? Will they humor? Will they dismiss?

"I'll check storage," he says. Firm. Decisive. Serious. "You keep going ahead. Find Tom."

"Okay."

Then he's gone. And Malorie kneels to pick up the clothing Tom has left behind.

"He shed his skin," she says. Or thinks. She doesn't know.

But what if his skin is all that protects him from the new world?

She can barely stop from falling apart. The train rocks. Dean's footsteps grow quiet behind her before she hears a door open and close. She's alone again. Looking for her son. No, not *looking*. Never looking. Never looking at all.

And isn't that exactly why Tom wants to get away from her? From this life? Isn't that exactly why anybody, even those born into it, would want to shed their skin?

She continues. She calls out his name. She knocks on the nearest door, and a voice from within says they don't need anything. She tells them she's looking for her son. The voice, a woman, tells her he's not in there with her.

Malorie continues.

The train sways.

She knocks on the next door. Nobody responds this time. She imagines Tom standing silently inside. She tries the door. It won't slide. It's locked. Now a voice comes. Tells her they don't need anything. She says she's looking for her son. We're on a train. First time ever. Please. Help. Is he in there? No, they say. No, go away. Please.

Malorie continues. She reaches the door. Near to shaking now, she steps between the cars. But before entering the next one, she checks how much space is here, how much room. Could a sixteen-year-old boy fit through the space between cars? Could he jump from here?

The wind crawls up the long sleeves of her sweatshirt. Like the fingers of the creatures she's never been allowed to look at.

If they have fingers. If they have anything at all.

She doesn't know. Doesn't know a thing about them.

Still.

She enters the next car.

Has Dean found anything in storage? An empty casket? Or worse, much worse, a creature in a box, and Dean Watts too proud of his train to be careful when he opened it?

Has Malorie sent Dean to his madness? Has she sentenced them all?

It's not difficult to imagine Dean beside her again. Suddenly. Forcefully. He'd be saying the same things he was saying before. Using the right words. But she'd hear it. The madness in him. Possibly before he heard it himself.

She knocks on the nearest door in the next car.

"Yes?" It's a young woman. She sounds scared. Malorie hears her whisper to someone. Is it Tom?

"I'm looking for my son," she says. "He's sixteen. Is he in there? Have you seen him?"

"Please, go away," the woman says.

Malorie feels a sudden stab of rage. She wants to tear the door down, wants to storm into the young woman's room and ask her how she could possibly only be thinking of herself at a time like this.

"Please," the woman says. Firm. "Go away."

And she sounds a lot like Malorie used to. Back when a man on a boat approached her and the kids on the river. Back when people knocked on the door to their room at the school for the blind. Even as recently as when the census man came.

"I'm sorry," Malorie says. And it feels like she's saying it to herself, telling herself she's sorry for losing sight of Tom. Sorry for slapping her son. Sorry for turning into the paranoid person she's become.

She stumbles from the door, visions of herself and Tom and Olympia tucked safely inside. As if she's leaving that possibility now. Leaving security and safety at last. Becoming, in the end, unsafe.

If they'd run for the train a year earlier, would this be happening? Would Tom have reached his end with her?

And her with him?

She can't think about that. Not now. The names of her parents burn bright in her head, burn the very pages they appeared upon, and Tom vanishing into the darkness of a moving train cannot eclipse this.

Yet, everything, *everything* feels wrong. The movement, the voices, the smells, the fact that they are in the hands of other people, Olympia alone in their room, Tom alone and angry, Malorie alone and searching.

The caskets in storage. Dean checking them.

How? How can he possibly know if one is in there or not without looking?

Absolutely everything feels wrong, everything *is* wrong, like it's *gone wrong*, like she fucked up something that was once precious to her. She's struggling to get a grip, to find purchase in the pitch-black present.

Jesus.

She should've stayed home.

She knocks on the next door. A man slides it open. When he speaks, his voice comes from above. He's tall. He sounds like what people used to refer to as conservative, though that word doesn't apply to the new world. Not to Malorie. There are only those who are safe and those who are not, and today she was not.

"My son," she says.

Before she says any more, the man speaks.

"Young man? Teenager? Black hair like yours?"

"Yes." She hears the light, the hope in her voice. It startles her.

"Saw him go down the hall. Closed my eyes when he made it to the end there."

"Okay. Thank you."

This is something.

"But he stood between the cars for a long time."

"How would you know that?"

"Because I listen closely, ma'am. And I didn't hear that second door, the door to the next car, open for a long, long time."

"How long?"

"Two, three minutes."

"But you heard it open?"

"Yes."

"So you know he went through?"

"Me?" the man says. "What do I know? I think we're out of our minds for taking a blind train in the first place. Could've been a creature that opened the next door for all I know."

"But, you—"

"I'm sorry, ma'am," he says. "That's all I know."

Firm. Final.

She understands. She thanks him as the door slides closed again.

Two or three minutes.

Between cars.

What was he doing there? No hoodie. No gloves. No fold.

Malorie hurries to the door, slides it open herself.

She stands where he stood.

She listens.

She thinks.

She feels.

Wind. The openness. Is that all? Or did Tom leave from here, from this very spot? It's not hard to imagine him doing it. Tom jumped from the roof of Cabin Two, landing on a pile of mattresses he'd prearranged himself. Once, he rolled down a particularly steep hill in the woods bordering Camp Yadin. He swam the lake, eyes closed. He's been injured, broken bones, spent weeks laid up in his bunk. His whole life he's dared, been daring, tried new things, pushed back against his lot, their lot, the new world in full. It's not hard to see him making a decision, his face still red from where Malorie struck him. It's not hard to see him smiling even as he leaps from the moving train, the gravel cutting into his elbows, his bare hands splintered by the tracks.

But then what? Where from there? And while Tom might flee Malorie and her rules, would he ever go without saying goodbye to his sister?

She can't help but think of her own sister. Shannon, dead upstairs, a glimpse of something she shouldn't have seen from the upstairs bedroom window. A bedroom they fought over when they moved in together.

Malorie enters the next car and knocks on the first door she comes to. Silence from within.

Someone's coming up the hall. A woman speaks.

"Is everything okay?"

Malorie stands still, just like she would've had someone asked her the same thing, suddenly, in Camp Yadin.

But the truth is, this train is *not* home. And sometimes the clearest path to safety is through other people.

"Did you see a teenager ahead?" she asks. "A young man. About my height. Dark hair. Short-sleeved shirt?"

"Did you lose someone?"

The way she says it, Malorie wants to reach out into the dark and grab her.

NO, I DIDN'T LOSE SOMEONE. SOMEONE LEFT ME.

"Yes," she says.

"No. I didn't see anyone like that at all."

"Not in the dining car? Not seated? Think."

"I'm thinking." She sounds like the people from the school for the blind. No doubt she is questioning why Malorie is wearing her sweatshirt, gloves, a blindfold, in a place they were told is secure. "I didn't see him, no."

Malorie walks. She knocks on the next room. There's movement within. The door slides open.

"Is someone there?" a voice asks. Maybe this is the blind woman Dean spoke of.

"My son is missing," Malorie says.

"Oh, no."

"He's sixteen. Did you . . . see . . . or hear a young man, dark hair . . ."

"I'm wearing my blindfold."

This steals Malorie's breath. In a place where they've been told it's okay to look, this woman still lives by the fold.

Lives like Malorie does.

"Please," the woman says. "Don't ask me to look."

"I wouldn't dare. I understand."

There's a moment of silence between them. Malorie feels it, a kinship. Something deeper than personality or character or even worldview.

Instincts.

The word doesn't feel as good to her as it normally does. She has trusted her instincts since the world went mad, and so far it has served her well. She is alive. Her teens are alive. Despite abhorrent tragedy erupting around them, they have survived. Yet, only days ago, Malorie abandoned those instincts for the first time. Even as her parents' names flared bright from the page, even as images of the people they once were and the people they might've become rose like colored fog in her personal darkness, Malorie's gut told her to stay. Her gut told her she'd been doing it right, that it was the only way to do it, and that to leave, in a rush, to run for a train run by who knows who, to be accompanied by who knows who, was all much worse than simply being unsafe; it was playing too many games of cards at once, too many chances to lose.

And now she faces her old self. Her strict, instinctual self. And she feels shame for having come.

"It's the only thing in the world I'd remove my fold for," the woman says.

"What is?" Malorie asks.

"My boy." Then, "I'm sorry I couldn't help you."

The woman slides the door closed, and the clicking of the latch severs their worlds.

Malorie is alone again.

She breathes in. She holds it. She breathes out.

She steps to the next door and knocks. She waits. She tries the handle. The door slides open.

She steps inside.

The train is rocking as she enters somebody else's room. She stands still. She listens.

Is the stirring coming from the wheels beyond the wall she faces? Or does somebody move in this very space?

"I'm looking for my son," she says. Surely whoever is in this room, if they were to see her, blindfolded, scared, hooded, surely they would empathize, understand, respond.

She steps deeper into the room, arms extended. Her gloved fingertips come into contact with what she thinks is the mirror.

Motion behind her. The door slides closed.

She doesn't move. She waits.

The train hums. The wheels whir. Is Dean uncovering a creature as she stands here? Are his eyes open, allowing the unfathomable in? Does the lid to the second box creak open as he checks the first?

Is Dean, mad, in this room?

"Is anybody there?" she asks.

It's impossible not to imagine everything, every kind of thing, every potential danger, in this darkness. People, expressions, features, feelings, animals, smells, rivers, homes, schools, cabins, trains, madness.

But there is no answer.

Malorie steps forward, checks the bench.

Tom wouldn't be waiting here in the quiet, would he? Tom wouldn't intentionally hide, would he?

She moves quick now to the bunk beds. She swipes across the upper bunk, feeling nothing but a blanket. She bends and reaches across the lower bed.

Someone grabs her wrist.

"Get out," the person says. Malorie can't tell if it's a man or a woman. Her heart is thundering. This isn't Tom. And whoever it is now yells. *"GET OUT!!"*

Malorie is either shoved or kicked. Either way she's falling, suddenly, backward, tumbling through many darknesses. The train jolts, hard, and when she lands, she lands funny, so that her shoulder hits first, then her chin.

"GET OUT!!" the person yells. And they're no longer hiding, no longer curled up in a lower bunk in the dark.

They're coming out now. Coming for her.

She scrambles, disoriented, afraid. She isn't sure where the door is, where it's not. Hands pull her by the hood, drag her toward the sound of a sliding door. Then she's up. Before they can throw her out, she's up.

"I'm sorry," she says. But what she wants to say is, *FUCK YOU! MY SON IS LOST IN THE NEW WORLD!*

The door slams closed.

Malorie turns to continue up the hall.

Someone is there.

"I've seen him," a man says. "Back this way."

"What? My son?"

"Yes," he says. "Come on. I'll show you."

Malorie tries to determine, in seconds, what the man might look like. How old he is. If he's safe. But she's moving, following him, back the way she came. Through the doors, car to car, passing the people she no doubt scared with her search for her son.

"He's up here," the man says.

He takes her by the hand. She thinks to pull away, but she wants to get there. Wants to get to Tom.

"He's okay? He's alive?"

"Yes," the man says. "He's absolutely fine. This way."

Malorie is partially dragged now, partially jogs alongside the man. They pass through another car, walk another hall.

"Are we in storage now?" she asks.

Have they come that far?

"He's right here," the man says. "One more car up."

"Are you sure you saw—"

"One hundred percent sure."

He's tugging on her, drags her to the next set of doors.

Malorie reaches out with her other hand, feels for anything familiar. What car is she in? How deep back into the train have they come?

She hears movement to her right. Someone in storage?

"Just on the other side of these doors," the man says.

Malorie pulls her hand from his.

"A teenager? Black hair?"

The man laughs. "Ma'am. I told you I saw him. Right through here."

His hands on her shoulders now, through sliding doors, out into the open air.

She can't see it, but she knows this is where she boarded the train. The platform her teens pulled her onto, as the safety of Camp Yadin receded.

"Tom?" Malorie asks.

It's a different voice that responds. Not her son. Not the man who took her here.

But a voice she recognizes all the same.

"Take her, Nate," the second man says. Malorie imagines a beard. A briefcase. Hands tearing down the drapes in the house in which she gave birth to her son.

"No," she says.

But it's so obviously yes.

The blindfold is torn from her face.

"I'll meet you at Athena's," the second man says to the first.

"*No,*" Malorie says.

But it's so irreversibly yes.

She turns to reach for the train's back door, but her hands only find other hands. Hands that grip her hard.

Before pushing her off the train.

She thinks she hears one of them leaping, too, just before she hits the tracks, headfirst, just before she blacks out and sinks into a darkness no blindfold on Earth could provide.

TWENTY-ONE

Dean is in the first storage car, the very back of the train, when he hears what sounds like people moving by the train's back door, the door Malorie came through when she and her two teens boarded. He knows his mind is piqued by the things Malorie has been saying. A missing son. A creature in storage.

And the fact that she believes touch can drive someone mad.

This worries him. Not because he believes everything he hears, but Malorie is especially believable. She's sharp. She's dedicated. And, most of all, her kids have survived this long. Dean has nothing but unfathomable respect for any parent who pulled that off.

He didn't.

Blindfolded, he steps through the boxes of canned goods and clothing, his palms out, moving slow, lest something was jostled loose by the motion of the train, something that would hurt to run into.

He thinks of something touching his hand. He imagines going insane.

In his version, he doesn't act stealthily. There's nothing cunning about his vision of madness. Rather, he's embarrassed by what he does: he sees himself, frothing, wild-eyed, racing the halls of this train with an axe.

He shakes his head no. He doesn't need to be thinking this way. Not while searching for a casket that the woman Malorie thinks may be harboring a creature.

Who told her this? It doesn't matter. Rumors abound on a blind train. A lot of scared people. But if safety is truly his top priority, then he must look into this now. Only, *look* is the one thing he won't do.

Or perhaps one of two things.

"She's really gotten into your head," he says.

She has.

He doesn't know yet how he's going to search the casket for what's inside.

His first idea was to open the lid and reach in. Nobody knows any more about the creatures now than they did seventeen years ago, but Dean believes some things must be assumed. For example, the space they take up. If Dean opens the casket and feels a dead body within, it stands to reason that there wouldn't be space for a creature as well.

But Malorie has him questioning *reason*.

Is there any? Any more?

Who's to know if they occupy any space, any of what people know space to be, at all?

He knocks a box off a table with his hip and bends to pick it up. He can tell by its weight that it's clothing. He sets it on the table just as the train jolts, and he reaches out for balance. Finding none, he imagines the fingers of something that can drive him mad.

He opens the box of clothing.

Scarves. Winter hats. No gloves. That's okay. Hats will do.

He uses two as gloves and, still blind, continues deeper into storage. The coffins are the first to be loaded in as they are typically the heaviest and can be used as a tabletop if need be. For this, he has to go all the way in.

"Malorie," he says, "I hope you realize I'm braving this for you."

He thinks of his staff, if such a word applies. David, Tanya, Michael, and Renee are only people looking for progress, no different than Dean. They're more family than workmates, as they've done the impossible together: got a train running in the new world. He can't have them getting hurt. He couldn't live with that. It'd be like reliving the loss of his children, but possibly worse for not having learned the first time around.

He bumps a second table and, his hands covered with hats, he discovers he's reached the coffins.

Two of them. To be delivered to Mackinaw City. Those who have asked for them will take them from there and bury them wherever they want them to be buried.

Dean breathes in. Holds it. Breathes out.

In a world without pills or therapy, it's as effective an anti-anxiety treatment as any he could imagine.

He feels along the wide wood surface of the first coffin.

It's clear.

He opens the wood lid.

The smell is strong. Too strong. Dean turns his head and gags. He brings one of the hats to his mouth and gags again. Eyes closed, he can easily imagine what makes this smell. A decomposing body without what was once modern science to stave off the stench.

"Malorie," he says again. "Thanks a lot."

He reaches into the box and feels an arm. A chest. A second arm. Legs.

Then, the head.

He closes the lid.

He takes a few steps from the box and allows his breathing to return to normal.

The second coffin is deeper into the space, boxed in by the first. He climbs up onto the first and feels the lid of the second. Two boxes have somehow ended up here. Dean doesn't doubt it was the motion of the train, but it's not difficult to imagine someone or something else rearranging things in here for reasons he knows nothing about.

Reason.

On his knees, the hats still over his hands, he lifts the second lid. He's prepared this time, breathing only out his mouth, and he gets to work checking it immediately.

He feels legs. Fingers. Arms. This man is naked.

Dean's hands move fast, too fast, and the hat slips from his left.

He yanks his arm back.

"Jesus," he says.

He doesn't want to reach back in for the hat. Doesn't want to touch the dead body

(*something else?*)

bare-handed.

"She's *really* gotten into your head, man," he says.

But maybe what Malorie speaks is the truth. In a world without shared experiences, who knows what laws she's discovered on her own?

He begins to close the lid. But he hasn't felt the head yet.

He doesn't know why this matters. But it does. As if, in the end, it's the head that separates sanity from madness.

One hand on the lid, he reaches in with the other, his fingers covered in wool. He touches the tip of the nose first and imagines something other than a face, something that looks back up at him.

Something with fingers that can touch.

He moves quick, running his hand over the rest of the face.

Satisfied, or something like it, he pulls his arm out and lets the lid slam closed.

Then he hears what can only be commotion in the hall. Nobody hurrying this time. He heard voices. More than one. Possibly even somebody yelling.

Eyes closed, still anxious, Dean lowers himself from the first coffin and makes his way back to the door. He's moving too fast, and he knocks another box to the ground, but this time doesn't bend to retrieve it.

In the hall, the door closed behind him, he opens his eyes.

And sees a familiar face walking toward him.

"Gary," he says. "Hi."

Gary's silver hair and gray stubble glisten under the car light, and he looks momentarily insane.

Then Gary smiles and wipes his hands on his sweater.

"Needed some air," he says.

Dean, still shaken, nods. He likes Gary. Gary has ridden the train before. Numerous times. He always gets off at Indian River.

"Close to your stop," Dean says. It's supposed to be funny, as the train doesn't actually stop for Indian River, but Gary will get off all the same.

"Yes," Gary says, stopping a few feet away. "Can't wait."

"And Nathan?" Dean asks.

Gary thumbs toward the train's back door.

"He just got off. Gonna walk the rest of the way himself. Knows of a man who makes his own ice cream around here. He has a sweet tooth."

Dean nods again. He can't tell if it's because Malorie has piqued his mind with her talk of boxed creatures or it's because he literally just searched two dead bodies in storage, but he doesn't feel right about this encounter. It feels like Gary is hiding something.

"Wanna walk with me back to my room?" Gary says.

Dean doesn't want to, but doesn't know exactly why.

"Thanks, but I got some work to do," Dean says. He thinks of Malorie, no doubt waiting for word on what was in the coffins.

Gary smiles. "If I don't see you again, thank you," he says. "It's a pleasure as always."

"Be careful getting off," Dean says. It worries him. And maybe that's it. It worries him that Gary and his friend Nathan get off the train whenever they feel like it. At this speed, it's not unsafe, but Dean worries.

"Always am," Gary says.

He passes Dean, and Dean watches him go, vanishing into the next car.

"She's really gotten into your head," he says.

He brings a hand to his head, to run his fingers through his hair, but feels wool against his skin instead. Wool that just touched dead bodies.

He shakes the hat off his hand and thinks how crazy it is that for a second there he felt like he'd been touched after all, like he'd somehow ended up in the presence of real, actual madness.

TWENTY-TWO

When Gary reaches the spot between cars where Tom sits, cross-legged, eyes hidden behind strange glasses, looking as content as any teenager ever has, he pauses.

"Tom," he says, loud over the wind. "Are you enjoying the ride?"

Tom looks surprised for having been caught. No doubt shocked that Gary is looking at him, here, between cars, without a fold.

"Yes, what are you . . . how are you . . ."

Gary smiles.

"Helluva thing. A train."

Tom gets up.

"Henry," he says, "how are you—"

But Gary interrupts him.

"Hey, I'd love to show you something. Come to my room?"

To Gary it looks like Tom hears his mother's voice in the deep, dark distance. She's telling him to put on his gloves. His sweatshirt. His blindfold. She's telling him not to go into the room of a stranger.

But in a way, Gary has watched this boy grow up. Numerous trips to Camp Yadin fortified his belief that Malorie would never move again. Once he stayed three winter weeks in the shed that housed the boating equipment. Once he even entered Cabin Three as they slept.

He was there when Tom asked the census man to leave the papers on the porch. And he knows what Tom's going to say now before he says it.

"Sure, Henry," Tom says. "I'd love to."

TWENTY-THREE

Tom isn't used to the motion of the train yet, and he can't imagine he ever will be. This is his first time in the big world and, here, now, his first time sitting with a stranger without Malorie perched on his shoulder.

Screw Malorie.

Henry looks like a big child to him, the way he's sitting just barely on the edge of the mattress on the lower bunk. The way his big hands lay flat on his knees. The sparkle in his eyes, too. It's the first time Tom has ever thought this way about an adult before.

"Welcome," Henry says.

Tom sits on the bench. Between them is a small table. And on that table is a notebook.

"Where's your friend Nathan?" Tom asks.

"Nate? He got off."

"Got off . . . the train?"

Henry smiles. "We can do that any time we want. Even you."

Tom looks to the notebook just as Henry points at it.

"It's just my thoughts, really," Henry says. He acts bashful, but Tom can see the man is proud of what he has written down. "Who am I to think anybody else would give a hoot about what I have to say . . . Yet, after seventeen years of observations, one begins to find their own important. Especially in a world where one is told not to look."

Observations.

Tom likes the word. He thinks of himself between cars, looking at the world through glasses he fashioned himself out of material from the office at Camp Yadin.

"I'd like to read it," Tom says.

Truth be told, he was hoping for something a little more interesting than a notebook. Olympia would probably like this more than he would. But the pages left by the census man have done something to change Tom's tune about the written word. And the power therein.

"Really?" Henry says. Again, a big kid. A genuine smile. Wide eyes. And those big hands that now reach for the book and slide it Tom's way. "Feel free."

Tom didn't necessarily expect the man wanted him to read it right now, but where else does he have to be? Mom doesn't know he's in here, and that's good enough for now. If Henry wants Tom to know his thoughts on the creatures, on the world, why not? He can tell Henry doesn't think like Malorie does. Not at all. For starters, he's not wearing a fold and hasn't asked Tom about one yet. Then there's the lack of anxiety, ever present in Malorie. That stiff sense of rules.

Tom flips the notebook open. As he does, he hears Malorie standbys.

Even a drawing might drive you insane.

Are there photos in this book? Should Tom wear his glasses?

"Don't worry," Henry says, as if he's completely read Tom's mind. "No pictures in there. Only words."

Still, Malorie would be worried.

Even a description might do it, Tom.

He tries to shake off thoughts of Malorie as Henry reads his mind again.

"A mother like the one you described upon entering my room sounds like one who is perhaps not made for the new world. Please, I don't mean to offend when I speak this way, but I've always talked openly and honestly and I'm not going to change that now. It sounds to me your mother would be better off as a hermit."

Tom thinks Henry's exactly right. On the first page of the open notebook he reads:

THOUGHTS ON HOW THIS ALL BEGAN: HYSTERIA IN DROVES

Tom can't tell if the words make him uneasy or if he's just so excited to be here, talking to a stranger about the creatures, that his stomach is turning.

He reads on. But what he reads must be impossible. Henry writes as if he's seen one, a creature, before.

Tom looks to him. To the big kid who is no longer smiling but whose face seems to be all eyes beneath the shadow of the upper bunk.

"No doubt some of the observations therein will be difficult to believe, given the upbringing you've had," Henry says. "But the more you read, and the more you experience the *concept* that they are, in fact, observable, the less unfathomable they become. And isn't that just it? Doesn't your mother tell you that you can't look at them because you can't understand them, that your mind is too small to do it?"

"Yes."

"Well, Tom," Henry says. He leans forward, his features emerging from those shadows. "I'm allowed. Do you know what that words means, given this context?"

Allowed. Tom thinks of the woman Athena Hantz in Indian River. She claimed to simply accept the creatures. Even to live with one. Has Henry done the same?

"Yes."

Henry nods.

"And my permission doesn't stem from some biological lottery." He points a finger to his right temple. "It's born up in here."

Tom, electrified, understands.

"So," Tom says, "then . . . you've seen one?"

Henry smiles. But his eyes do not.

"Many."

For the first time in his life, Tom can't believe his ears.

"What . . ." he starts, then he's out with it. "What are they like?"

Henry holds Tom's gaze for what feels like a long time. Tom expects the man to break out with enthusiasm, to stand up, to gesticulate as he describes them. Instead, it feels like something frosty occurs within Henry's head, and his eyes go cold with it.

"Why don't you try your glasses?" Henry says.

Tom laughs. Nervously. Here he's in this stranger's room, a man who repudiates every fiber of Malorie's being, a man who breaks another rule with every single thing he does and says, a man who somehow intuited the glasses were more than old-world eyewear.

"You wore them between cars," Henry says. "I saw you. As you looked at the world *your* way. And did you see anything out there to drive you mad? Are you mad, Tom?"

"I'm not. No."

"Of course you're not. Let's imagine for a moment that I'd been raised without the knowledge of the existence of whales.

Would the sight of one, a leviathan rising from the deep, have been enough to drive me insane? If I were to encounter one, alone, out in a dinghy, the beast coming up beneath me, would that have been enough to have stolen my sanity?"

"I don't—"

"I think it might've been. The fear alone, the moment of disbelief, reality forever cracked. But you see, Tom, I *do* know about whales. I was raised with the knowledge of them. We all were. So when the creatures came and people lost their minds, I reminded myself of this, I saw things *this way*. As if I'd always known them. And that's all there was to it. I wouldn't allow them to surprise me. I didn't let them confuse me. You and your sister, you two were raised in a world where they exist. Doesn't that make them fathomable?"

"Yeah."

"More than that even, huh. As commonplace as trees. You ever hear how, in the old world, the older generations didn't know what to make of new technology? And so they quit using it or didn't ever start in the first place? It's not that they were actually incapable of using a video camera. It's that they chose not to. This," Henry waves a hand, "all this is a choice. Your mother doesn't have to live by the fold, as modern people have come to call it. And she certainly doesn't need to force *you* to live by it at all. Can I see those glasses?"

The question comes suddenly, but Tom isn't put off. Everything Henry says is making sense to him. The man is connecting with Tom on a level nobody ever has. Is this what Indian River is like?

"Here," he says. He hands over the glasses. Henry examines them, flips them over, tries them on. When he looks at Tom, Tom smiles. But Henry doesn't. His face is stone behind Tom's invention.

Henry removes the glasses.

"Have you tried them yet? Have you really gone out with them, stared out the window, anything of that nature?"

Tom reddens. He's embarrassed. Why hasn't he tried them out?

Malorie.

"Well," Henry says, "I have a surprise for you. But you cannot tell a soul!" He raises a finger.

"Promise," Tom says.

Henry hands Tom his glasses back, gets up from the lower bunk, and steps to the wall. Where there was once a window is now a slate of black metal. Henry places his hands flat to the metal, looks to Tom, then shifts the plate so that a triangle of sunlight enters the cabin.

"Here's your chance," Henry says. "The big world, waiting for you to take a look."

Tom hears a hundred warnings in Malorie's voice. As if she were sitting inside his head.

I'm the only person you can trust. The house you were born in went mad. The school we thought was safe went mad. And wherever we go, if there are other people there, that place will go mad, too. Do you understand?

Yes, Mommy. (Always yes, always.)

Because there are men and women out there who maybe once lived like we do but got sick of it and so they gave up. And there are men and women out there who never believed it in the first place. Do you understand?

Yes.

Good. Because those are the people who got lazy. Some after the creatures arrived. And some long before.

"Tom?" Henry says.

From where he sits Tom can't see the window, can't see outside. But he sees the light.

Malorie, in his head, louder:

There's a way to go about what you're trying to do. The man you were named after pushed back, too. But never without the fold. He never got lazy. Do you understand?

"Yes," he says, actually, out loud.

Henry smiles. And opens a palm to the glass.

"Carpe diem, Tom."

Tom feels like his whole life has led up to this moment. Here's a man, an adult, not Malorie, whose philosophy rings true. Here's a man who is able to articulate the things Tom has never been able to. Here's a man giving him the chance to test not only his glasses, but his resolve, his spine, his perspective of what Malorie calls the new world but is the only one to Tom.

He puts the glasses on.

Malorie stands up in his head.

Maybe she shouldn't have slapped him. But Tom's glad she did. Glad because it was the slap he needed to leave the room, leave her side, to cut the apron strings, to set off alone. And maybe he was supposed to meet Henry. And maybe Henry was supposed to meet him. And maybe Tom was meant to walk up to this window, right now, and to look out, to see whatever it is Henry sees, to prove to himself that all these feelings, all these ideas, have come from a true place after all.

"What is it?" Henry asks. He's looking at Tom. Tom sees him through his own glasses. Glasses that suddenly feel strange on his face. Like a mask. Like something silly that Olympia would roll her eyes at.

But Tom wants this moment. He wants to look out this window before Malorie comes to this room and drags him back into her way of life forever. If he doesn't act now, right now, when will he?

Tom steps to the glass.

Henry steps out of the way.

Tom leans toward the window.

And he hears them outside.

A lot of them.

"What is it?" Henry asks.

Tom doesn't know what to say. He wants to try his invention, but not when he knows . . . so many . . . outside . . .

Henry shifts the plate over the glass again.

"Tell you what," he says. "Why don't we go somewhere where this type of thing is not only tolerated, but encouraged." He steps closer to Tom. "Do you know where we are . . . right now?"

Tom shakes his head no. He has no idea. He's spent the last ten years in a former summer camp.

Henry makes a mitten of his hand, shaped like Michigan, and points to the center of his middle finger.

"Indian River," he says.

He smiles.

Tom's heart is beating too hard. This is too much.

"You've heard of it?" Henry asks.

"Yes!" Breathless.

Henry nods.

"I could guide you there. You can show them your glasses. People who will appreciate what you've done."

"Have . . . have you been?" Tom asks.

Henry laughs.

"I've lived there." Then, "What do you say, Tom? Change your life? Start living your own . . . no longer your mother's?"

Tom brings a hand to his face, to where Malorie slapped him.

"Yes," Tom says. "I wanna do that. I wanna start living my own. Right now."

TWENTY-FOUR

Olympia doesn't have to look out a window to know the train is nearly surrounded by creatures.

She hears them.

There's a difference, she's learned, between the steps of a deer and those of the things that have nearly driven her mother insane the old way. It isn't so much the weight as it is the width, the breadth of a step and the intent (or lack thereof) within.

Yes, she knows they're surrounded. It sounds like hundreds outside the train. Enough to be heard above the wheels.

Malorie is not back. This doesn't mean she hasn't found Tom yet, but it probably does. Olympia doesn't want to believe her brother could've left the train, but she also understands that Malorie has never slapped him before, either. What might Tom be thinking right now?

It's impossible for her not to compare real life with the words and pages of writers from the old world. And adding to this is the number of "coming of age" stories she's found. Dozens of novels in which the boy or girl found themselves by the end, their purpose, their future. Is Tom on a similar precipice?

And if so, could he step into a wholly new future without them?

Voices outside the room. People sound worried. Maybe they suspect something's outside, too. She needs to tell everyone what she's heard. If there's one horror Malorie has underscored more than any other, it's that it only takes a single person to look, one to see, one madman to set the entire matchbook aflame.

She slides open the cabin door, half expecting to see the man Henry who, if she's honest with herself, reminded her of Malorie's description of Gary. Malorie's boogeyman. In the hall. With an axe.

GOTCHA!

But, no. In his stead are a half dozen scared people, looking to her, a sixteen-year-old girl, for guidance, information, hope.

"What's going on?" a woman asks.

"Like Dean warned us," she says, "we're passing through an area with a lot of them."

Them.

Nobody needs further clarification in the new world.

But the people only stare at her.

"Please," Olympia says. Then she adopts her mother's voice. "Stick in your cabins, close your eyes, till we get past them."

Leading. Guiding. Olympia has been doing variations of this for years.

She heads up the hall. The doors to each room are open. People sense something is up.

"Close your eyes," she tells each she passes. "Sit tight."

When she reaches the end of the car, she does the same. She slides the door open and steps through.

Here, more people. More conversation. They all look so confused. So vulnerable. Don't they know there's only one rule to live by? Don't they understand that any time they feel like something is up they should close their eyes?

"Hey!" she calls, gaining confidence in giving directions. "Everybody close your eyes. Lots of them outside."

A man stops her.

"What do you know?" he asks, suspicion in his eyes. Olympia thinks of something Malorie taught her long ago.

Whoever you meet, whoever we encounter, you have to remember that they've experienced loss. Whether it was their parents, their kids, their friends . . . they've lost someone to the new world. And you need to keep that in mind when they talk to you, when they sound like they don't trust you, when they eye you like you're the danger.

"There are many outside the train," she says.

The man closes his eyes.

"Thank you," he says.

Olympia is moving again. Thinking of Tom. Thinking of Malorie. Where are they?

"Hey," Olympia says to a woman who stands facing the black metal slate that was once a window. "You should close your eyes."

By way of the woman's profile, Olympia sees a sadness she has not encountered before. When the creatures arrived, Malorie, Olympia knows, got angry. She got scared. But she never let the sadness of the new world rule her.

Mom, Olympia thinks. *I'm coming.*

Malorie thought her parents dead for seventeen years, for longer than Olympia has been alive! Yet she found the energy to raise her kids. She's found the resolve to repeat her rules, over and over again, to pound safety into their heads, always. What would Olympia do if she'd read her birth mother's name on that list of survivors? Would she have reacted as swiftly as Malorie did? Or would she have withdrawn?

"It's over," the woman says. But she doesn't seem to be speaking directly to Olympia.

Olympia begins to tell her to close her eyes again but stops herself.

The woman has painted open eyes on her closed lids.

"It's over," the woman says again.

A cabin door opens. A man peers out.

"Close your eyes," Olympia says. "A lot of creatures outside."

The man does more than that; he vanishes back into his room and slides the door closed. Olympia hears him moving something in front of the door.

Good, she thinks. And she knows Malorie would think the same. And it feels good, God, it feels good, to play the part of Malorie. To step into her shoes, Mom, who must be losing her mind, looking for Tom, thinking of her parents, so long believed dead.

Dead!

Olympia reaches the end of the car. She slides the door open, steps through. No sign of Malorie or Tom yet. Maybe they're in the dining car. Maybe they're fine.

But why hasn't Malorie come back to check on her?

It strikes Olympia that the people they are going to see, Sam and Mary Walsh, the people she wants so badly to be alive, are the people who checked on Malorie her whole life, too.

Until the creatures came.

Creatures that, Olympia can hear, number in the hundreds. As if the entire landscape is made up of them. As if this very spot, here in the middle of Michigan, U.S.A., as if this is where they came from, broke through, entered the old world, making it the new.

A door slides open to her left. A kid looks out.

"No, no," Olympia says. "Back in. And close your eyes."

"Why?"

It's a little boy. He reminds Olympia of Tom. Dark-haired. Fierce-eyed.

"Because we're passing through a dangerous area and we may as well be extra safe. Right?"

But the boy, so much younger than Olympia, looks at her the same way she imagines she once looked at Malorie. There's less severity in his reaction than hers. Less horror. This child is growing up in a world where the creatures are commonplace. For all Olympia knows he's stood beside a thousand in his lifetime thus far. For all she knows, he's completely unafraid.

Is it possible? And will every generation feel more and more comfortable until . . .

Until what?

"Inside," she repeats. Then, "Where are your parents? Are they with you?"

As she asks this, a hand emerges behind the boy, takes him by the arm, and pulls him back into the room. The door slides shut.

Olympia moves on.

Still, she wonders . . . until what?

Malorie would say that so long as the creatures remain here, the world must wear a blindfold. But Tom would argue that eventually someone is going to figure out a way to beat them. But to that little boy in the room . . . what does "beating them" mean?

She reaches the end of the car, slides open the door, enters the next one.

There's Dean. Okay. Good. Maybe he's seen Malorie. But he asks her before she asks him.

"Have you seen your mother?"

He looks anxious. Olympia knows he has piloted the train through this concentrated stretch many times.

Does something other than the creatures worry him?

"No. Maybe she's in the dining car?"

Dean holds her eyes a beat. Yes, there's worry there.

A lot.

"I don't want to frighten you," he says, "but I've searched the entire train for both your mom and your brother. And . . ."

Olympia feels something break inside her. Whatever this is, it's bad.

"And they're simply not on the train."

Olympia feels younger than she's felt in a long time. She's a child again, leaving the school for the blind. Maybe even younger.

"They have to be here," she says. "They—"

"There's someone else missing," Dean says.

Olympia knows who it is.

Henry. The man Malorie would've killed them for talking to.

As Dean says his name, as he begins to describe him, Olympia is already heading the other way. The length of one car, then another, her heart is beating too hard. Too heavy. Malorie's always telling her to breathe when she feels afraid, that oxygen, simple as it is, is actually the best medicine for fear.

But she can't do it.

Gary.

Dean didn't call him "Henry." He called him Gary.

"*TOM!*" she screams. "*MOM!*"

Gary is missing, too.

Into a storage car. No cabin doors here. Dean is somewhere behind, calling out. Olympia doesn't stop.

The second storage car. The end of the train.

Beyond the door ahead is the big open world.

And that world is teeming with creatures.

Olympia opens the door, passes through, stands on the metal platform, feels the wind rush to meet her.

Dean's out here, too, now. Telling her to be careful. Not to worry. This can't be as bad as Olympia thinks it is.

But Olympia hears something else, buried beneath his voice.

A fluttering at her feet.

She kneels and discovers the source of the sound is a singular piece of fabric, flapping in a grate where the platform meets the door.

She's touched this particular piece of cloth so many times that she doesn't question what it is.

As the train carries her farther north, she rises and faces south.

"Mom," she says.

Because if there's one single item that Malorie Walsh would never lose, would not let off her person, if there's one object in all this mad world that defines her more than any other, Olympia holds it now.

She knows the worst has come. Something has happened to Malorie.

The proof is not in Malorie's absence . . . but in what Olympia holds, what flaps, black and angry, in her hand.

Her mother's blindfold.

SAFER ROOMS

TWENTY-FIVE

Malorie hides in a cluster of trees at the far end of her home's property. The pond is between her and the house where her parents and Shannon are, hopefully, desperately looking for her.

She's upset.

Mom and Dad insist she read the kids' book for class, the book the teacher assigned her, but she doesn't want to read the kids' book, she wants to read the adult book, the one Mom is reading, the book written by an adult woman with an adult brain. She doesn't like the idea of what she calls a pretend book, a book geared for someone who's supposedly not as developed, not as smart, as her parents. And isn't she? Isn't Malorie as smart as her parents? And what's worse than them denying her is the fact that Mom and Dad are usually so encouraging. Yes, that's what bothers Malorie most of all. It's that they're siding with Mrs. Cohn when it's so obvious that Malorie is right.

It's why she ran away. No, she didn't get far, but it's far enough to let them know that what they're doing, what they're saying, is wrong.

From where she hides, she can't hear them anymore. Can't see them at all.

That's good. They can't see or hear her, either.

She sits on the fallen needles and cones but discovers it's too wet, so she gets up.

Does Mom know where she is? If she does, she's going to have to walk out here and scold Malorie to her face. Malorie isn't going back inside. Not for anything in the world.

She hears a stick crack, and she thinks aha, Shannon is coming to talk. An ambassador for their parents. Shannon will come and say come on, Mal, come on, they're just doing what's right, it's just Mom and Dad, you know them, come on. But Malorie won't come. This is the moment she's growing up. The exact moment. Can't they see that? Can't everybody tell that the world has changed?

But when Malorie peers between the trees she doesn't see Shannon or her parents at all. She sees no one. Nothing. Not even an animal.

So what's made the sound? Something surely stepped just outside the cluster. It was clear as day, even as day wanes, as the sun goes down, as it gets colder yet where she stands and has her thinking momentarily about the comfort of her coat inside, her blankets, the couch, the heat of the house.

But no. She's not going. Not right now. Not until Mom and Dad say she can read an adult book for her book report and not the one about the dog who travels to outer space.

Another crack and Malorie actually steps out of the cluster. Shannon's got to be here, about to leap out, scare her. Or maybe it's Mom or Dad, come to talk after all. Maybe they're watching her, spying, waiting to see what she does.

Should she run farther from home?

"Shannon," she says, because her sister has got to be messing with her. It's just like Shannon to pick a weak moment, to come out all smiles, to scare her, to poke fun, to roll her eyes at the meager distance Malorie actually got away.

But Shannon isn't there.

Nobody is.

And nothing.

Malorie feels a chill. Is the sun going down faster than it normally does?

"Damn you all," she says. It's a phrase she heard on TV. It struck her. It feels like the exact kind of thing she wants to say to her parents right now.

She sits down again, just as the sky gets really dark. She hugs her knees to her chest.

She should've worn something warmer, should've taken the fifteen seconds to pack. Gosh, why did she leave in such a rush? And do Mom and Dad even know she's left? Or do they think she's only in her bedroom, quietly stewing?

She should've told them she was leaving. Yes. For full effect. But it felt like her anger was enough, felt like the whole world could feel it.

A crack. Again. This one so close Malorie gasps a little and turns to face it. She has no doubt something is about to leap through the trees, a hand coming for her, a face, barely lit, in the dark.

She's seen stuff like that on TV, too. Scary stuff. Ghosts and demons and, for Malorie, worst of all, *creatures*.

The inexplicable kind, the ones that don't fit neatly into boxes like vampires or werewolves, goblins or ghouls. It's the abstractions that scare her deeply, for she has no reference for these.

"Go away," she says. Then, "Please."

Because who knows? Maybe whatever inches closer will listen to her just as Mom and Dad will not. Maybe whatever is out here with her will honor her wishes. Maybe, maybe, maybe—

"Mal."

She leaps to standing, arms out, ready to box whatever's close, a thing that must've watched her run away, followed her to the far end of the property.

"Can I come in?"

Her instinct is to say no, *no,* but she recognizes the voice.

"I'm not in the mood for a lecture, Dad."

It's almost like she can hear him smiling, just past the trees, in the dark.

"And I promise not to give you one," Sam Walsh says.

Then the trees are parting and, for a second, she can see the sky, see there's some light left, and Dad is painted purple and orange with the setting sun as he steps into the clearing and is swallowed by the very darkness she stands in.

"So," he says. "This is a neat little place. I've never actually come in here. Didn't realize it made a little room like this."

Malorie thinks of it as hers, already, a clubhouse, a fort, a place where only people who think like she does are allowed entrance.

"I get it," Dad says. "And I respect the hell out of what you're asking for."

She doesn't know if she should trust this. Does he really get it? Does Mom?

"Yeah, well, why can't I read Mom's book then?"

"You can," Dad says. "Any time you want to. Even right now."

"I can?"

"Of course. You can even do a book report on it. But you gotta write about the other one, too."

"Why?"

"Because," Dad says, his silhouette comforting in the small cold space, "there's a way to do both things at once."

"Both?"

"Yes. A way to follow the rules and break them at the same time. Some people would call it 'paying your dues,' you know, you read the kids' book so you can read the other one. But I've never liked that phrase. To me it's more like, hey, you can actually learn something, even something big, by doing the things you don't think you should have to. Like mowing the lawn. You think I wanna do that every week? But meanwhile, every time I mow the lawn my mind wanders and I end up happier for having done it."

"But, Dad . . ."

"What?"

"I'm too big for that book."

"Then write the biggest book report ever, Malorie. And hand in the one about Mom's book a week later. Trust me . . . Mrs. Cohn will never look at you the same way again."

Footsteps near, someone on the lawn. The trees part, and Malorie sees Mom.

"Found her," Mary Walsh says.

She steps into the darkness, too. It's comforting, in its way, being in the dark with the two of them. They can't see her face, can't see that she's embarrassed. At the same time, she can say exactly what she wants to, how she feels, without worrying what she looks like while doing it.

"Cold out here," Mom says.

"I was gonna sleep here," Malorie says.

"Were you?" Then, "Well, I hope you thought to bring a flashlight."

Malorie feels what she at first thinks is her mom's hand against her own. But it's not. It's the book. The adult one.

She takes it.

"Can't imagine us ever telling you not to read a book," Mom says. "And it's a good one."

"Thanks," Malorie says. She doesn't want to cry. Doesn't want them to think she's weak.

The trees part again.

Shannon.

"What's up, Mal?" she says. "You ran away to the backyard?"

"Shut up," Malorie says.

But Dad laughs. And then Mom laughs. And then Malorie laughs, too. She can't help it and she can't stop it. Even more, she doesn't want to.

"I read the kids' book while you were hiding," Shannon says.

"It sucks," Malorie says.

"You haven't read it!"

It's true.

"Is it good?" she asks.

"No," Shannon says. "It's really not."

They laugh again.

Dad sits down, cross-legged, in the pine needles and dirt.

Mom joins him.

Shannon, too.

Then, thinking these three are the only three she'll ever let into her new clubhouse, Malorie sits, too.

And they talk.

And Malorie, a young girl yet, thinks how a parent will always find their kid. Even if they run away. Even if they're hiding in the dark. And she knows, without a teacher telling her so, that this lesson will stick with her for the rest of her life.

TWENTY-SIX

Malorie wakes.

Smells dirt.

An old-world instinct tells her to open her eyes.

A sense of cold air, of being outside, tells her not to.

"What . . ."

She feels the cold air on her eyelids. She hasn't felt this in a decade or more.

The outside world on her naked eyes.

"What . . ."

She raises her arms, feels nothing above her. She reaches out to her sides. Feels dirt.

She smells it. The dirt. A cellar smell.

Her head hurts in a way it hasn't before. This isn't a headache. This isn't lack of sleep. This is an injury.

And she's not wearing her fold.

She sits up, arms extended, as though prepared to strike whoever must be near.

Someone put her where she is.

But nobody moves. Nobody breathes. Nobody speaks.

She crawls far enough to discover a dirt wall. She stands. Her head aches. She reaches up the length of the wall but can't find the top.

Dizzy, she stumbles across the space. The lack of the fold is horrible. The sense of a sky above. The vulnerability.

She gets to a second wall and reaches for the top. Can't find it.

It's damp here. Cellar damp.

She remembers a familiar voice at the back of the train.

"No," she says. Because it's too terrible. The voice she believes she heard. How many times has she been wrong about hearing that same cadence of speech? How often did she wake to discover it was only Gary speaking from the other side of partially opened doors in dreams?

"No."

But maybe. Maybe.

She touches her head, feels a lump. She was struck. On the platform. She remembers it.

"Oh, God."

The train. And Tom and Olympia still on it.

Traveling away from her now.

"HEY!" she calls. She has to.

She was struck. Hit in the head. Thrown off the train.

Right?

She breathes in, but she can't hold it. She can't calm down.

She hurries across the space, finds a third wall. Can't reach the top.

All dirt.

A hole in the ground?

Words from the census pages rise to her mind's eye.

Safer Rooms.

Efforts by men and women to build bunkers in the event the creatures completely take over.

Have they taken over? Is she the last sane woman alive?

She moves faster. Finds a fourth wall. She scrambles to touch all four again.

The space is big. Bigger than any grave. But a hole in the ground all the same.

"Help!" she calls. But she doesn't want to do this, doesn't want to give herself away. She needs to listen. She needs to think.

Whatever's happened . . . she's survived.

She digs at the walls. She has to get out of here. Has to find her teens. Has to get back to the train.

Now.

She tries to tell herself it's one thing at a time. Get out of this hole first. Then find her kids.

She can't breathe steady. Can't control it.

"Tom!"

She shouldn't do this. There could be anybody above. The people who've trapped her. She remembers the name Nathan. She remembers Gary's voice.

Or does she?

And does he wait above? Does he look down on her in the hole?

Or did they put her here to get her out of the way?

"TOM! OLYMPIA!"

She scrambles up the wall but finds no purchase.

She remembers Tom leaving the train cabin, his face red from where she slapped him.

"Oh, no," she says.

Because whatever this is, whatever's happened, it suddenly feels like she's the reason it did.

"Tom," she says, as if her son were in this room (safer room?)

with her. "Tom, please. Don't be angry. Don't do anything unsafe. Please, Tom, don't be unsafe."

Please,

Tom

don't go mad.

She recalls the name *Indian River,* spoken in a familiar voice. Just before being shoved from the train. But the moment she thinks it was Gary, the voice shrinks further into her head, a spider avoiding detection.

Indian River, she knows, is no place for her. It doesn't matter if they've caught a creature there or not. The kind of community that would celebrate something like that is . . .

"Fucking insane," she says. And her voice is rising with panic and guilt.

Her breathing picks up again. She can't sit still. She tries climbing the walls.

Oh, Malorie shouldn't have brought Tom and Olympia to the train. She shouldn't have let them taste the new world. Certainly not a train. She didn't have to bring them. There were options. She could've searched for her parents on her own.

But now . . .

This is Malorie's fault.

The things people say about her are true. Paranoid. Overbearing. A helicopter mom. And here she thought there was no other way to be. Here she couldn't be any other way.

She remembers swatting a two-year-old Tom with a flyswatter when he woke with his open eyes. She remembers slapping his face in the cabin on the train. She remembers yelling, so much yelling, so much saying no no no, Tom, *NO!*

But if you tell someone no enough times, they start thinking yes, just to hear something else, just to hear a different word, they start thinking *yes.*

Malorie imagines Tom's young face standing before a group of new-world lunatics, the lot of them excited to pull back a tarp, to show him what they've caught. That's the world Tom wants. Like the one in Indian River. She sees his blue eyes, huge now in her mind, his black hair, hair like hers. Young Tom bracing himself for that fabulous rebellion, making small fists to fool himself into feeling bigger than he actually is. She sees something in his mind, his brain, the spot where actual insanity begins. She hears it flutter, coming alive.

She imagines the tarp pulled back.

She sees Tom's eyes go wide, wider.

Because that's why they'd want Malorie out of the way, right? The people who put her here? Why else if not to get to her kids?

She opens her mouth to say the name *Gary*, but she won't do it. Can't.

She scrambles up the wall, imagining Tom as he tilts his head with curiosity toward the thing under the tarp, Tom's last stand, the last attempt at assimilation, as the origin of insanity takes flight, a bird as black as his hair and as blue as his eyes, flying up into the infinity of his own mind. He attempts to grab it, to put it back in its box, to stop the sound of those fluttering wings, insanity afoot, a young man gone mad, a mind not yet mature enough to recognize his thoughts as being wrong, as cracked, as flown. She imagines him thinking he's succeeded, that he beat the creatures that have held him down so long, the thieving entities that stole views, any views, all views, them all.

And at exactly the moment he believes he's done it, that he's stopped himself from going insane, he brings his fingers to his face.

And he rips.

And he tears.

And he screams the awful scream of a man made mad. Not

even old enough to understand what's being taken in the feet of that bird, taken out of reach, so high, out of sight now, out of earshot, too.

Even for Tom.

Malorie digs at the dirt. She has to get out of here. Now.

She thinks of the housemates, Felix and Cheryl, Olympia and Don. She thinks of Victor barking at blackened drapes.

She digs.

Whose voice did she hear? One of the housemates?

She feels naked without her fold. Completely exposed. She remembers Annette turning that corner, knife in hand, her red hair like blood from her head exploding back, back toward what drove her mad.

She digs at the walls. She jumps.

She cannot calm down.

"TOM!"

All he does is listen! All he does is hear! He's done it better than anybody else for sixteen years!

He'll hear her. He must.

Except . . . he's on a train. With . . . with . . .

She walks right, too fast, and strikes a dirt wall. She flattens her hands to it and reaches up, up, up.

She imagines a square, high in the sky, an exit from the hole she's fallen into.

She thinks, *Safer Room.*

Are there ways out of these rooms? Or is the idea . . . to die on your own terms . . . without going mad?

A stirring behind her and Malorie spins, eyes tight, arms up. She's shaking. Breathing too hard.

She listens.

It moves.

"Stay away!" She yells.

And her voice is hysteria. A black and blue bird considering flight.

Either she's heard this sound before or she's so scared (*Tom, Tom and Olympia, Olympia*) that she's mistaking this sound for one like it, one she heard behind her in an attic, as she gave birth to the very boy she now desperately wants to find.

Motion close to her right side. Malorie spins, backs up.

"Oh, please, no," she says. Because she believes it now. Because she *knows* it.

This isn't a person down here with her.

"*Stay away.*"

She flattens herself to the closest dirt wall.

She doesn't imagine a man. She doesn't imagine a woman. She doesn't allow herself to imagine at all. Rather, in her mind's eye, she sees an uncovered tarp and beneath it, a thing she has been raising her children to avoid at all costs, in every way, at every moment of every day.

"*Stay away.*"

Malorie is not alone down here, no.

"*STAY AWAY!*"

She pulls the hood tighter over her head.

There's no recorded instance of a creature initiating contact, forcing someone to look at it.

But what if one were to fall into the same hole you were thrown into?

"*Don't come near me.*"

Over time, Malorie has come to believe the creatures aren't saddled with the same limitations human beings are. Would a falling tree crush one? How about a car driven by a blindfolded woman? Because she's never heard proof of a dead body, a creature deceased, it's impossible to imagine one in a perilous state. But now, here . . . is it as stuck in the Safer Room as she is?

This means something to her. Something bigger than this moment allows for.

It moves across the hole, Malorie tracks it, and she turns to the wall, tries to climb again.

She jumps but touches no edge.

A deeper stirring. Something sliding across the dirt. Something wet? A bright sound? She wishes Tom were here to tell her what it is. Oh, how many times did *he* teach *her* when they were out in the world? How many times did his ears save them, guide them, tell them what to do?

"Please," Malorie says. But this thing deserves no pleading.

Something brushes against the sleeve of her sweatshirt.

She screams, falls to the ground, her gloved hands over her face.

Would it try to take her hood? Her gloves? Her last vestiges of armor?

The thing retracts, back to the far side of the Safer Room.

Malorie remains still. And it feels like Tom and Olympia are slipping away.

Forever.

How long could she have been expected to protect the kids? As if Malorie herself is a walking blindfold. Malorie made of black fabric, her dark hair the fount by which she springs. How long could she have been expected to keep Tom and Olympia safe? One year? One day? Ten years? Ten afternoons? There is no right and there is no wrong anymore. She knows this. Motherhood isn't what it was seventeen years ago, when it was the last thing in the world she considered. Motherhood isn't even what it was ten years ago, when the toll of surviving began weighing on those who survived so that their sanity would be tested the old way, brutal, cruel, and slow.

Now, folded up in the corner of the space, Malorie feels like she's her own blindfold, worn so long she's become it, discarded in a hole, never to be used again.

People in Indian River claim to have caught one . . . trapped . . .

Oh, yeah? Malorie thinks. *I caught one, too.*

Right here.

In this Safer Room.

She lowers her hands. She listens. There's silence from the far end of the hole.

What does it do? Does it observe her passively like Tom the man once theorized? Does it wait for her to look?

She stands up. Because she has to. Because she'll die if she remains folded in the corner of this grave.

"You've got to leave," Malorie says. "You've got to find a way out. I can't die with you near. You've already taken so much."

She thinks of the housemates. Cynical Don, who she can still see in the cellar as Tom the man put his hand on Don's shoulder and asked him to come upstairs for one last round of rum. Cheryl's voice down the hall after she got scared feeding the birds. The birds that hung like an alarm system. Jules, who loved his dog, Victor, so much. Felix, who got paler and paler the longer Tom was out of the house. Tom.

Tom.

She's tried to close the door on these thoughts. She tries now. She makes to shove the housemates into the attic. But they keep showing up around the table again, glasses of rum before them.

That's the way she likes them best. Happy as they were allowed to be.

Tom's wearing a makeshift helmet. Maybe he's at the piano. Maybe they don't have a phone book yet and so haven't begun the process of getting out, because once that began it was like the wheels were set in motion, from point A to point B, phone book to now, Yellow Pages to Safer Room, like Tom had called Fate and said, *We're ready. Do with us what you will.*

And Fate has.

Done with her.

She tries to close her already closed eyes to the memory of the bodies in the halls, upstairs and down, the living room, by the cellar door. But it's hard. How far is she from a creature right now? The same wretched thing Olympia the woman saw as Olympia the baby was born?

And is it the very same one?

Malorie shudders. The idea. Each a private demon. To each a creature comes. Waiting for you to slip, to get lazy, to look . . .

DON'T GET LAZY.

Don't look.

She tries to close her eyes a third time, a fourth. A creaking door on each layer, each chain of thought that rises from the hole she's in. How many times can a person close their eyes? How dark can one's personal darkness get?

"You . . ." she says. She thinks of the voice at the back of the train. Two men, right? One spoke to another? One spoke, one pushed? She shudders. No stopping that. Not right now. And never again. Not when she thinks of Rick at the school for the blind and the people there who, before Malorie arrived, gouged their eyes out to guarantee a lifetime of safety.

A lifetime of darkness, too, she thinks. *Where memories overlap. Where one begins to forget where the old world ended and the new one began.*

She presses against the wall. No space for these thoughts right now. Not in this room, not in her head. How high is the ledge?

"I'm not going to look," she says, her voice betraying every ounce of fear she feels. "I'm never going to look."

Then, an insane thought: the temptation to look.

She steps from the wall. She holds her arms out, as if telling the thing to take her. Tear off her sleeves. Touch her. Try to make her look.

She stands this way long enough to lose her nerve. She lowers her arms. She backs up to the dirt.

Did it take a step forward as well?

Malorie breathes in. She holds it. She breathes out.

She feels like she's losing her mind. The old way.

She opens her eyes. Not her actual eyes, but the eyes she's closed behind those eyes, and the eyes behind those, and those, and more. She feels a fluttering, a fanning of doors opening, in rhythm with her heart.

This, she knows, is how Tom thinks, always. Because she can't hide down here. Because there's no other choice but to *do* something.

She needs to push back.

"You're caught," she says. "No better off than I am. But you don't deserve to watch me fail. You showed up uninvited and you took everything from us. You stole our sisters, our parents, our kids. You took the sky, the view, you took day and night. A look across a street. A glance out a window. You've taken a view, every view, and with that, perspective. Who do you think you are, coming here, taking, then sitting silent, watching me go mad? I hope you're hurt. I hope you're stuck in here. I hope you get taken from you what you've taken from us. How can I be a mother in this world, your world? How am I supposed to feel, ever, in a world where my kids aren't allowed to look? They don't know me. My kids. They know a weathered, paranoid woman who cringes at every suggestion they make. They know a woman who says *no* so many more times than she says *yes*. A thousand times no. A hundred thousand times no. They know a woman who tells them what they're doing is wrong, every day, all night. I was different before you. My kids will never know that person. I'll never know that person again. Because even if you left now, even if you vanished as suddenly as you came... I've been through it. You dragged me through it. You dragged us all so that we don't resemble who we used to be and, Goddammit, who we were *supposed* to be. What's worse? Robbing someone of their childhood or taking away the person they were on their way to becoming? Because I can't tell! I can't tell who has it worse between me and my kids." Her voice grows hoarse. Half defeat. But half not, too. "There is no ignorance anymore and there is no bliss. We've all been scarred. This woman before you? *This isn't me!* This woman who lives in darkness, who cries behind closed eyes, who hasn't had *fun* in seventeen years. *This isn't... me.* This woman who can hardly call herself a woman at all because she feels more like a living blindfold. A machine that says no no no no *no no no no.* You wanna go outside, Tom? No. You wanna make a joke, Tom? No. Because *what's there to laugh about?* What's there to smile about? What's there to turn on its head, other than... you? *You.* I caught them playing 'creature' once. Running between cabins, saying, *Don't look at me!* I should've let them do it. I should've let them have *fun.* But I couldn't. And I can't be sure that, given the chance, I'd let them do it now. I'm a machine. Because you took the human. You took the glances, the winks, the eye-to-eye knowledge, the seeing somebody in a park, on a walk, on a drive. You took every relationship we were ever supposed to have and now you sit in this *fucking* hole with me and watch me go mad. Well, fuck you! Fuck you all! Get out! Go on and let me die alone. You don't deserve to watch the end of me just like I didn't deserve to be there at the beginning of you. *Leave!* Get out of here! Stop watching us go mad! Stop standing in plain sight so we have to close our fucking eyes, *stop!* Go back where you came from! You've seen what you do to us! It's been seventeen years, *seventeen years.* What more do you need? Can't you see that you hurt us? That you take from us? That you've ruined this place you've come to? I'm a mother! But I can't do anything except keep them away from you. *You.* You're terrible. You're greedy. How much can you take? When is it enough? You want and you want and you take and you take and now my son is left with no choice but to want to beat you, my daughter with no choice but to accept you, and me . . ."

She doesn't think she can finish. But she feels like she must.

"And me . . . I'm the one who survived long enough to go mad in the end."

Malorie doesn't remember falling back down to the dirt. She doesn't remember lying curled up where two dirt walls meet. But here she is. Above her, the ledge could be as high as a hundred feet. Taller than the house she gave birth in.

She cries. She punches the ground. And she feels it, too, when something is near again.

"Stay away."

She remembers a silly game Shannon loved to play. Her sister called it the *third-eye test.* You closed your eyes and someone slowly brought their finger to the space between your eyes and you said when you could feel it. The farther the person's fingertip was from your skin proved how active your third eye was. How liable you were to feel things that aren't of this world. Malorie feels the thing now. But it's not a fingertip. It's an entire presence, big as her own, maybe bigger, filling the rest of the Safer Room so that she has no choice but to remain curled up on the dirt. She's hot and cold with it, and she thinks of Shannon's fingertip, belonging to the same finger, the same hand that gripped a pair of scissors she drove into her own body.

"STAY AWAY!"

Her voice cracks; she's reached her limit. She can't speak or scream anymore. And while she still cries, her eyes have gone dry.

The presence gets closer yet, loaded air presses, and she can't breathe evenly. She's hyperventilating. She gets up because she's too afraid to stay down. And she's flatter this way, against the wall of dirt.

This creature may as well be the only creature on the planet, all of them the same thing, the point of perspective, the one place Malorie can't look.

Everywhere.

She turns to the wall, tries to steady herself. Tries to calm down.

It's close. Too close. Against her? Is it pressing against her?

It's going to kill her.

Right now.

It's going to rip the fold from her face.

Right now.

It's going to force her to look.

LOOK.

Right now.

She wants to scream, but she can't. She wants to run, but she can't.

She raises an arm, reaching for the same ledge she hasn't been able to reach yet.

And she cries out when a hand takes her own.

Malorie, nearly delirious, almost pulls away. But no, this is skin. This is bone. This is human. This is help.

"Mom!"

She recognizes the voice, because in an unfair way, this is not out of context. She's heard this same voice with her eyes closed too many times to count.

"There's a root to the left of you," Olympia says. "You can use it for your left foot. Then I'll pull and you should be able to—"

What is Olympia saying? What the *fuck* is Olympia saying?

Malorie feels to the left, finds the root. How did she not feel this before?

And how does Olympia know where it is?

"Ready, Mom?"

"No, Olympia . . . what's happening . . . how did you . . ."

"Come on, Mom. You step up and I'll pull and you'll be able to—"

When Malorie cuts her off, her voice comes much calmer than she means for it to sound.

"How did you see the root, Olympia?"

There is a creature with Malorie in this hole. This grave. This Safer Room.

"Mom . . ." Then . . . the loaded silence of a sixteen-year-old girl who has been keeping secrets.

"Olympia. I need you to tell me how you knew this was here. And I need you to tell me now."

Malorie, parenting. Still.

"Mom," Olympia says, "there's no creature in there with you."

What?

"You do *not* know that."

"I do. You're alone down there."

"You can't know that!"

Quiet from above. The sound of a daughter about to tell her mother the truth.

"I'm looking into the hole, Mom. I can do that. I can look."

Malorie pulls her hands away.

"Olympia . . ."

As if learning Olympia is able to see could drive Malorie mad all on its own.

Then, tears from above. Olympia is crying. And Malorie recognizes this brand of cry.

Shame.

She reaches up again and finds Olympia's hand. She uses the root as her daughter pulls. Malorie feels the ledge, just out of reach this whole time.

Her fingers dig into the lip of the hole and Olympia grabs both her wrists. Before Malorie has time to process what Olympia's just told her (but already accepting it because it rings a bell, doesn't it? Rings many), she is flat to the ledge, pulling herself forward.

With an effort and a strength she did not know she still has, Malorie is fully out of the Safer Room at last.

She spends hardly any time at all on the ground, exhausted, before she gets up. Again, Olympia's hand is there to help. A hand that has helped Malorie thousands of times over the course of what feels like thousands of years.

"You . . ."

She hugs Olympia hard.

"I thought you would be upset," Olympia says. Crying still. "I thought you would be scared. I thought people would be afraid of me."

Malorie, eyes closed, grips both Olympia's shoulders.

"You've seen them?"

"Yes."

"How many?"

"All of them."

"What does that mean? What does that *mean*?"

"Every one of them that was near enough for me to see."

"Olympia . . . how long have you been able to look?"

In her mind's eye, Malorie sees Olympia's mother in the attic. She witnesses the woman's face as she sees the creature standing behind Malorie. Hears it as Olympia the woman tells the creature it's not so bad. Sees the baby still connected to the mom between the mother's legs, the mother who begins to lose her mind.

"Always," Olympia says. "I'm so sorry."

Malorie takes her daughter's face in her hands.

Was she really all alone in the hole? Was she so close to going mad . . .

. . . the old way?

"Oh, my God, Olympia. Don't say you're sorry."

What has Olympia seen over the years? What has she been shouldering?

"I think it has to do with my mom," Olympia says. Crying still. "And what you told me about me being born when she saw one."

Malorie agrees. But she's too stunned to say so.

"You've seen everything. For years."

"Yes."

"And you followed me here."

"Yes." Trepidation in her voice. "Sort of. I found you."

"How?"

"Dean said you weren't on the train."

"So you got off . . ."

"Yes."

"Where's Tom? Where is he?"

It's too much to fathom at once. Olympia is immune.

Tom . . .

"He wasn't on the train, either."

"Oh, God."

"Dean said he might be with a man . . ."

"What man, Olympia? *What man?*"

She hears Olympia swallow, as if bracing herself to speak a hard truth.

"Henry."

"Who?"

"It's a man who . . ."

But it doesn't matter what Olympia says next. It doesn't matter that her daughter's words line up with what she knows to be true.

. . . he was just like the man you always talk about, the man named . . .

"I heard his voice just before being shoved from the train," Malorie says. Her voice is steel. Her voice is unbreakable. "Gary."

Her own private boogeyman, hiding, these sixteen years.

"Did you ever see him around camp?" Malorie asks. And her voice is flint.

She is already preparing herself to murder this man.

"No."

Malorie breathes in, she holds it, she breathes out.

"Listen to me," she says. "I heard him mention Indian River. Do you know what that place is?"

"Yes."

"Because Tom told you?"

"Yes, mostly. I read some myself."

"Okay."

But it's not okay. Because whether Gary has been watching them or not for all this time, whether he called a corner of Camp Yadin home or slept in the damp cellar of the lodge, he's never lost track of Malorie.

She knows this now.

"You're immune," Malorie says. "Just like he is."

"Mom, don't say I'm like—"

Malorie cuts her off, her mind light-years from where she stands.

"No, this is good. This makes us even. Do you know where Indian River is?"

"No. But we can find it. Mom, I don't like how you sound. We can't—"

"We can, Olympia. We can do absolutely anything we want to."

She's standing, Olympia's hand in hers.

"You're not wearing sleeves," Malorie says.

"We don't need to."

"But . . ."

"We don't need to. I promise."

"How could you let me think we did?"

Immediately after asking it, Malorie wishes she hadn't. She wants to know everything, all of it, all at once. But for now, she needs to find her son.

"Lead me," she says. "Take us to Indian River."

"Mom . . ."

"Olympia, we need to go this second."

"That's not what I meant."

Malorie feels hands at her neck. Olympia is pulling her face closer.

"Here," her daughter says.

Then Olympia is tying fabric around Malorie's eyes. Tying the fold, her fold, tight to her head.

"I've never killed anyone before," Malorie says, speaking her thoughts.

"Mom, we don't have to do this."

"We do." And her voice is resolve. Her voice is truth. "Because if we don't, he'll hide in the dark, our dark, forever."

Malorie turns once toward the hole.

Olympia is immune. Olympia can see. And she says the hole was empty.

But Malorie doesn't feel mad anymore. Doesn't feel like she could ever go mad in any way ever again.

"We have to hurry," she says. "The real monster's got Tom."

TWENTY-SEVEN

"Well, they're really just a pair of glasses," Tom says, his voice shaking with nervousness. "I made them out of this . . . this . . . do you know what a two-way mirror is?"

The woman sitting before him on a stool nods. She sits on the very edge of the wood, her veined hands gripping her knees, a long brown ponytail with streaks of gray reaching past her shoulders.

Tom hasn't seen her enormous eyes blink since Henry brought him into the tent.

This is Athena Hantz.

"Okay. Good," Tom says. "Yeah . . . in the office of the camp we lived in, we lived there forever, it felt like. You ever feel like that? Yeah? Okay. Well, in the office was this two-way mirror so that the camp director could look down at the campers eating or at whatever was happening in the main lodge area without everyone being able to see him."

He pauses. Is she following this? Are any of them?

Two men younger than Malorie sit on the ground, flanking Athena. There are others in the tent, too.

Tom hears constant motion outside the tent. Indian River is active.

"Go on," Athena says. "This is interesting."

"Yeah, okay," Tom says. He pauses again because he wants to make sure he words this next part right. "So . . . my mom, she told me those two-way mirrors were in grocery stores, back when people could look around freely, you know? And she said they were in a lot of movies. Detective movies? I can't be sure. Anyway, she also told me that the man I was named after, Tom, he sounds like a cool guy actually. Like someone I would've been friends with. Well . . . he was the first to tell my mom that maybe the creatures are . . . infinity. It's hard to explain."

"We know the theory," Athena says.

"Yeah, okay," Tom says. "Well . . . so . . . if the creatures are something we can't understand, because our heads can't comprehend what they are . . . what if we could like . . . what if we could make them do something we can relate to? That's what I was thinking. If we could make them do something, anything, that makes sense to us, or is familiar to us . . . well, maybe then we could understand them. Even if it's only a little bit."

The two seated men exchange a look. Tom thinks they probably think he's crazy. Or not smart. But when they look back to him, both appear to be wholly interested.

Athena reaches out, taps Tom's knee.

"Go on," she says.

"So . . . one thing I was thinking was . . . one day I was in the office and I thought, man, what if I looked through the glass and saw a creature in the lodge. Right? Well, I guess I'd go mad. Mom would say so, anyway. I think most people would. And my sister, she has this idea that the creatures have no face . . .

not like ours, I guess? She says they're all face and all not at the same time. That's her theory anyway. So it struck me that . . . if a creature was in the lodge . . . and if it was reflected, right? If it looked at the glass . . . which, if it's all face, on all sides, then if it was reflected at all it would be looking, right? Well, in this case, it wouldn't see *me*. You know? It would see itself. In the mirror."

The people in the tent are silent. Henry smiles as if he thought of this idea himself.

Athena's eyes seem to be frozen on Tom. As if he's talking to a photograph.

"And I got to thinking . . . if a creature saw itself . . . wouldn't it . . . couldn't it maybe . . . *consider* itself? I don't know if that's the right word exactly. But . . . maybe it would look at itself and be forced to consider what it is. And while it did look . . . at itself . . . while it did consider . . . what it is . . . maybe *that's* something I could understand. That's something I could relate to. Making it . . . you know . . . safe . . . to . . . to look at it."

He could talk for hours about this subject, but for now, he feels done. Or like he's told them what the glasses are supposed to do, and either they think he's crazy or they don't.

"So I cut up the two-way mirror and made glasses out of them."

He feels like he can hear the seconds ticking. Then:

"Genius," Athena says. "Absolutely genius."

"Like I said," Henry says.

One of the seated men raises a finger, as if about to debate. Then he lowers it.

"Well, I think that's one of the brightest ideas I've ever heard," he says.

"Really?" Tom says. "You do?"

"Have you tried them out?" Athena asks.

"No." He feels ashamed of this answer.

"That's okay," she says. "You're going to."

Her face looks like one large smile. As if she has a second, hidden smile behind her lips.

"May I?" she asks, reaching for the glasses.

Tom hands them to her. She hands them to the man seated to her right. Her eyes remain fixed on Tom.

You're going to.

What did she mean?

The man tries the glasses on.

"We'll have to modify these," he says. "Make sure there's no peripheral vision."

"They're the safety brigade," Athena says to Tom. "I rather liked them the way you had them. Risky. And do you have the rest of the mirror?"

"No," Tom says. He wishes he did.

"We do," a man standing deeper in the tent says.

"Where?" Athena asks.

"The old Farmer Jack. The grocery store office, just like the kid's mom said."

A moment of silence follows. Athena looks to the glasses. Tom does, too, sees her eyes reflected in them.

She looks happier than Malorie ever has.

"Do you have one here?" Tom suddenly asks. He can't help but ask it. The census papers said the people of Indian River claimed to have caught one.

He doesn't need to explain what he means. These people understand.

"If you mean do we have one locked up in some sort of cage, then no," Athena says. "But there's no shortage of creatures in Indian River."

Tom hears heavier activity outside. Malorie's words begin to rise in his head and he cuts them off, can almost see the blood of them, slashed.

"Get the mirror from the grocery store," Athena says. She hasn't taken her eyes off Tom, and for a second he thinks she's telling him to do it. But a man near the back of the tent moves to the door.

Are they going to test his glasses? Right now?

You're going to.

"So this is how it works," Athena says. "We have volunteers. A long list of them. People who have decided it's wiser to risk their lives than to hide behind a blanket. People like you, Tom."

"Someone's gonna look through my glasses?" Tom asks. "I don't want someone to get hurt because of me."

Athena doesn't laugh, doesn't smile, doesn't move to calm his fears, either.

"These two"—she fans palms toward the men seated on either side of her—"are up next."

Tom doesn't know what to say. It's one thing to reveal his invention, and it feels good for it to be received this way. Yet . . . these men right here?

They're already standing up. Already getting ready.

"Don't worry," Henry says, suddenly at Tom's side. "This is what they live for here."

Athena rises from the stool and offers Tom her hand.

"I'd like to thank you for coming to Indian River," she says. "And for having the balls to present your theory." Then, smiling: "Make them do something we can relate to. Make them consider themselves . . . make them look within . . . like we do. What's more relatable than self-reflection? Absolutely brilliant, Tom. You belong here. With us. Did you know that? Don't answer. This is a big moment for you. For me, too. Welcome, Tom. Welcome to Indian River."

TWENTY-EIGHT

The warring emotions within her are so extreme that Olympia endures actual, physical pain.

She's told her mom her secret.

She told her!

And Malorie reacted with . . . pride? She reacted well. As well as she could have, given the circumstances. And it's those circumstances that cause the war within.

Tom.

Gary.

Olympia doesn't think Tom will have enough time in Indian River for something truly terrible to happen. They're on their way, after all; it's not like Tom vanished years ago and they just discovered his name on the census as being accounted for in a notoriously unsafe town. No. He's just ahead. Out of sight, yes. But he can't be too far.

The people there will have to get to know him before they can ask him to be a part of anything perilous.

But then again, what does she know? Tom could walk into the very building in which they've caught one, if they actually have done so. Olympia doesn't think that's possible. She's seen them. Most of her life. And, to her, they don't look like something to be caught.

"This way," she says, gripping Malorie's gloved hand and leading her around a dead body in the road. It's an old man. He looks like he could be a hundred years old. There's a tent twenty feet away. She thinks the man lived there. There's no sign of self-immolation.

Old age, she thinks. But she does not say. Now isn't the time.

And when is? When has it ever been the time?

"Do you see him?" Malorie asks.

Tom.

Tom left the train.

This is too much. This is bad.

"No," she says. "But he can't be far."

"How long?" Malorie asks.

They're moving fast, Malorie's words are breathless, but Olympia knows what she means.

"Since I was six."

Yes. At the school for the blind. It was her first time, and she can see it today, in her mind's eye, as if it's happening again. The man Rick who called the night Olympia and Tom were born, he'd just asked her to get a basket from the room everyone called "the supply shed." Just a regular classroom down one of the many brick halls in the school she was just beginning to call home. They kept paper and tools and a ladder and scissors and just about everything in that room. Olympia was happy to be asked to do it.

Are you big enough to get me a basket? Rick had said. And Olympia was all smiles. It didn't matter that Rick couldn't see that smile or that most of the people in the building would never see her face at all. She was glad to play a part, any part, at all.

But on the way to the room, at the far end of the hall, she saw one.

She knew what it was right away. Even at six she understood it was the thing Malorie had raised her to fear. Yet, gazing upon it, she didn't feel any worse than she did when she woke up that morning. She was scared. But that was all. And the fear never quite eclipsed any she'd known before. Not even the fear she felt when Malorie told her they were taking a river they'd never even swam in.

More importantly: she didn't feel crazy. Nothing like that at all. Maybe she was too young to know what mad might feel like, but she wasn't too young to think.

In fact, the only thing she was worried about, really, was the idea that someone else might see it, too. That someone else would come around the corner and go mad and hurt everybody. Malorie talked about that potentiality all the time.

Then someone did come.

Annette.

Olympia had long wondered about the red-haired woman who told everyone she was blind. She wondered because one night, late, Olympia left their bedroom (a converted classroom like all the rest) to use the bathroom alone. And there, in the stall, seated, she heard someone else enter. Someone who thought they were alone, too.

Olympia, embarrassed, already keeping secrets even then, though not of the magnitude she soon would, heard a match strike and saw a candle come to light, illuminating a sphere in the otherwise pitch-black darkness of the restroom. She peered through the stall door and saw the woman holding the candle to the mirror; saw Annette looking at herself.

Annette. Blind.

But looking.

So why pretend? Even then, so young, she guessed it had something to do with wanting to be unbothered. Wanting people to leave her alone. Wanting people to consider her safe in a world where anybody who can see is liability. Malorie herself spoke of Annette without fear. This meant something. In what Malorie called "the new world," going unnoticed was good. For this, after a time, Olympia came to believe that Annette was simply still trying to be good.

In a world without personal possessions, secrets were precious indeed.

She saw the woman's face clearly in the glass, floating features in the otherwise dark space. Olympia's heart hammered in her young chest as she watched the woman's eyes for the first time, saw them connect with her reflection in the glass, saw the relief in Annette's face for being allowed to look, here, where she was sure she was alone.

Then Annette looked at Olympia.

Olympia wanted to gasp, wanted to cry out, wanted to say oh, no, don't worry, I'd never, I'd never ever, I'd never ever tell a soul that you aren't blind!

But Annette only stared. Then she blew out the candle, and the face seemed to vanish, a wisp of smoke, features swallowed by darkness once again.

Olympia didn't move. Nor did she hear the woman, who was much older than Malorie, move. The two remained still in the darkness for what felt to Olympia like a very long time.

When Annette did move again, Olympia steeled herself, ready for the stall door to be thrust open, or worse, to creak slowly, as the old woman's wrinkled hands entered the dark rectangle, searching for the body belonging to the pair of eyes that had caught her.

The girl who knew her secret.

But Annette did not come. Rather, her bare feet slapped the tiled floor on the way out of the bathroom, and Olympia remained still long after that same door swung closed.

"Don't look," she said to Annette, later, months later, as she set out to get the basket for Rick. As Annette rounded the corner. "There's one at the end of the hall."

Annette's red hair hung vibrant to a powder-blue robe.

"Look?" she asked. "But I'm blind."

"Oh," Olympia said, because she didn't know what else to say and because, too, she'd just seen a creature for the first time in her life. Even the word *creature* was starting to feel like the wrong name for what lurked at the end of the hall.

Then Annette looked.

Years later, now, leading Malorie up the road to Indian River, as her body seems to physically swell with the uncertainty of a brother who has fled and a mother who now knows she is immune, Olympia finds the room within herself to feel that lack of closure, that lack of understanding, once more: *why* did Annette look when someone told her not to?

Was it because Annette had seen her in the glass in the bathroom and wanted to discredit what Olympia knew to be true? Was it because the voice that warned her was young and Annette, so old, had simply had enough of taking orders, of living the way people had to in the new world?

Or maybe, Olympia still thinks, maybe the woman was curious. And nothing more.

She tells Malorie this story now. But saying it out loud doesn't add any clarity. And Malorie doesn't give her any opinions.

Mom, Olympia knows, is only thinking of Tom.

"You saw the massacre at the school for the blind," Malorie says.

"I did."

Olympia guides Malorie around another turn. Still no sign of Tom ahead. It's possible Gary knows a shortcut to the community. Malorie said so.

"I'm so sorry," Malorie says. "I should've helped you with that. I could've."

She hears the sorrow in her mom's voice, and she doesn't like it. The last thing she wants is to make Malorie feel worse. About anything.

Here, they rush to her son.

Here, they've gotten off the train that might take them to her parents.

Malorie, Olympia knows, has suffered enough.

"No," Olympia says. "Honestly, Mom. You've been the best mom in the world to us."

Malorie grips her hand, and Olympia squeezes back.

Around the next turn, she sees it. Just as she's seen so many of them through the years. There were dozens on the rudderless hike from the school for the blind to Camp Yadin. That journey remains the most frightening of Olympia's life. It marked the beginning of guiding her family in secret.

This way, guys.

Look out, guys.

Uphill now.

I'll go ahead a little. Don't worry, I like doing it.

You hear that, Tom? So do I.

But she hadn't heard it. She'd seen it. All of it.

Her ears are no match for her brother's. Another secret.

"Anything?" Malorie asks.

Olympia still considers that first walk, six years old, as the time she became a woman. She's read enough books to know that the good ones tell of a character who experiences something that changes their life. For her, it was coming to grips with immunity alone.

And how many more did she see once they got there? Really, how many through the years? How many creatures, if that's what they must be called, stood outside their cabin, stood within others, roamed the lodge and its kitchen? How many did she find in the basement of the lodge as Malorie fished for canned goods on the shelves, believing her daughter to be blindfolded, too?

Oh, there were so many times she wanted to tell Malorie about Annette; wanted her mom to know the woman was not touched, that they didn't have to wear sleeves, hoods, gloves. Oh, how she wanted Malorie to know her secret. The truth.

But even now, as they turn with the road, as a creature is revealed to be standing ahead, Olympia's instinct is to say nothing, only to guide.

But things have changed. And maybe people experience more than one life-changing event.

"There's one about forty feet away, Mom."

Malorie comes to a stop.

"Close your eyes," she says.

But Olympia doesn't close them. Instead, she eyes a way around the thing, just as she has done so many times before.

The path curves this way, when it did not.

There's an object in the road, when it was everything Malorie feared.

"Olympia," Malorie says.

But this is something Malorie will have to get used to.

"It's in the center of the road," Olympia says. "Follow me, we'll go around it."

She hears Malorie's breathing intensify. She knows her mom is as afraid as she's ever been.

"I won't go mad," Olympia says. "I promise."

It sounds so silly to say, yet Malorie squeezes her hand again.

And Olympia leads.

She guides Malorie around it, but near it, coming as close as Olympia's ever come, emboldened by her reveal.

"Okay," she says. "It's behind us. But . . ."

"There are more ahead," Malorie says.

"Yes," Olympia says. "So many that we're going to have to take this slow."

"Olympia." Malorie pulls on her arm.

But Olympia understands Malorie is only scared.

And if she's not keeping secrets anymore, she may as well admit that she's scared, too.

She pulls back on Malorie's hand.

"Tom," she says.

Malorie breathes in, holds it, breathes out.

"All right," she says. "Guide us."

Then Olympia, with pride, new, changed, does that.

TWENTY-NINE

This is everything Tom has ever wanted. The opposite of the life he's lived.

A community where people are *trying*.

It's all he's ever asked Malorie to be okay with. Trying. New things. New ways. He knows not to look. And here he won't be told what he already knows ever again.

Henry understands. Oh, boy, does he. It was Henry who said go, go to where the people think like you do. Be bold as you were born to be! And how those words connected with Tom. They electrified him in a way Malorie never could. Nobody has ever spoken to him like Henry does. Not Mom, not Olympia, not anybody at the school for the blind. The more Tom thinks about it, the more he believes the train was an intervention of Fate. Olympia's told him about Fate before. Without that knock on the door by the census man, and without Tom asking him to leave the papers, he never would've heard about Indian River, Malorie never would've seen her parents' names on the page, and he never would've met Henry. It scares him how close he was to spending the rest of his life at Camp Yadin, never knowing there was a whole world that felt like he does.

And they really, really do.

The man, Allan, has already retrieved the two-way mirror. He and some others are testing it out inside a large ten-person tent right now. Tom is in the next tent over, where the two volunteers, Jacob and Calvin, have been discussing the philosophy of Tom's invention for a while. They're next on the list, Henry reminds Tom, and the people of Indian River can't wait to try new ideas.

Tom knows why. It's because they want to be a part of something bigger than the life Tom was leading. It's because they understand that, yes, someone might get hurt, but someone might also not. The people of Indian River want to be the ones to break down the door, the ones who discover a safe way to look, who return sight and seeing to a world that's already mourned the loss of both.

Doesn't Malorie get it? Could she really stand where Tom stands now, mere feet from the people who discuss what might be their last moments alive? Could she be this close to a breakthrough and not feel the excitement Tom feels? He knows the answer to this, and it makes him feel sick. If Malorie were here, it wouldn't be happening. She'd get hysterical. She'd demand everyone close their eyes. She'd take him by the arm and drag him out of this tent, one gloved hand over his face.

Maybe she'd even hit him again.

"Your mother," Henry says, once again seeming to sense where Tom's head is at, once again proving he already knows Tom better than his own mom does, "wouldn't get any of this at all, would she?"

"Not at all," Tom says.

But he doesn't want Henry bringing Malorie up right now. He doesn't want to think of her at all.

"She'd scream bloody murder at every single person in this town," Henry goes on. "She'd call them all crazy, and she'd include you in that assessment."

Tom nods. But he really doesn't want to talk about this right now. He just wants to listen to Jacob and Calvin, hear what they have to say, add to their conversation. Their ideas. Their bravery.

Jacob says, "It's different than looking at the reflection of one in the mirror because, for starters, you might see something in your peripheral vision that isn't reflected in the limited shape of the glass."

Calvin says, "In this case it's all about forcing the creature to do something fathomable."

They're talking about his ideas!

It's everything Tom's ever wanted.

"God, it's like I can hear her voice already," Henry says. "The shrill bemoaning of the new world. The endless rules. You'll see." He plants a heavy hand on Tom's shoulder, and Tom wants him to remove it. "When you finally get to view one, you'll see just how paranoid your mother has been."

Jacob and Calvin are discussing mirrors. Reflections. The possible mind of impossible creatures. Tom wants to get lost in their words. He could listen to them for weeks.

But Malorie, as is her nature, keeps coming back up.

"She'd go for me first," Henry says with a chuckle. "She'd ask who took you here, and when I raised my hand . . ."

"She wouldn't see it," Tom says.

"That's right!" Henry says. His laughter is louder than the discussion between the two volunteers.

He thinks this is funny, but it's not. Not right now.

"Eventually she'd find out," Henry says. "And she'd come for me. Except . . . like you bring up, where would she know to look? And doesn't that sum everything up, Tom? Here, a woman so righteous, yet completely inert. Well, she's done it to herself, I say. She's so deep in the dark she wouldn't know if safety were sitting right beside her."

Not now, Tom thinks. *Not now.*

"My God, if she had her way, you'd be locked in a crate like veal. She ever tell you what veal is, and how it was raised? Probably not. She probably didn't want you knowing that's what was happening to you."

Allan enters the tent. He says the two-way mirror is ready. He says something about a park. Jacob and Calvin stop talking.

Tom can't help but imagine them mad.

". . . like a caged animal, Tom. And what kind of life is that? And who, then, would have put you in a worse position? The things outside . . . or your very own mother?"

Jacob and Calvin smile Tom's way as Allan escorts them outside.

"Wait," Tom says, but they're already out of the tent.

"Who indeed?" Henry says. "And it makes you wonder, it makes you ask, who is the monster? Not I, Tom. Not us. Indian River has accepted me. Just as it accepts everyone. Your mother would say a place like this must draw the psychos. And maybe it has. But a madman at ease is safer than a sane woman unsettled. The creatures may be monsters, but as evidenced by your mother and the life she deemed fit for you . . . those nasty things are not the problem. Man is the creature he fears."

The words rattle in Tom's head like broken sticks outside Cabin Three at Camp Yadin. Tom hears them, yes, thinks he even knows what they are, yes, but his mind is on other things.

Amazing things.

Outside, Athena Hantz calls for him. And beyond her voice, the sound of a community celebrating.

Already, Tom thinks.

Before even trying it.

And isn't that everything he's ever wanted? To celebrate the effort? The results be damned?

"Best be going," Henry says. But his hand is still on Tom's shoulder, keeping him rooted to the ground. "You thought you cut the apron strings by leaving the train . . ." Henry laughs. Not the happy kind. "You're about to positively slash them."

THIRTY

Malorie smells rot seconds before Olympia tugs on her arm.

"Mom . . ."

Malorie stops walking. It's harrowing enough to grasp the reality that her daughter can *look*, but the gravity in Olympia's voice chills her.

"How bad is it?"

They've reached Indian River. It's as black as it's ever been behind Malorie's blindfold.

"Well," she says, "in sight, from where we stand, and we're just at the border, literally . . ."

"Olympia. Out with it."

"Bodies, Mom. So many bodies."

Malorie knows that, right now, this moment, she has to be as strong as she's ever been.

"And there's . . ." Olympia's voice trails off the way it does when someone is observing something bad. "Flags. Plastic flags . . . pinned to each of their chests."

"What do you mean?" But it doesn't matter. Whatever Hell unfolds before them, they must go through it.

"Heroes," Olympia says. "Tributes, I think. To the fallen."

Malorie thinks, *Sacrifices*.

"It's bad," Olympia says. "I've never seen . . . so much . . ."

It smells to Malorie like an entire graveyard's worth of bodies never buried.

"Okay," Malorie says. She's trying to remain calm. She must. "Do you see your brother?"

"No," Olympia says, her voice shaken. "It's not like that. The road leads toward buildings. Bodies in the road."

"Don't look at them. Don't think of them. Do you see Tom ahead?"

Malorie hardly recognizes the stability in her own voice. A thought flutters distantly; all her paranoid preparations, all her rules, have led to this moment in time.

Is she ready? Has she done right by herself, by her teens?

"No." Olympia stifles a cry. "Oh, Mom. These people killed themselves. Their faces are torn apart. These people . . ."

"They went mad," Malorie says. She breathes in. She holds it. She breathes out. "But we need to move. We need to go. *Now*."

She feels Olympia's hand in her own. The sun, still up, gets hotter. The smell gets worse.

They walk. And every time Olympia squeezes her hand, Malorie imagines another atrocity in the road.

"So now," Olympia says, audibly shaking, "there are . . . things, too."

Malorie stiffens.

"Creatures?"

"No. Like . . . makeshift things. Things Tom would've made. I don't know what any of them are. Things made of wood and plastic, rope . . . metal . . ."

Malorie wants to move faster, to whip through this insanity, to find Tom *now*. The census papers talked about the risks this community is willing to take. She knows these broken objects are failed experiments left to decay with those who went mad.

"What do you see?" Malorie asks. "Talk to me."

"Street signs. A gas station. Storefronts. I don't know. Mom. No people. Wait . . ."

Olympia stops.

"What is it?"

"Can you hear that?" she asks.

Malorie listens. Hard.

"No. What do you hear?"

"People. Cheering. I think."

Malorie starts walking again, and Olympia guides her along a curve in the road.

The stench is worse. Yet, somehow, this suddenly feels horribly right to Malorie. How long has it felt like she's been walking through Hell? How many years? And how long has she seen the new world as a place of death and decay from the darkness behind the fold?

In its terrible way, this is exactly where she's supposed to be. Indian River. An eventual point in time, a location in space, where the last seventeen years have carried her.

"So many bodies," Olympia says. *"So many . . ."*

Are the failures so commonplace that the people who sacrifice their sanity and lives are simply wheeled to the lawn and dumped at the city gates, left to rot under the sun?

"Bones," Olympia says.

Malorie was expecting this. The closer they get to town, the older the corpses. Like all graveyards, this one grows out.

And at the center of it, its source, she hears the voices now, too.

Cheering. There is no doubt.

"It's going to be okay," Malorie says. But she hears the lie in her voice.

Who waits for them downtown in a community like this? Who stands guard?

In her memory, she hears Victor the dog destroying himself in the emptiness of a dive bar.

"It's going to be okay," Malorie says.

"Bones," Olympia repeats.

Malorie's never heard this level of fear in her daughter's voice. She doesn't want to know what Olympia sees. Yet she'd rather see it *for* her. She'd willingly carry these memories herself.

A crowd cheers. A central voice erupts. A woman speaking through a megaphone.

Malorie thinks of the name from the census pages: Athena Hantz.

The amalgamation of barker and bad sound reminds Malorie of the Marquette County Fair.

Possibly the most unsettling aspect of all, for Malorie, is that, despite what Olympia sees . . . it sounds festive.

"Ahead," Olympia says. "The buildings, the sidewalks, lined with more bodies. Oh, Mom. Oh, no. A kid."

Malorie wants to demand why, *why*? What kind of community dumps the dead in the streets?

But she knows the answer.

One gone mad.

Altogether.

Unsafe.

An explosion of cheers tells Malorie the crowd is to the right of her, but the sound is still muffled. Distance to go.

"Step down," Olympia says.

"It's going to be okay," Malorie says again. It's all she can say. For all the preparations and hard work, for all the surviving she's done, she has no better words for her daughter at this time.

She's shaking.

But she tries. Because when they get to this crowd of people, when they finally reach the heart of Indian River, she's going to need her wits.

They're here for Tom.

"Up again," Olympia says. "Onto the sidewalk."

Her daughter guides her serpentine, and Malorie knows it's because they're avoiding the dead. How many have scissors in their chests? How many are surrounded by puddles of blood?

The crowd is more emphatic now. The woman's voice through the megaphone. They sound hungry for whatever's about to happen.

What's about to happen?

Malorie can't make out the words. Her mind is barely able to keep these elements together: the dead, a crowd, Gary, this town, her son.

Indian River is everything she is not and has never been.

People laugh. An eruption of genuine laughter. People jeer . . . a joke? The voice again. Riling up the crowd. Do the people wear folds?

Is everyone in Indian River out of their fucking minds?

"Stop," Olympia says.

She pulls Malorie to the side of a building.

"What is it?" Malorie asks, shocked by the calm in her own voice. A calm she does not feel.

"So . . . Okay. So . . ."

"What is it?"

"It's a park in the center of town. And a lot of people are in the park. Blindfolded."

"Calm down, Olympia. We're going to get your brother. We can do this."

"Okay. And . . . and there's a stage. Flags. Banners."

Malorie's heart breaks before Olympia says the words.

"And Tom's on the stage," Olympia says. "He's standing next to . . . a mirror."

The words feel plucked from Malorie's personal darkness. As if they are made of the dark itself.

"Is he blindfolded?"

She didn't mean to yell it.

"I can't tell."

"You *what?*"

"Mom, I can't tell . . ."

"Okay we need to—"

"There's a creature on the lawn in front of the stage. I don't know how to explain this, Mom. Like it's . . . waiting to see what happens."

Malorie is already moving before Olympia finishes.

She doesn't grab her daughter by the wrist, doesn't want her to follow. She doesn't attempt to look strong, to appear dangerous, to threaten. She only walks, arms out, stabilizing herself, readying herself for a curb, a gradation, a hill, a body.

People clap around her. People call out. Someone yells something about breaking through. Someone praises God. So many voices. Hysterical, absurd, convinced.

"TOM!"

Malorie yells his name but others are doing it, too.

Calling for Tom.

Tom on a stage, a creature in the crowd.

"TOM!"

She knows he can hear her. She knows he could've heard them at the gates of town if he'd wanted to listen that far.

So many people. Infinite voices.

"TOM!"

She trips on what feels like a curb, almost falls, rights herself. Someone says something about freedom.

"TOM!"

Like she's calling out to Tom the man, telling him to get up into the attic, don't stay downstairs where Gary . . . Gary . . . Gary . . .

"Malorie."

A voice, at her side. At her ear.

"Get away from me!"

She shoves him. Kicks the open air.

Then, a sea of people. Chants. Cheers.

"Malorie," Gary says (she knows it's him, it's always been him, behind the fold with her, always, forever), "Tom doesn't want you here. Tom is growing up now. Right now."

"TOM!"

She shoves but can't find him. She kicks but he's not there.

"He's looking at one right now," Gary says. "It's incredible, Malorie. Looking through a device of his own making."

Malorie moves fast, too fast, swings at Gary, misses, as the voice of the one she believes to be Athena Hantz speaks through the megaphone, tells the people of Indian River that Tom is looking at the creature, that he and the creature *look at each other right now.*

"TOM!"

But Malorie is falling. As Gary's laughter is swallowed by a burst of unbridled cheer from the people around her.

And from the stage . . . suddenly, softly, somehow heard by Malorie as she hits the ground.

"Mom?"

Tom.

He's heard her.

And he sounds . . .

"Sane," she says, planting her palms on the grass, getting to her knees. Her elbows shake, her wrists shake, her entire body rumbles with the horror of her son gone mad and the unfathomable possibility that he hasn't.

"Mom?" he says. Then, "Malorie!"

Malorie is up. But the crowd is too loud. She's losing track of him in a wash of lazy, dangerous strangers.

Someone is at her by the elbow, forcing her back the way she came.

Gary

Gary Gary Gary

Malorie makes to push but Olympia's voice stops her.

"Mom, *Mom*. He's okay. Tom. He's looking . . . and he's okay."

The people around her explode with a cheer Malorie has long thought reserved for the day human beings discover a way to look at the creatures safely.

And has that happened?

And is today that day?

And is Tom the one to have done it?

Tom the man appears in her mind's eye. A man who so desperately wanted the world to cheer just like this.

"CLOSE YOUR EYES!" Malorie yells. And her voice is torn fabric.

Olympia guides her, but even Olympia seems enamored with what has happened.

Where's Gary?

"Where's Gary?"

"Mom!" Olympia is crying. Elation in her voice. "Mom! Tom did it!"

"*Where's Gary?*"

Then . . . a voice.

A man's. But not Gary's. As if in a dream tortured so long it's become a nightmare, Malorie hears the voice of her father.

It comes from deep within the darkness, *her* darkness, a depth even she has never been. She tries to repudiate it, to shove back, to refuse it just as she tried to shove Gary moments ago.

Now isn't the time for false hope. Now isn't the time to dream again.

"Malorie?"

But it *is* Dad's voice. Real or imagined.

"Who . . ." Olympia begins to ask.

"What's going on?" Malorie asks.

"Who . . ." Olympia says again.

"Malorie Walsh?" the man asks.

Dad's voice again. Out of the darkness. Close to her ear.

"Oh, my God . . ." Malorie says. She grips Olympia's arm for support.

When it becomes real, the truth of it, Sam Walsh, here, his fingers to her face, it hurts. It's so powerful, the implications of this voice, this real voice, that it turns the light on behind her fold for the first time in seventeen years.

"Help," she says. Because she can't take it. All of this. At once.

Sam Walsh speaks again.

"I heard the boy call your name," he says. "And your voice . . . I recognize your voice . . ."

Fingers again, on her face.

"Mal?"

Malorie breathes in. She holds it.

She hopes.

"Dad?"

The familiar hands are on her shoulders now. Olympia is saying something impossible, telling her this could be her dad.

And Olympia can see him.

"Oh, my God, Mom," Olympia says. "Oh, my God . . ."

"I'm Sam Walsh," her father's voice says. "Are you Malorie?"

Malorie falls to her knees. This can't be. It's simply too much. There are so many voices out here. Tom's on a stage. Olympia's by her side.

And her father . . .

She wants to tear the fold from her face.

But even now . . . she lives by it.

The man is beside her, low. He's on his knees. Olympia describes the impossible scene. She tells Malorie yes, *yes,* as a crowd who leaves their dead unburied cheer for her son, her son who may be going mad, even as Olympia tells her he's not, even as Olympia sounds excited by all of this, by Tom, but also by this man, this familiar touch and smell and sound, beside her, the two of them together on their knees in an impossible street in Hell.

"Mal," her father says, this time with confidence. "Oh, my God. Malorie."

They're hugging. Malorie's fold is wet with tears. Her fingers don't feel strong enough to grip his shoulders, but that's what they're doing. They're digging into him, deep as she can make them go.

"Dad . . ."

"Malorie."

Sam Walsh is crying. He's trying to talk, and she feels a fold on his face, and she laughs because Dad has lived by the fold, too. Because Dad is *alive.*

"We knew it," Sam says. And his voice is unfathomable relief. "We knew if we came here we'd find you."

Olympia is talking. Then, so is Tom, near now. He's asking if Malorie is okay. He's telling Olympia his idea worked. He's asking

Olympia why her eyes are open. "I saw them open from the stage," he's saying, "from behind the mirror. I saw your eyes were open."

And a creature, too. He's telling Olympia he saw a creature.

But through all this, a chaos more confusing even than the arrival of the creatures themselves, Malorie still hears what her father, her impossible, living father just said.

We knew if we came here we'd find you.

"Dad," she says, her lips touching the fabric that's wrapped around his face. "Dad, why did you come here?"

Sam laughs, and in his laughter she hears boundless, painful reprieve.

"You were always our rebel," he says. "You took risks we were always too afraid to take."

He's hugging her, hard. And Malorie thinks, *I was once the kind of person who took risks . . .*

Where did that person go?

She hears dignity, elation in Tom's voice. Astonishment in Olympia's. The community surrounding them is getting louder, and Malorie realizes that, despite what Tom claims to have done, despite the unadulterated, unsafe joy of this crowd, she isn't scared.

For the first time in seventeen years, she isn't scared.

And for a second, a flash, she remembers the girl her father described. She remembers pushing back against a world she felt was unfair.

She remembers being like Tom.

"Your mother," Sam says. And the pause worries her. "She would've . . ."

"Mom . . ." But Malorie can't finish the sentence out loud.

Mom is dead.

Sam rises and makes to help her up. Then Olympia's and Tom's hands are upon her, too.

Together, they're trying to help her to standing. But as Dad speaks again of Mom, as Dad stands with her two teens, as the most dangerous community Malorie's ever known celebrates on high, Malorie, here, unable to process this new reality, unable to see it as anything but a fantastic variety of madness, Malorie passes out in the arms of those she loves.

THIRTY-ONE

When Malorie wakes, she does so with her eyes closed. She is lying on something soft. A blanket covers her to her chest.

She can tell there are people in the room.

"Mom?"

It's Tom. Tom is here.

"You can open your eyes."

It's Olympia. Olympia is here.

But when Malorie does open her eyes, the first face she sees is her father's.

"Oh . . . Dad . . ."

The vision of him is blurred by sudden tears. A joy she once believed impossible.

"Hey," he says. But his eyes are wet, too.

He looks older, but good. White hair. Bright eyes. The same smile she remembers from before the world went mad. His clothes are different; a flannel shirt and sweats. Clothes she doesn't remember him ever wearing. He looks like someone who has walked instead of driven for seventeen years. Like someone who hasn't seen a television, hasn't used a computer, hasn't eaten at a restaurant for that time, too.

There's something else in his eyes. Malorie can see enormous emotions, memories, knowledge, there.

She looks to Tom. Because she remembers now. His name cheered by a lunatic crowd. Olympia saying her brother's eyes were open.

Facing a creature.

"Tom . . ."

She makes to sit up but doesn't get very far.

Tom is watching her. Sane.

Olympia. Sane.

"Your kids are amazing," Sam says.

Malorie looks to him and can barely get the words out through fresh tears. "Your grandkids."

"I'll get you some water," Olympia says. Then she's up and out the door.

Malorie looks about the room. Blankets over the windows. Wood-paneled walls. She's in a small bed in what feels like a guest bedroom.

It's clean. It's nice.

Dad is here.

Malorie looks to Tom again.

"What happened?"

Tom looks older, too. But not in the same way Dad does. Her son has the tranquil look of someone who has achieved something he set out to do.

The look of success, possible even here in the new world.

"Seems my grandson invented a way to look at them," Sam says.

Malorie starts to sit up again, but Sam is up and out of his chair, kneeling beside her.

"You don't have to hear it all at once," he says. "But you definitely have to hear it."

"Where are we?"

Sam smiles.

"It's what I've called home for a few years now. Your mother and I worked our way south after they arrived. I have enough stories to fill a library."

Malorie smiles. But while Tom may have invented a way to look at the creatures, some still roam the horizons of her mind.

"Oh, Dad . . . me, too," she says.

"We're in a house about as far from the maddening crowd as you can get," he says. He looks to the blanketed window, and Malorie easily remembers him doing the same in her youth. Only then he looked pensively out at the world. And now? "Mary insisted you'd come here. I can't tell you how often we argued this."

"And she's . . . ?"

"Yep."

No grieving in his voice. Sam has already gone through that. Just as Malorie went through it for him.

"Shannon . . ." Malorie says.

Sam nods and holds a finger to his lips.

"Olympia filled us in."

He still smiles. Malorie knows it's because her parents accepted the deaths of their daughters a long, long time ago.

"Us?" she says.

"Just because your mother has moved on doesn't mean I don't keep her up to date. She's buried in the backyard."

"Oh God, Dad. I'm so sorry."

Sam only nods, raises a hand to say he's okay.

"I'd like to see her," Malorie says.

Sam gets up and holds out a hand to help her do the same.

"She would love that."

Malorie breathes deep before exiting the home's back door. She holds Sam's hand.

Despite the fact that the people of Indian River are currently fashioning visors out of two-way mirrors, both are blindfolded.

"How long have you guys been here?" Malorie asks.

"Close to three years."

"Did a census man ever come to your door?"

Sam seems to think about this. Malorie hears the wind through the leaves on the trees. Hears leaves gently swept across the lawn.

"Yes," Sam says. "A little man. Very dangerous what he was doing. Your mother said it was noble. We offered him our place to stay for the night, but he said he had a lot of work to do."

Malorie feels fresh tears behind her fold. She wants to find this man. Wants to let him know that what he did, what he does, it works.

"Let's go see Mary," Sam says.

He guides Malorie down concrete steps to the lawn. She can hear a fence rattling by that same wind. The fold is tight to her face.

"Here," Sam says. "It's not much. But I dug it myself and that means something to me."

"How did she . . ."

"In her sleep, Mal. Thank God it wasn't the creatures." He kneels, guiding Malorie to do the same. She feels stone beneath her fingers. A large block of it. Leaves and grass, too. "Here."

Then his hand slips from hers and Malorie is left alone with Mary Walsh. Until now, she believed she'd already lamented the death of her mother. But it strikes her, in full, here, that she's never been allowed to grieve.

The creatures stole the time to do so.

"I missed you so much," Malorie finally says.

Then she's crying too hard to speak.

Malorie visits Mary every day for the two weeks they've stayed in this house. Not all of Indian River is as progressive as what she witnessed, without sight, in the town square. She understands why Sam didn't leave. Despite the behavior by some that she considered unfathomably dangerous only fourteen days ago, she also gets it. People in the new world fall into two categories: safe and unsafe.

But who's to say which lives the better, fuller life?

She thinks of Gary a lot. Too much.

She is preparing herself, she knows.

Olympia is on watch.

The teens join her at Mary's graveside often. They tell her stories, about the river, about the school for the blind, about Camp Yadin, and the Blind Train. Malorie talks about Shannon. It feels good to do it. She describes the people she met in the house. About Tom's namesake. About Olympia the woman. Felix, Jules, Cheryl, Don. Even Victor. And she can tell by the looks on her teens' faces when they get back inside that they're hearing a lot of this for the first time. Has it really been so difficult for her to relive the house? The people she met, loved, and lost?

Sam tells her of his crossbow kept in the home's front closet. He says he's killed numerous deer with it. Blind.

There are moments, wonderful hours, in which Malorie feels like she's home in the Upper Peninsula where she grew up. As if this were the house she was raised in. As if far in the backyard is a cluster of trees she once ran away to, a place where Sam and Mary Walsh knew she would go.

While they eat canned goods in the kitchen, Tom tells Malorie what happened. He'd made the glasses all the way back in Camp Yadin but was too afraid to try them out. He brought them with him despite her telling him not to. Here, in Indian River, on stage, two men attempted to view a creature from the other side of the glass, the two-way mirror from a local grocery store. They didn't go mad. About the time Malorie arrived is when Tom tried it himself.

He saw a creature through the glass. Yes. He saw Malorie, too.

Every time he tells the story, Malorie thinks she's going to be horrified by the ending.

But she just isn't.

Tom's here. He's sane. And maybe, *maybe,* he's done something to change the world.

The people of Indian River are attempting to mass-produce the visors, Tom says. People have been sent to find more material from neighboring towns.

Olympia and Tom spend time outside. They *look* out there. Neither is mad. And when they're inside again they tell and retell their stories to Malorie and Sam.

Sam takes Malorie's hand often. He silently tells her it's okay.

And it is.

Her teens are living, for the first time in their lives. One by way of genetics, the other by the creativity of his own mind.

Malorie endured. She delivered them to this moment in time. Dad and Mom endured. Many people in Indian River have, too.

Even those who didn't deserve it.

"Teach me how to use that bow," Malorie says one morning, alone with Sam in the living room. She's ready now.

Sam nods.

"Of course."

Olympia and Tom guide her as Malorie carries the weapon. She didn't outright tell Sam what she's doing, but he knows.

She hasn't been able to bring herself to use Tom's visor. It would be what feels like a seventeen-year leap. Yet, getting this done requires being able to see.

So she uses the eyes of her children.

This is the fourth time they've gone into town, looking for him, the man Tom still mistakenly calls Henry. The man Olympia knew, instinctively, was wrong from the start.

With each trip out, Malorie steels herself for change. She has never killed anybody. She has never had to pull a trigger, slit a throat, strangle an intruder. None of the dangerous people they encountered on their myriad journeys. Not even the uncommon strangers discovered in Camp Yadin, the place she last called home.

But killing Gary will mean more than just becoming a killer. She will also be leveling the loose ends of her time spent in the house with the housemates. The very friends she buried, finding everybody's body but his.

They find him outside a former liquor store not far from where they stay with Sam. Olympia spots him and taps Malorie on the shoulder in the manner she's been instructed to do.

"He's sleeping against the outside wall," Olympia says.

"It's him," Tom says.

The bow is formidable. But after seventeen years of living to protect, Malorie is the strongest she's ever been.

"A little higher," Tom says.

He's at Malorie's shoulder, helping her aim.

"A little more," Olympia says. She adjusts the angle of the bow.

If they miss, they will have to think fast.

She can almost hear the door closing. The clicking of a lock. The past put away.

It strikes her as somewhat incredible that, in a way, Gary was right.

Man was the creature she and the housemates had to fear most.

"All right," Tom says.

Malorie pulls the trigger. Gary makes no sound.

"It hit him right in his chest," Tom says.

"His heart," Olympia says.

The three walk cautiously to his dead body.

"Eat shit," Tom says.

"Watch your mouth," Malorie says. Then, "For someone who talked too much, he had no last words."

Olympia guides Malorie's hand to check Gary's pulse.

He's dead.

"Don't remove that arrow," Malorie says. "I want him to stay forever this way."

The teens are asleep. Sam is asleep.

Malorie has spoken long with her dad about what he wants to do and how he wants to do it. Neither of them believes they ought to live here, in this home, in this community, forever. Sam often speaks of wanting to return to where Malorie was raised. It would be a long journey, one Malorie believes her dad can endure, one they both want to take, but neither of them has declared today the day to do it.

Now, six in the morning, the world still dark outside, Malorie takes the stairs to the first floor. There, in the kitchen, she dunks a glass in a wooden bucket of water and drinks.

On the kitchen table is the visor the people of Indian River fashioned out of Tom's two-way mirror. Some of those people have come to the house, hoping to speak to Tom about his invention. It used to be that Malorie wouldn't let anyone in. Now, she picks and chooses. When she denied Athena Hantz entrance, the local legend was offended. When she asked for an explanation, Malorie told her she got lucky. Lucky that Tom came up with what he did. Because if something had happened to him . . .

Malorie picks up the visor. She eyes it. She considers.

She puts it on.

She stands by one of the blanketed windows, facing the darkness for many minutes, before she takes her coat from the rack beside the back door, closes her eyes, and steps outside.

It's autumn now. Malorie hears leaves crushed beneath her boots.

Her head is lowered as she waits for the heat of the sun to warm her. She likes standing here, beside Mary's grave. She likes talking to her still. She repeats stories about Shannon, her head lowered, eyes closed.

She tells Mary about Dean Watts. She says that maybe, when they finally do head north, Malorie will make a point of checking Mackinaw City for the man who brought back the train.

And just when the sun prickles her neck, just as she senses that some semblance of light has begun anew, Malorie, for the first time in over ten years, opens her eyes outside.

It surprises her how familiar the colors are. Old friends, back again. At her feet is Mary's grave; yellow, orange, and red with leaves. When she looks up, she sees a creature stands twenty feet farther into the yard.

Malorie does not move.

She senses a bird attempting to take flight somewhere in her head, a thing as black as her hair and as blue as her eyes.

But, despite the sound of flapping feathers, whatever is trying to get away doesn't quite get there.

Malorie breathes in. She holds it. She breathes out.

She looks.

She sees.

Infinity considering itself. Eternity facing its own endless journey.

And despite the thousand various words that rise to describe it, and the struggle to name it, she knows that by looking, now, beside her mother's grave, with her father and her teens asleep and safe inside, she has bridged some gap, she is losing no more, nothing more is being taken. And something has been returned.

AFTERWORD/ACKNOWLEDGMENTS

I've got a thing for rough drafts. Some might call it a fetish. In a slightly different reality I consider the rough draft/demo of a book or a song a finished thing. I've even gone so far as to consider outlines realized stories, albeit oddly told. Thing is, before getting my first book deal I had no real reason to rewrite at all. I'd wrapped a dozen rough drafts by then (in those days I only called them *books*), and, to me, they were as complete as any hardcovers on my shelves. I shared them with everyone; bands we, The High Strung, toured with, friends and family, strangers. In the '90s, my songwriting partner, Mark Owen, and I had a list of names we'd send cassette dubs to, generation-loss copies of already lo-fi albums. Those twenty people were enough. They made the group of songs real. By virtue of mailing out *Bid Me Off* and *A Lot of Old Reasons*, Mark and I could move on to the next batch, as yet unwritten, relieved to have another album in our bag, enthused for the next one. It was in those days that I learned to love the initial go-round, the first try, the stab at it when nobody was watching. Do you like live music? The rough drafts and demos were and still are like that. A performance. Fluctuating speed, some miffed notes, a forgotten lyric here and there.

And I *love* them.

Hello, I'm Josh Malerman. And I'm a Prolific.

It's a word that comes under some fire, and the common dismissals go like this: *If you write so much, how can any one book or song be truly meaningful to you?* Or: *It sounds like you're more interested in having finished a book than you are the actual book itself.* Or, this: *With all your stuff, I don't know where to begin.* But what the Prolific understands, deeply, is that you can start anywhere in a Prolific's catalog and work your way in either direction from there. For us, that's a thrilling prospect, and it's not unlike "prospecting" insomuch as, either way you dig, toward the earlier work or along the path of what followed, you're always looking for similar gold. What the Prolific cherishes above all things is not the singular work of art but the *canon.* The oeuvre. The arc of a creative mind unable to stop itself, the waves created by endless ideas. Have I mentioned that the Prolific believes anything he or she does, at any time, is a snapshot of the whole? That to wait years between projects is akin to having misplaced a thousand photographs from an era that, in hindsight, was much cooler than it felt at the time?

Who wants to miss out on those photos, that time?

I bring this up here for a reason.

The rough draft for *Bird Box* was written in a twenty-six-day frenzy in October of the year 2006. At the time, and certainly when I started it, it was only *the next story to be written.* I had the image of a blindfolded mother, two blindfolded children, navigating a river. Nothing more. Where were they going? What were they fleeing? Why couldn't they ... look? All these questions were answered as I went; what began as a possiblity became blood, sweat, and fears, and it's the closest I've ever come to reading a book as I wrote it. And the spirit of such a thing, the idea that I ought to write every day, to get the story done, to add another book to the growing stack of drafts in my office, was unquestionably born of the philosophy of the Prolific. Like the band Guided by Voices and people like Alfred Hitchcock, there was a sense that to stop, to slow down, to (gasp) wait for inspiration, was the equivalent of creative death. You can easily picture the imagination standing on the edge of a cliff, alone, eyeing the abyss below, weighing whether or not to leap. Because the Prolific knows, above all things, that the artist can't be expected to know which of his or her works are the good ones, which might resonate with other people, and certainly not which idea would be done best when plucked from the field of growing conceits.

Nothing scares the Prolific more than an Idea Graveyard. Not even the ones for the bodies.

So why not write . . . everything?

In this spirit, *Bird Box* was begun. She was finished within a storm of songs, tours, shows, and a thousand conversations that, had they been recorded, I might've slapped titles on them and described each as small works of their own. Following *Bird Box*, I simply wrote the next book, a complex 600-pager called *Bring Me the Map*. But while I was working on *Map*, and as The High Strung began that next tour, I started getting reactions from the friends and family to whom I'd sent *Bird Box*.

This is where the acknowledgments come in.

Can you imagine how many people there are to thank, those who encouraged and helped, over the fourteen years between the rough draft of *Bird Box* and releasing the final, official version of *Malorie*?

In a word (and, not so coincidentally the title of a High Strung song): *legion.*

I'll start with Mom, Debbie Sullivan, who read *Bird Box* at a dog trial in Indiana and called to tell me there was something to the then 113,000 words that were not broken up into chapters, were not indented, and were written entirely in italics. She liked it. My stepdad, Dave, called me, too. My friend Matt Sekedat, too. My sister-in-law Alissa. I printed the book up for my friend/landlady June Huchingson, gave it to her at night, and found her finished by morning. Her reaction remains vivid with me today.

To these early readers, I scream thank you. For, if it weren't for a handful reading Malorie's story in its earliest incarnation, I might not have pointed to it when, later, I met Ryan Lewis and Candace Lake, a managing duo who had read *Goblin* but knew we ought to begin with something other than a collection of novellas. It was by way of Ryan and Candace, along with the help of the brilliant lawyer Wayne Alexander, that I rewrote *Bird Box* in a significant way in the year 2010. I chopped the story in half, gutted what felt like repetition, broke the story into chapters, indented the paragraphs, and removed the italics that had, until then, essentially laminated the story in what felt like a dreamlike hue. Ryan, Candace, and Wayne shopped the book to agent Kristin Nelson, whose website, at the time, said she wasn't interested in horror. And suddenly, it seemed, the book, and myself, had a team. From there, Kristin shopped *Bird Box*, it was picked up in 2012, I rewrote the book once more entirely from scratch (one of the benefits of being a Prolific is the gumption to write the same book a second time), Universal Studios bought the film rights, and the book was published in 2014. And so began, for me, Malorie's story occupying a larger place in my life than I could have ever predicted.

Thank you Candace, Ryan, Wayne, Kristin, and Lee Boudreaux, who edited *Bird Box* and who must've been able to tell I'd never worked in a professional landscape before but had the heart not to tell me so at the time.

Still, no self-respecting Prolific will slow down his or her pace just for having experienced some level of success with a single book or song. He or she is constantly looking for windows, a partially open door, feeling for the breeze of a hole in the wall where a story might get in.

But what happened in the case of *Malorie* was, one got *out*.

In chopping *Bird Box* up, I'd removed a thread of the novel that no longer fit. Or to put it better: The book would've remained twice as long upon publication had I not removed a certain idea that, after time, I started to consider as its own novel. But before deciding whether or not to do something about that, Netflix bought the film rights from Universal and, really, any plans I had, the list of what should be written next and what could be a book and what wasn't, were blown apart, jumbled, and sunk, as if something like a tidal wave had come through the keyhole of my office door. Because, at the conclusion of watching the movie for the first time, I leaned over to my fiancée, Allison, and asked, "What happens to Malorie now?"

Thank you to the producers of the movie: Chris Morgan, Ainsley Davies, Scott Stuber, and Dylan Clark, for getting me to that place. And thank you Michael Clear for bringing the book to the producers to begin with. Thank you to Netflix and the movie's crew and to the friends I made on set, especially, but not limited to, members of the cast: Happy Anderson, Pruitt Taylor Vince, Julian Edwards, Vivian Lyra Blair, and the amazing David Dastmalchian.

Thank you Susanne Bier and Eric Heisserer.

And thank you (with a bow) to Sandra Bullock, for showing me what Malorie might look like outside my head.

And so . . . from Malorie to *Malorie*, fourteen years after first writing her into a rough draft, finding myself infused with the same ardor I held then, renting out the same space I once called home, June's place, the desk I'd written the rough draft of *Bird Box* at, the third floor of a gorgeous home in Detroit's Boston-Edison district, letting myself in every morning, heading upstairs, writing *Malorie,* and writing *about* Malorie and Tom and Olympia with the experience of a Prolific who had traveled through dozens of stories (novels, songs, movies), only to bring it all back to her, back to the character who had meant so much to me long before she was introduced to the world.

Malorie.

And in doing so, in understanding that there was ample room to tell more of her story without touching the original book in any significant way, I realized, completely, that any follow-up to *Bird Box* couldn't be about another man or woman who had dealt with the creatures in their own way, couldn't be about the world at large, but had to center on Malorie herself; *Bird Box* wasn't an apocalyptic story as much as it was the tale of one woman's reaction to the world gone dark.

Bird Box, in any form, will always be Malorie's story.

Del Rey Books gave me the chance to write about her again.

The conversations I had with editor Tricia Narwani were immeasurable; fuel enough to carry me through the "out to sea" weeks that occur during every rewrite, when you're not convinced you're gonna reach the other end of things, but you always do.

To all those at Del Rey who worked on *Malorie,* thank you so:

Tricia Narwani
Scott Shannon
Keith Clayton
Alex Larned
Julie Leung
Ashleigh Heaton
David Moench
Mary Moates

David Stevenson
Aaron Blank
Nancy Delia
Erich Schoeneweiss
Edwin Vazquez
Rebecca Maines

There were other factors, other moments along the way, outside the realm of notes: For this I thank Allison Laakko and Kristin Nelson. Allison is the one who brought up how, due to the tracks, a train might be the safest mode of travel in a world gone dark. We talked about how one might work, so long as the tracks were clear and nobody nefarious was on board. . . .

And Kristin gave me key direction when she reminded me that, despite having the spirit of a Prolific, and therefore the natural inclination to never return to the scene of the magic, it was not only okay for *Malorie* to resemble *Bird Box* in spirit but that maybe it *should*.

To Allison, to Kristin, to all, thank you.

To Dave Simmer, always, thank you.

And so you see, the power of a rough draft is not only in having outlined what you wish to do, it's not only about the potential therein: The first draft can be *magic*, no matter how "right" or "wrong" it felt while writing it, if you choose to look at it this way, a snapshot of who you were when you wrote it, whether you were inspired or not, and how you can later look at that photo and say:

Ah, yes, that was me just prior to meeting all these people to thank, all these incredible people, both real and imagined.

JOSH MALERMAN
MICHIGAN, 2020

ABOUT THE AUTHOR

JOSH MALERMAN is a *New York Times* bestselling author and one of two singer-songwriters for the rock band The High Strung. His debut novel, *Bird Box,* is the inspiration for the hit Netflix film of the same name. His other novels include *Unbury Carol* and *Inspection*. Malerman lives in Michigan with his fiancée, the artist-musician Allison Laakko.

Joshmalerman.com
Facebook.com/JoshMalerman
Twitter: @JoshMalerman
Instagram: @joshmalerman

INSPECTION

Boys are being trained at one school
for geniuses, girls at another.
Neither knows the other exists – until now . . .

Like every other boy in his school, J has never seen a girl.

Like every other girl in her school, K has never seen a boy.

But unlike the other students, J and K have questions
which nobody wants to answer.

Both of them suspect their teachers are hiding something from
them beyond the vast pine forests that separates their schools.

As K and J try to solve the secrets that have defined their lives, they
may discover something even more mysterious: each other.

UNBURY CAROL

She has died many times before.
But she's never been buried alive ...

Only three people know Carol Evers' secret.

Her best friend, who's dead.

Her husband, who hates her.

Her ex-lover, who left her.

Carol suffers from a dreadful affliction which makes her fall into long comas: waking slumbers indistinguishable from death.

Her husband Dwight wants her next 'death' to be her last. He will claim her fortune by pronouncing her dead ... and burying her alive.

The infamous outlaw James Moxie, once Carol's lover, rides the Trail again – pursued by murder and mayhem – to save the woman he loves.

And all the while, Carol is a prisoner in her own body, hearing her funeral plans, summoning every ounce of will to survive ...